I0678974

ALSO BY LYNN RODOLICO

TWO SEAS

HEART AND SOUL

INTIMATES

Lynn Rodolico

Eccolo Editions

First printing—February 1984
ISBN: 0-440-14066-8

Second printing—May 2012

Published by
Eccolo Editions
ISBN: 978-88-906986-8-2
Epub ISBN: 978-88-906986-0-6

Eccolo Editions

For Antonino—for every single day

CHAPTER ONE

From the rail of the quarterdeck Vanessa Ansel watched the sunlight in the wake of the ship; it turned the sea-froth luminous, almost neon, before it dissolved back into the black depths of the Atlantic. Up ahead she saw the Verrazano Bridge, which spanned the narrows between Brooklyn and Staten Island. This wasn't the first landfall she'd seen since leaving Denmark, but it was the first she recognized. She glanced sideways at her father, quickly taking in the strong brow and contemplative purse of his lips framed by the full white beard. He, too, looked ahead to the stretch of land, as if wondering what possibilities it would present him.

"We'll be in New York in half an hour," said Clemens Ansel, the accent of a childhood in Copenhagen barely evident after fifty years of gypsying around the world with his cameras.

Vanessa smiled to herself. She had been about to speak those exact words. They were so close that they often uttered what was in each other's mind, noticed the same detail at the same moment. They had to be close, they were each other's only family. More than that, she was terribly proud to be working with him.

"And after your opening tomorrow we'll be on our way to Mexico."

Her father cleared his throat. "No, Vanessa, I don't

think so," he said.

Startled, she turned and searched his face for clues. "What do you mean?" she asked tentatively. He continued gazing out over the water. "Haven't we been hired to photograph the Portillo family?"

"Vanessa . . ." His voice dropped off into a silence she at once found ominous. It sent a chill down her spine.

"What's wrong, Clemens? What is it?"

"I've decided to go to Mexico alone." He cleared his throat again.

She gripped the rail with her hands until her knuckles turned white, but there was no feeling in them. Her hands, like the rest of her body, had suddenly turned numb.

"I don't understand. What is the problem?"

"There's no problem. I'd just prefer to take this assignment alone."

Vanessa fought back a siege of tears. She was a woman of twenty-six, mature and sophisticated by anyone's standards, but suddenly she felt like a six-year-old; the same six-year-old child who had lost her mother and had been left a long time ago to a father who didn't have time for her. Once she'd convinced him not to send her away to live with an aunt, they had fashioned a kind of life together. His work had become her life; his travels, her home; his clients, her family. He had introduced her to hundreds of famous people during their travels. Now it felt as if their journey together had never commenced, and she had to convince him all over again not to abandon her.

"Isn't my work up to par?" she managed to ask.

"It's not that, Vanessa," he said, shaking his head

2

wearily. He hesitated. "As a matter of fact, your work is exceptional."

Vanessa hardly heard the compliment. "Then, why, Father? Why?"

He faltered. "Because . . . it's time, that's all. Time you were on your own. "

"I see." Her words sounded hollow. She brushed a handful of heavy black hair away from her face, and the sting of the wind dried her brimming tears before they could fall.

"You're good, Vanessa. With the reputation you've built with all the people you know—you'll have no trouble establishing a career of your own, if you want one. Especially after your spread in *Time* magazine." He looked down at the dark sea, thinking of what he wanted to say next. "I've never understood why you've stayed with me so long," he confessed.

Vanessa's answer came automatically. "Because there's still more you can teach me."

He shook his head. "No, I've taught you all I can," he answered.

"But—"

His voice grew deep, tinged with impatience. "Listen," he said sharply, turning to face her for the first time. "I've done what I could for you since you were a child. I've taken you with me against my better judgment. I've taught you my trade, even when I didn't have time for explanations." He stopped himself, as if censoring a thought.

"But there comes a time, Vanessa, when you must strike out on your own."

The tears that had filled her eyes rolled down her

cheeks. She hated the display of emotion but couldn't help herself, and turned away.

So, she thought, he'd been waiting for her to leave, and because he couldn't stand to wait any longer, had decided to act himself.

"You should be out mixing with people your own age, moving in your own circles, finding your own place in the world, perhaps a place to settle down, not constantly on the go with an old relic like me."

Her anger shot through her unhappiness. "Right, I should get married, have children, and do the laundry like a good girl." Her head snapped back, her violet-blue eyes brilliant in a pool of tears. "Is that what you see for my future? After growing up the way I have, do you think I can turn into a housewife?"

"It wouldn't be the worst fate to befall you."

She laughed ironically. "What do I know about family life?" Or about being a woman, she added silently to herself.

Clemens folded his hands and leaned his weight forward against the rail. "I did what I could," he repeated softly. "I know it wasn't much of a home life."

She expelled a breath and began again on a different course. "I'm not blaming you, Father. I'm just trying to understand why you don't want me anymore. I pull my own weight. I always have. You'll never find another assistant who knows the angles, the kind of lighting you prefer—"

"That's just the point." He turned to face her again.

His gray brows knit deeply over his pale blue eyes. They were eyes that looked sad even when the rest of his face shone with happiness. "You are too helpful! You

4

have everything set up before I can even analyze the situation," he said, "and to be truthful, I miss doing things for myself."

"Go on," she said formally.

"And I'm afraid if we continue working together any longer, I'll become little more than an appendage to you."

"Oh, Father," she mocked. "The great Clemens Ansel? That's laughable."

He didn't see the humor. "Perhaps someday you'll understand. I am no longer a young man. In many ways I have said what I have to say. My only hope of staying alive in my art, Vanessa, is at this point to go it alone."

She was jolted out of her anger by an unaccustomed plea in his voice. Those pale eyes, which had captured some of the most startling and revealing images of their time, seemed to fade; they appeared almost colorless now, and she had never before noticed how tired he looked.

"Naturally, if you feel that way, you should continue on your own."

He seemed encouraged and spoke to her enthusiastically.

"Vanessa, you know you're good. In fact, your work is better than good, it's exceptional. Rick Jacobs at *Time* already has you at the top of his list. If you stay true to what you know—no, to what you *want* you can do no wrong."

Her strength dissolved as quickly as it had come. Again she felt like the child being left behind. "But I want to be with you!" she cried.

"No. No, you can't be with me!" His determination rallied to match hers. "I need time now to be by myself. If you want to be a photographer, then go out and be a great one. Make your work eclipse mine. Believe me, I am doing this for your sake as well as my own."

Then, having said what had been on his mind, he turned on his heels and started inside.

"Father?" a thin, uncertain voice called after him.

"Yes." He stopped but hardly turned.

"What is it?"

It took all her courage to speak.

"I'm going to miss you."

He didn't answer right away. The only sound was the water rushing against the huge ship. She waited for him to return the sentiment, to say that he loved her and would miss her, too. But when he finally spoke, he merely told her he was going below to get his bags, and left her standing alone at the rail.

It was hard to believe that only ten days before they had left Copenhagen in fine spirits, pleased with the work they had done. Clemens had wanted to make the return crossing by sea, had told her he needed the rest. They would arrive in New York a day before the opening of his retrospective at the Steichen Gallery, then the next day they would fly to Mexico City.

She had thought the crossing by ship was a wonderful idea, never suspecting that what he needed was time in which to plot their separation.

She felt foolish now as she recalled how happy she'd been during the trip, even through the days of turbulent seas. One morning she'd braved a violent storm, trying to capture on film its raw power, until the captain had finally ordered her below. It was too dangerous, he had insisted.

Yet that danger seemed minor compared to the fear that gripped her now.

She heard the rhythmic thrum of the engines and the sound of the water churning as the ship cut through it, but all she could think about was that before long she'd be on her own in New York City.

The sounds of laughter drifted out from the mess in the June air, and she resented the reminder that elsewhere people were happy. At the other end of the deck a couple stopped by the railing, their arms intertwined. Suddenly she shivered, not quite sure if it was the cold or her heightened sense of aloneness that was giving her a chill.

She drew her jacket closer around her thin shoulders and hurried inside, slipping past her father's cabin and into her own.

If he wanted her out of his life, she'd oblige him. He wouldn't have to bother with her again. Quickly she threw her clothes into her suitcase.

Vanessa and Clemens appeared on deck after the ship had passed quarantine, and by four o'clock the S.S. *Dansk* was nestled safely in her slip below the Promenade in downtown Brooklyn. A customs officer came aboard to examine the passengers' passports and luggage. He recognized Clemens Ansel's name at once and treated him and his daughter with a respect bordering on obsequiousness.

Vanessa remained formal, almost detached, throughout the proceedings. She would not be reduced again to helpless pleading.

Both she and Clemens had their own suitcase, but a third bag, the one that contained their equipment, they carried between them, each holding a handle, so that the bag united them. Past warehouses full of stevedores and forklifts, to the far end of the pier, they crossed through a gate and onto a street. In unison they set down their luggage.

Clemens took a sealed white envelope out of the pocket of his cloth coat. "I want you to have this," he said gravely. He handed it to her, but avoided her eyes.

"What is it?"

"Enough for you to settle in, to decide what you want to do."

Abruptly he raised his hand and waved for a passing taxi. It screeched to a halt at their feet, and he opened the door and gestured for her to get in.

She pushed her suitcase in before her, and he hoisted the camera bag in after her, but made no move to follow.

"I hope everything goes well for you," he said at last.

"Aren't you coming, too?"

He shook his head.

"But where will you stay?"

"I've arranged to stay with a friend."

The formality of their words pained her. She had to say something more, even if she didn't know what. Smiling to cover the misery she felt, she added, "I'm sure your show will be a great success."

He nodded. "Which reminds me . . . after you've had a chance to separate your equipment from mine, would you get the case back to me?"

She shrugged, trying to act nonchalant. "Sure, where are you staying?"

Again he avoided her question. "I'll see you at the opening tomorrow, won't I?"

"You want me there?"

"Just because it's time for you to go out on your own doesn't mean you are no longer my daughter." He changed the direction of his thought. "And it's probably simplest if you leave my equipment at the desk of the Pierre."

She nodded, waiting for him to say more.

"If you need any"—he paused, to consider what it was he had to offer—"any more money, you have my address in Mexico, and you can always reach me through *Time Magazine*."

She looked at him sadly, but he only seemed to harden under her gaze. What if she needed comfort or advice? What if she simply needed *him*?

All right, if that was the extent of his offer, she'd make certain she didn't need anything more from him, ever.

"Good-bye, Clemens," she said solemnly and, reaching over, she pulled the door shut between them.

"Where to, lady?" the man behind the wheel asked, switching on the meter and beginning to move forward.

"Over the bridge, into Manhattan," she said.

She slipped a finger under the sealed tab, and opened the envelope, finding the check she had expected. He had paid her off, she mused bitterly, feeling the worse for the generous amount he had given her.

Reflexively, she looked back at the pier. Through the window of the cab she caught a last glimpse of her father. The great photographer was gazing distractedly around him, as if he didn't know what in the world to do next with himself.

CHAPTER TWO

It wasn't until they were crossing the Brooklyn Bridge that the driver, a middle-aged Israeli, turned to ask Vanessa where she was going.

"The Pierre," she said automatically.

"Hotel Pierre, missus?"

"Yes, please."

She knew what he was thinking. As distraught as she must have appeared when he picked her up, he probably figured her for the Upper East Side or Murray Hill. Vanessa wanted to tell him that she wasn't really a spoiled rich girl, that she had also spent time in the Golan and in West Beirut; but she decided not to. Perhaps people were better off left alone with their assumptions.

Though she looked naive, she could not rid herself of the image of those big black eyes she had photographed in the Near East, staring out at a world in rubble. She had called the photo-essay "Children of Anger, Children of Scorn," and, if she could believe her editor, Rick, the magazine copy should be awaiting her inspection in her hotel room.

"Been away long?" The cabbie tried to make light conversation as they threaded their way on to the northbound entrance to the FDR Drive.

"Seems like years," Vanessa mused.

"New York your home?"

"Sometimes." She turned her attention to the oil barge making its way up the East River. The air was so clear, even the clouds had edges. Was Manhattan home? She pondered, studying the unyielding rise of concrete.

The name of Ansel was not unknown here. Nor was his show at the Steichen Gallery the first Clemens had had. Even before Vanessa was born, her father had stunned the public with his World War II frontline photos. It was through the lens of Clemens Ansel that many Americans had viewed the retreat from Manila, and the final assault on Normandy. *Time* had published the grimy doughboy faces framed by steel helmets, the men carrying their wounded buddies, the lifeless bodies in a foxhole. In his thirties he had traveled with the famous newscaster Edward R. Murrow, and had given Western audiences their first published photographs of mysterious Tibet.

No, they were not strangers in New York. When she was a little girl they had lived in Manhattan, on East End Avenue overlooking the river. And after that, when her mother had died, they'd spent another six months at the Pierre while Clemens decided what to do with his daughter.

For six months she had gone to Walden School at the other side of Central Park, with the sons and daughters of New York's social elite. But she'd never made friends. *Time* maintained a suite of rooms at the Hotel Pierre for their VIPs, and Vanessa and her father had begun to think of the suite as their own. But living in a hotel wasn't really the same as having a home.

Had it been difficult to leave? Yes, but she'd hung on her father's arm through all the foreign cities, and eventually Europe had become a familiar place. But no one spot beckoned her any more than another . . . it had been the movement that had soothed her, the constant rhythm of the trains, the quick jump on a jet, the languorous journeys over water. Home, Vanessa realized, was the movement from one place to another. Perhaps it was time to redefine that word for herself.

But where? She wondered. The major galleries, magazines, museums, and portrait clientele were in New York, but that would mean a life packed with appointments, contracts, shows, parties—another kind of endless motion. Did she really want to trade one kind of movement for another? Did she want to trade at all? There were other alternatives, but could she remember how to stay in one place?

As an adolescent she had spent three years in Virginia while her father had been traveling through the southern states, shooting his photo essay on the sons and daughters of the Confederacy. She had enrolled in high school in Arlington, and odds against hope, she had made a friend. When Clemens was ready to move on, she, for the first time in her life, asked if she could stay behind.

Was it such a joyful memory because she'd been rooted in one place, or because in that place she had met Annie Durham?

It had been her new friend, Annie, who had first persuaded Clemens, then her own parents, that Vanessa should stay with her until graduation, and for three wonderful years Vanessa was accepted as one of the Durham family.

She and Annie had been inseparable, more like sisters than friends. They had held nothing back, were privy to each other's every secret, every doubt. It had been the fullest and happiest time in their lives, and they had tried to prolong it by applying together to Georgetown University.

Pretty blond Annie, with the clear blue eyes of a southern sky, majored in French and dreamed of living in Paris someday. Instead, it was Vanessa who would lunch with Sartre, Genet, and Truffaut before doing their portraits. Annie dropped out of school to marry a medical student and now lived in Vermont, where her husband practiced. Vanessa was godmother to their young son, Daniel. He was nearly six, and though she rarely saw him, the letters and postcards kept them close. He had built a stamp collection on their correspondence, and his letters to her always asked the same question: When would she visit them? One of Vanessa's regrets was that she'd never spent time with Annie in Vermont, and had had only a fleeting glimpse of her husband, Mark. Two years had passed since the last time she'd seen Daniel, when Annie had passed through New York on her way to visit her folks in Virginia. Vanessa had been in transit, too, but they had somehow managed to spend most of a day together. It still made her grin to think of Danny winning a game of tick-tack-toe with a chicken in a Chinatown arcade.

The light was turning dusky. Already the windows facing her along the side streets were reflecting the rosy glow of the newly set sun. The traffic around them grew denser as the cab approached Second Avenue and Sixty-First Street.

"Nice day like this, everybody heads out of the city,"

the cabdriver told her. The light changed and he edged his way across Second, weaving through traffic waiting to enter the lower level of the bridge.

Vanessa was suddenly aware of missing Annie, and longed for the comfort only a longtime friend could bring. As the taxi pulled up in front of the Hotel Pierre, she found herself wishing, instead that she were arriving at the door of her best friend's house.

"That's twenty on the meter, and I have to charge you for the trunk." The cabbie sounded apologetic.

Vanessa paid and tipped him, then went into the warm, mahogany lobby while the doorman wrestled with her bags.

"Will Mr. Ansel be staying with us?" the elderly clerk inquired at the front desk.

"No, John, he's staying with a friend."

A middle-aged bellboy carried her luggage through the lamp shaded glow of the lobby, up the elevator, and into her rooms. When she walked into the suite she found a cluster of white and yellow asters on the table, behind a bottle of Pouilly-Fuissé chilling in a bucket. The bellboy efficiently pulled the shades, turned on the lights, and placed the luggage on a rack.

When she was alone, she read the card accompanying the flowers.

Welcome Home, Vanessa.
Love, Rick.
P.S. How about dinner tomorrow, at eight?

She wasn't ready to see Rick, yet. But she *did* want to look at the advance printing he had sent her.

She spotted a stack of envelopes on the table by the entrance and hurried through each until she found her section in the glossy *Time* magazine.

Spread out on the bed a dozen sets of desperate eyes gazed back at her. Viewing them in her room in the Pierre, she found it hard to imagine them back in Golan, or huddled around the seaport of Beirut. They were transformed into something more domestic. They were the eyes of frightened children everywhere.

The phone rang.

"Vanessa?" Rick's voice echoed on the other end.

"Hello, Rick. I just got in."

"My spies are working. How are you?"

"Exhausted. Do you really have spies?"

"Yes, indeed. Have you seen the spread?"

"It's wonderful. Really, Rick, a fine job."

"It's your work. I'm just a lowly editor. For my money, Ansel the Younger takes the best shots of anyone today."

"You always were a sucker for a pretty face."

"Speaking of which, how about dinner tomorrow?"

Vanessa paused. She genuinely liked Rick. It was difficult not to. He was a handsome man, tall, with wryness beyond his thirty-odd years. In addition, he was both a successful editor and an intelligent human being. What made her hesitate?

"I don't know. Tomorrow is Clemens's opening. That will be a big deal. And I'm tired from the journey."

"What do you say I meet you at the Steichen, and we take it from there? You may be very glad to have some-one around to take you away from all the culture mavens."

"It's a deal. Oh—" She was glad she remembered: "The flowers are lovely."

"Glad you like them. I'll leave you together in peace."

"You really do have spies?"

"In case you didn't notice, the bellboy was wired. See you tomorrow. "

A nice guy, she thought as she unpacked. Too nice. That was the problem. Charming Rick had a dozen women on call at any given time, and he loved them all. Vanessa had no intention of letting their friendship, not to mention their business relationship, deteriorate into a grade B Don Juan scenario.

All the same, she was glad that he was there.

With her toilet articles on the sink, Vanessa filled the old porcelain tub. It was delicately veined with age, and otherwise immaculate down to its brass fittings.

Steam filled the room as she undressed and emptied oils into the water, then stepped in. As she soaked in the heat, she felt a tremendous wave of relief at being alone. For the first time that day she was glad her father had decided to stay with a friend.

But who? Vanessa tried to guess. Normally Clemens would have said, "I'm going to stay at the Plimptons', or the Vanderbilts'." But *a friend?* Well, that was certainly mysterious of him.

After her bath she ordered a light meal to be sent up to her room. The avocado stuffed with shrimp satisfied her appetite, and the cold white wine melted on her tongue. There was something nice about being overcome by exhaustion, giving into a tiredness that begged to be trusted. She abandoned herself to it, sliding in between sheets so clean they emitted the faint odor of soap. If her problems wouldn't solve themselves, at least they could wait, she thought, before drifting off to sleep.

*   *   *

The workday traffic had thinned along Madison Avenue by seven that next evening. Most of the stores had closed already. A few of the galleries were busy with the final openings of the season. In another ten days most would close for the summer, and the dealers and collectors would disappear to Europe, or the Hamptons.

She might spend her summer at the Hamptons, Vanessa considered. There were lots of people she knew in The Springs. Her father had done portraits of Pollack, de Kooning . . . many of the Abstract Expressionists. If she decided to open up a studio of her own, The Springs was the ideal place to drum up business.

The idea wearied her. She continued up Madison.

She could see people spilling out of the Steichen Gallery a half-block away, and her heart started to pound. In the golden light she tried to calm her nerves.

Vanessa had to elbow her way in through a door jammed with fashionable folk sipping Perrier-Jouet from paper cups.

"Excuse me, please," she found herself repeating.

A path opened in front of her and closed as quickly behind. She found herself greeting familiar faces that extracted a smile, a handshake, or a breezy hello. Fortunately, at openings, one never stopped for more than a second to talk; eyes met for an instant only before glancing away to see who else might be present. She picked out the face of Henry Geldzahler of the Metropolitan Museum, and the art critics Clement Greenberg and John Perreault.

Through the shifting bodies she could see the walls hung with her father's portraits, of Franz Kline in his Fourteenth Street loft, Henry Miller seated in a Montmartre cafe, Man Ray standing on the corner of Hollywood and Vine, Marcel Duchamp in his flat in Greenwich Village. How different their eyes were from those that looked out from Vanessa's pictures. She studied the shot of Picasso at Antibes, moved on to Tennessee Williams in Key West, Katherine Anne Porter at Yaddo; their eyes burned with an intense confidence. The eyes of those children gazed out at a chaos that was absolutely impenetrable.

"Vanessa, darling."

Vanessa recognized the watery blue eyes perched above the high cheekbones. It was the Princess Christina. They had met, briefly, aboard the yacht of the tycoon Alexis Myrapos.

"Princess Christina, how nice to see you."

"Such powerful work, don't you think?"

"Yes . . . Have you seen Clemens?"

"When I first came, darling. He is somewhere at the center of this mélange." She laughed. "Probably near the bar."

"Thanks." Vanessa pushed toward the rear of the room, the hum of conversation growing more intense as the bodies pressed more tightly together. She caught snatches of conversations, comparing her father's work to that of Cecil Beaton, Brassai, and Avedon; remarking on his brilliance.

Over, a bald pate she glimpsed her father's gray hair touching the shoulders of his unseasonable tweed jacket. She began to push toward him with renewed vigor, but stopped at the sight of a slim woman with silver hair standing beside him. She looked positively Junoesque in a long dark dress, a single strand of pearls around her throat. But it was the way she took his hand intimately in hers that brought tears to Vanessa's eyes. All around him people pressed to give an admiring word. Ansel turned his profile to her, and Vanessa could see his lips curl into a facsimile of a smile.

Vanessa turned back toward the entrance. Her father would never miss her, not with all those other faces and hands begging his attention. And after dinner there was the hard, feline beauty of his *friend*.

By the time she reached the street she felt dizzy. Leaning against the door to steady herself, she felt a hand on her shoulder, and heard Rick's voice.

"Hi. I'll bet you're glad to see me, huh?"

"Oh, Rick, it's a circus in there."

His smile stabilized her. As if sensing her condition, he took her by the arm and started walking slowly downtown.

Rick decided on a fashionable French restaurant in an old landmark building in Tribeca. It was the kind of out-of-the-way place someone like Rick, who traveled in the au courant set, would know.

The room was large, with high ceilings and overhead fans. Heavy bolster curtains were pinned back at the huge windows, giving the place an open, inviting appearance.

A curly-headed maître d' showed them to a table on a raised platform, sat them against a rail, and took their order. Rick ordered for both of them: starting with escargot and *moules,* he followed with a coq-au-vin and a red snapper, all of which they washed down with a vintage St. Veran.

At first Vanessa was quiet, and even apologized for being morose. Without going into detail, she managed to tell Rick about Clemens's decision to go separate ways.

"But that's marvelous," cried Rick.

"Then why don't *I* feel happy?"

"But don't you see what this means, Vanessa? You no longer have to live in his shadow." He shifted his weight. "I've watched you grow as a photographer. You have a sensitivity that I find missing in your father's work, as if you strive to make the camera delve beneath the surface. *And* your technique is certainly equal to that of any living photographer working with stills. I think it's great that you'll now have a chance to be truly on your own. "

To celebrate, he ordered a sauterne with dessert.

"Yet I feel lost," she confessed.

"I could always take you home with me."

There was a seriousness beneath the humorous tone of Rick's suggestion that overwhelmed the intended playfulness.

"It would only dull a valuable friendship, Rick." She watched him eye a passing waitress. "Besides, you have plenty of other fillies in your stable."

"No one like you, Vanessa."

"I wouldn't risk it, Rick. Particularly not now, while my life feels so precarious."

"Friendship can include a lot more than you think. Love doesn't always mean possession."

"I know that line of thought. For some, perhaps. I also know myself, Rick. I'm not a player. I'm not built for it."

"All I mean is if you need me, I'm here." He lifted his glass of sauterne as if to make a toast. "Now, my dear Vanessa, I have what I hope will be a more agreeable offer for you."

"I'll drink to that." She clinked his glass.

"Now that there is nothing holding you back, we want you to do a special on the refugees still trying to get out of Vietnam, and marooned in Laos and Cambodia. The world has forgotten that area, but the dynamics of a people still devastated by a long-ago war, the quotient of human misery, is still high. It's an assignment made for you, Vanessa. And the folks up at *Time* agree. We are willing to pay handsomely for your work."

Vanessa was silent. The offer was almost too much for her to consider right now. She said as much to Rick, told him that since she'd arrived in New York she'd been thinking for the first time in her adult life about staying in one place for a while and seeing how it felt.

"I can understand that impulse." He nodded. "But you'd only be gone a couple of months, and it's a golden opportunity."

"Which breeds another, and another. Rick, I have to say no at some point so I can figure out how I want to lead my life."

"This may be your life, Vanessa. Very few people on this earth have something important to say. You have a responsibility as well as a gift."

"What about my responsibility to myself?"

"I understand your point, and I won't push."

"Can I have some time to think about it?"

"Sure." He smiled. "Take a week or two to decide. In the meantime let's drink to your independence." Rick raised his glass and sipped.

In the cab back to the Pierre she felt the effects of the wine and allowed her head to rest on Rick's shoulder. He talked to her about the options before her. After this spread appeared, she would be able to pick and choose her jobs. If she decided to take the Cambodia-Laos assignment, she could expect the same success her father had had with the Second World War photographs. All she had to do was decide what it was she wanted, and it was hers for the asking. Was she sure she didn't want to come home with him?

Yes, she was sure.

He kissed her warmly on the cheek and watched her disappear into the Pierre.

Upstairs Rick's voice continued: it spoke of all the possibilities. The letters on the hall table spoke of more opportunities: invitations to do this book, these portraits, to lecture at this institute, to be a part of that colloquium.

It was all too much. Here, with all of the possibilities, in the midst of choices some would give everything to have, all she could feel was an abiding sense of loss buttressed by an ancient loneliness.

Out of the chaos of voices calling for her attention, an image emerged to her like a radiant source of energy. She saw Annie's face and knew that, of all her options, the one that spoke to her most urgently was the opportunity to visit her old friend. Perhaps there, in the familiar warmth of that relationship, she could find the self that was slowly slipping away from her. Yes, tomorrow she would call and tell her friend how much she needed to see her.

CHAPTER THREE

"Sure you won't change your mind and come along with us?" Mark asked, holding the back screen door open as his son raced through.

"Positive," Annie said, trying to maintain a smile. "Go ahead. I have things to do while you're away."

Her husband shrugged. "Okay," he said obligingly. "We'll try to catch something to bring home for dinner."

"Just make sure you clean it first," she answered. Last week they had proudly laid their catch on the kitchen table, entrails and all. She'd had to swallow hard to disguise her repulsion in front of her son. She didn't want to seem unappreciative, but she didn't think she could stand it again.

Mark's smile faded. "Sure, we'll clean them. See you at suppertime," he added simply. Grabbing up his rod and reel, he let the screen door slam shut before she could remind him not to.

Annie returned to the kitchen table and poured herself a second cup of tea. Her son's high-pitched glee chorused along with her husband's deep, rich chords of laughter, and momentarily she regretted her decision to stay behind. Since the beginning of spring Mark had been teaching Danny to fly-fish.

The Saturday excursions had been intended originally to include the entire family. But Annie had been bored sitting alone on the banks, attempting to read, while Danny tried hour after hour to hit a tin-can target with his fly.

His infrequent successes had interrupted the monotony for her—she smiled to recall his proud expression—but it hadn't been enough to compensate for a day-long attack of boredom and black flies.

She listened to the car start down the gravel driveway. Settling back against a thick cushion in the oversized white wicker chair she had refinished for the breakfast nook, she savored the first unrushed moment of the week. Picking at a frayed spot in the sunny yellow fabric she sat on, she wished she had time to recover the cushions. The chairs needed to be painted again, too. The luxury of the solitude lost its magic as she thought about the things she should be doing. All week long she was busy with Danny and the house. One day to herself did little more than frustrate her.

As she glanced around the kitchen, it wasn't the pretty decor she noticed, but the succession of unfinished projects, not to mention the clutter of dirty dishes.

Sighing resignedly, and leaving unfinished her cup of tea, she got up from the table and started to stack the breakfast dishes in a sink full of soapy water. She didn't dare waste her few precious hours of free time by sitting idle. If she hurried through the housework, she might have time to read a few chapters in the book she'd just started. Who knew, maybe she'd even have time to finish writing her article on the poet William Standard's upcoming reading. Jed Cummings, the editor of the *Sherbroke Weekly,* had been asking after it.

In half an hour the kitchen was straightened, and she headed into the living room, determined to make it as quick a job. Danny's pajamas in the middle of floor annoyed more than angered her; he was always leaving his clothes scattered around the house, a habit he had learned, no doubt, from his father. Gathering up the beer bottles from the previous evening, the piles of newspaper discarded on the sofa, she wondered if she'd spend the rest of her life cleaning up after her son and husband.

The futility of it gripped her. She had cleaned the entire house the previous day, and it looked as if it hadn't been straightened in a month. For an instant she imagined how orderly the house would be if she lived in it alone. A second image, that of the chaos that would engulf her "boys", if left alone to care for themselves, challenged the fantasy, and guiltily she dismissed it. What would happen, she wondered, if she didn't pick up at all, but let things stay where they had let them fall? They probably wouldn't even notice, she concluded.

The sound of the postman dropping the lid to the mail-box broke her reverie.

She sorted through the stack of letters one by one. As usual, all were addressed to either Dr. Abrams or "Occupant." Not even the bills belonged to her, she realized, not sure whether to be sad or relieved. At the bottom of the pile she found a familiar cream colored envelope, and without even pausing to study the return address, she knew it was from Vanessa. Slipping the envelope into the pocket of her calico skirt, she restrained her impulse to read it at once. It would be a reward to cherish when the housework was done.

By half past eleven the house was neat enough to satisfy Annie. She had picked up Danny's room by rote, throwing the scatter of toys into a brightly painted toy-box. Vacuuming could wait until midweek, when he was at his swimming lesson. So could laundry, she thought, spreading the nubby blue bedspread up over the sheet on his bed. She had fought the urge to clean Mark's study. Instead, she had simply removed the half-dozen coffee cups that had accumulated in the last two days, and closed the door, remembering that he preferred to find it as he'd left it.

How he could think in such disarray was beyond her comprehension. Fortunately, someone came into his office to clean twice a week; otherwise, she was sure he'd have no patients at all. His success as a physician and his popularity in the community had nothing to do with his tidiness.

Pouring herself a tall glass of ice-cold lemonade, Annie stepped outside of the house to relax with her letter. The midday sun was hot but a cool breeze ran through the huge sycamores at the edge of the lot, lifting the waves of shoulder-length blond hair from her neck as she crossed the patio. She didn't need to sit on some bug-infested riverbank to enjoy the glory of nature. She was more comfortable in her own backyard. Reclining into the chaise longue, she smoothed her skirt over her knees and set her drink on the nearby table before bringing the letter out of her pocket.

The postmark read Denmark but the contents explained that she had finished her work there, and was traveling to Mexico City next week with her father for the summer months. To photograph the president, no less! Vanessa spoke briefly of her father's retrospective at the Steichen Gallery, and her photographs in a forthcoming issue of *Time.*

She skimmed through the perfunctory inquiries about her life. Vanessa was always sure to ask after Mark, too, and she had dozens of questions about Danny's latest adventures.

Annie found a pad and pen in the drawer to her desk and began composing a reply in her mind before she returned to the chaise. She considered the past months' activities, but even the events that had seemed so important at the time felt insignificant now, compared to Vanessa's news. She felt silly writing about the loss of Danny's first baby tooth, though she knew Vanessa would like to know. And about Mark, she could tell— what? That he was working all the time? Her own news sounded even more dreary as she attempted to write it down. That she had signed up for a course in contemporary French poetry at the neighboring college to finish her degree seemed mundane, and she was too frustrated to convey in a letter the importance it had for her. Undoubtedly Vanessa would understand, would value Annie's news as thoroughly as if she had discovered gold in the foothills of Vermont. That wasn't the problem. Rather, Annie was bored with her life, and she couldn't help but envy her best friend's adventure. Why couldn't Annie have had a world-famous photographer for a father instead of an accountant? Why couldn't it be she who traveled to foreign places? Why should she spend her entire life making a home comfortable for her family, as much as she loved them, when she herself wasn't happy? She set down the pad and reached for her lem-

29

onade. She couldn't write what she was feeling in a letter the way she could in her journal; it sounded too self-pitying.

Glancing around the well-groomed yard, she wondered what reason she had to complain. If someone had asked her ten years ago what would make her happy, her answer would have been what she had now. Was she one of those people doomed to always want more, no matter how much they had? Her head throbbed. She felt like crying but couldn't—no, wouldn't—let herself. It was a beautiful day, she had a lovely home, a faithful, hard-working husband, a healthy son. She wouldn't give in to her irrational dissatisfactions.

"Stop being self-centered," she said aloud, as if someone had walked into the yard to lecture her. But even as she spoke, she was helpless to stop the tears from sliding down her cheeks and onto her freshly ironed blouse, like condensation from an iced drink. She knew she was acting absurdly, but she couldn't stop herself. Maybe she was due to start her period; that would explain her moodiness. She couldn't be pregnant. They hadn't made love in—how long? Ages, it seemed. Mark had talked about wanting another child, but Annie needed more time to consider. Children and lovemaking would have to wait.

From inside the house she heard the telephone. Drying her tears with the back of one hand, Annie hurried indoors, lifting the receiver off the hook before the third ring.

"Hello? Hello, Annie?"

"Vanessa? The connection is so clear, you sound just across the street."

"Not exactly," she answered, laughing with a lightness that sounded like wind chimes, "but close."

"I just got your letter today. I thought you were supposed to be in Mexico."

Some of the lightness disappeared from her voice. "I thought so, too," she said, punctuating her supposition with an ironic laugh. "Dad and I had a . . . a parting of the ways. He doesn't want me traveling with him anymore; says it's time for me to try working on my own."

Annie heard the seriousness of the situation, and was quick to sympathize. "Are you all right?"

"I'm sure I will be," Vanessa assured her, trying to speak from a confidence she didn't feel. "As soon as I get used to the idea."

"But what are you going to do?" Annie asked anxiously. Unsettled plans made her nervous, even when they weren't her own. "Where are you now?"

"Well, I'm at the Pierre, where we usually stay, but I can't remain here forever. I mean, I could extend my stay another week, I guess—the people at *Time* wouldn't mind—but I can't *live* here."

"Then you plan to remain in New York?" Annie felt her spirits rise at the prospect of having her friend close at hand.

"Oh, I don't know . . . it seems like the right thing to do, but I can't make up my mind. I've had an offer to photograph the refugees in Cambodia, but the thought of being a stranger in a strange land once again bothers me."

"Then, don't go."

"It's not that simple, Annie. It would be a marvelous opportunity —a good career decision. Or, I can lecture at

31

Sarah Lawrence, or open my own studio, or curate a show at the Whitney —I just opened my mail and the offers are all there."

"I don't understand. What's the problem?"

"I'm—I'm simply overwhelmed." Vanessa heard her voice quiver. She was getting dangerously close to losing control.

"Why not come up here? Everything's so green now you wouldn't believe it. You can walk around with bare feet— the world is a carpet. Come on up and relax. Those other things can wait until you're ready to deal with them."

"Oh, Annie . . ." She was glad her friend couldn't see the silent tears that stained her cheeks.

"It sounds like you need to let yourself be cared for a little." She could hear her friend stifling back tears and it touched her. "Vanessa, I've missed you. It would be a great gift for me to have your company. Please, say you'll come up."

"Are you sure you don't mind?"

"Mind?" Annie's voice turned light with laughter. "I wish you were here right now."

Vanessa sighed. "Once again you provide me with a home. You're a lifesaver."

"Don't talk such foolishness. What are friends for, after all?" She didn't wait for an answer. "How soon can you be here?"

"I have a couple of calls to make and one quick errand, but they won't take long," she answered, impatient to see Annie. "I take the train into Albany?"

"That's right."

"I'll call you again when I know what time it leaves."

Annie's excitement burgeoned at the promise of seeing her friend. *"Well, hurry,"* she said, anxious to begin their reunion.

* * *

While Mark unloaded the gear from the car, Danny ran ahead to give his mother news of the afternoon's success. Annie listened patiently for as long as she could, but when he started repeating himself, she interrupted with her own good news.

Her enthusiasm wasn't lost on the boy. Immediately he forgot the victories of his day. "When? When is 'Nessa coming?" he cried, jumping up and down as if he'd burst if he didn't know at once.

For once Annie didn't mind her son's unrestrained energy. "Vanessa will be here tonight," she answered, with equal enthusiasm.

"Hurray!" he exclaimed, as his father called for someone to open the door.

Mark labored inside under the weight of a full day's fishing gear and, Annie noticed, their trophies: a half-dozen neatly filleted fish. "What's all the excitement about?" he asked, looking from mother to son.

"'Nessa's coming to visit," Danny sang, his dark eyes bright with joy.

"Vanessa Ansel," she told him, closing her journal and putting it away for the moment.

"Of course," he said, unloading the equipment into the corner of the kitchen. "Is she staying long?"

Annie frowned. "Probably not. Maybe a week. Is that all right with you?"

"Fine," he said. "I'm glad she's able to come up. I haven't seen her since Danny was born." And then he'd been so distracted he couldn't remember her, really.

He studied Annie's face and realized he hadn't seen her so happy in how long? As he had done so many times over the past few months, he tried to trace back to the source of her unhappiness, but he could never find it. She had simply faded, and because her initial radiance filled his mind long after it was gone, he had missed the point at which it had begun to pale. He wondered if all marriages dulled after the first years, but he refused to think so. Whatever the cause, he hadn't seen her shine like this for a long time, and he was glad that her friend Vanessa could bring back the smile.

"What time will she be here?" he asked.

"Her train comes into Albany at eight o'clock."

Danny's eyes glistened. "The train!" In the common world of automobiles, he approved of his godmother's choice to travel by train. "Can I go to the station, too?"

"You know what your bedtime is as well as I do."

"But—"

Mark intervened on his son's behalf. "He'll never sleep tonight if he has to wait till morning to see her." He hated to interfere, but the look of his son's disappointment was more than he could bear. It couldn't hurt to let him skip an hour or two of sleep. "Let's make an exception, this once, all right?"

Annie hesitated. She hated it when Mark countered her decisions, especially in front of Danny. Besides, she wanted those first moments of seeing Vanessa to herself, and if this was selfish, well, she had a right to greet her best friend alone. She looked from her bearded husband to her son, both of them waiting expectantly for her answer. "If you *promise* to go to bed *without fuss* the minute I say it's time, you can stay up until she gets here."

Danny squealed his delight, until he realized that her decision hadn't included a trip to the train station. He looked back to his father, but he had turned away, a tight smile on his lips, as if he thought he had succeeded in getting Danny his way. Maybe they hadn't understood. "But what about the train?" he tried, shyly.

Annie sighed heavily. Her look told him not to push the issue. The boy turned to his father for support, but he, too, looked distracted, as if he were no longer listening.

CHAPTER FOUR

The train was only twenty minutes late. The engine tooted a half mile down the track, then again as it drew into the station. There were six silver cars that would continue all the way to Montreal, but only one of them held Vanessa, and Annie found herself walking furiously up the platform until she found the first car discharging passengers.

For a moment they stood on the platform a few feet from each other, too moved to speak. Vanessa looked more radiant than ever, Annie thought, appraising the sleek figure and chic travel outfit. Vanessa couldn't help but smile at what the years of domesticity had done for Annie: Everything about her seemed to speak of solidity and comfort. The shock of recognition lasted only seconds, and they ran to each other and embraced, speaking the other's name as if it were a magic incantation.

"Oh, I feel so much better just for the sight of you," Annie enthused, picking up Vanessa's leather suitcase in one hand and slipping the other through her friend's arm.

"Me, too." Vanessa smiled. "The minute I got on the train, I breathed a sigh of relief."

"You look better than ever." Over two years had passed since their last meeting. "How do you stay so thin?"

"Worry," Vanessa teased.

Annie smiled. "Funny, worry makes me hungry!"

Once they were in the car, Annie asked Vanessa about her confrontation with her father.

"He said he needed to work alone at this point . . . and that it was time I find my own direction." She shook her head sadly. "And all the time I thought I was an asset to him."

"I'm sure you were an asset," Annie assured her. "But your father was always a bit of a curmudgeon."

"That's probably true, but I still feel like I've been fired. He said that wasn't it at all, that he was doing it for my own good."

"Maybe he was."

"There was so much to learn yet, Annie. Things *only he* could teach me. "

"Look at the other side of it. Now you will learn things you couldn't learn with him."

Her friend's words were comforting, but Vanessa couldn't shake off the sense of failure. "The truth is simple." She exhaled. "He had grown tired of my company. Some parents really like their kids . . ."

"You mean smother them," Annie interrupted, thinking of her own.

"Your parents? Wanna trade?" Vanessa offered.

As difficult as her parents could be, she could understand how much Vanessa had suffered for never having had a home of her own. Annie would make it up to her. She would make sure she felt at home.

They cleared Albany's city limits and climbed the rolling hills of southwestern Vermont.

"No matter where I've been," said Vanessa, "I'm never as taken with a landscape as I am in New England."

"Oh, come now. You've been to much more exotic places."

"Sure . . . the Riviera is exclusive, the Black Forest mysterious, the Pyrenees are quaint, and the English countryside looks like a picture post card, but New England"—she looked around again at the warm glow of twilight—"Annie, take my word for it, it has all of those elements rolled into one."

"I guess it's like anything else . . . when you live here all the time, you stop seeing it."

"I don't think I'd ever stop seeing it."

They had turned off the highway and were traversing a smaller country road that began to wind and ascend, waves of green foliage turning to black silhouette as night descended around them. Vanessa could smell the woods, their rich earth, the dampness in which hid myrtle and morels. They turned off onto a still smaller gravel road, and then past a white picket fence and up into a driveway.

"Is this it?" Vanessa's voice was full of excitement.

"This is the place," mugged Annie.

The light was sufficient for her to see a broad green lawn, as smooth and soft as the felt of a billiard table. It extended up, on a slight incline, to a white wooden house of several stories, with a broad red-brick chimney on one side. The windows were all large, framed by dark shutters, and the light from inside looked inviting.

"It's just how I pictured it," whispered Vanessa.

Without a word Annie drove up the gravel driveway and into the white wooden garage attached to the south side of the house.

"Come." Annie took her hand. "I want to show you something."

In the first light of a full moon they walked around to the north side, past the stone chimney, to where the land fell off into a valley, bordered all around by lush woodland.

"Beyond," Annie pointed at the distance, "are the Green Mountains."

"Breathtaking." Vanessa stared in awe. For a minute the silence reverberated with all the good feelings in life.

The two women turned, arms once again interlocked, and walked back to the house.

" 'Nessa! 'Nessa!" came the falsetto shout of pure delight. It was followed by the vision of a blond-haired boy racing the length of the long hallway. He stopped just short of collision. "I thought you'd never get here!"

She set down her shoulder bag and camera, and swung him up into her arms. "The train was late," she explained, smoothing his thick hair out of his huge brown eyes and noticing that it lay long against the collar of his little red sweater, probably the only one of the gifts she had sent him from Quebec last year that still fit. She held him at arm's length, examining his face. His features were much better defined now, but the expression was still the same. The surge of love she felt for him was as intense as if she'd watched him grow day by day. She was glad they had kept in touch, if only by letter and phone. She could see from the joy in his eyes that their long separation hadn't dulled his feelings for her, either.

"You promised to stop growing," she said, staggering

under the weight of his squirming body.

"Why aren't you in your pajamas yet?" Annie asked sharply.

"Oh," Danny said, recalling her last words before she left the house.

"The one thing I asked Mark to do while I was gone," she explained to Vanessa, barely able to conceal the impatience in her voice.

"He forgot, too," added Danny, not wanting his father to be in trouble, either. "But Mrs. Colby came over to say Belle was about to have a baby," he continued, hoping his explanation would make everything better. "They went to the Colby's' barn."

Annie didn't wait to hear any more, but hurried through the house, stopping only to deposit Vanessa's suitcase at the foot of the stairs before heading out the back door.

Vanessa grabbed her camera and hurried to catch up with her. Danny ran along at her side all the way to the barn on the far side of the sloping field behind their house.

"Go back," his mother ordered him when they reached the barn door. "I want you changed into your pajamas. *Now,*" she added, when he started to protest. She wasn't sure what she'd find in the barn, and she didn't want him witnessing the traumas of birth.

"Let him stay," a male voice resonated from within the dark, cool barn. "He might never see this again." Danny hesitated at the open door. He never knew which parent to listen to, they so often told him different things. He had tried obeying the decision he liked best, but that had often proven to be the wrong move. He edged in, "Mommy?"

Annie's eyes had adjusted to the shadowy light, and the sound of a mare tossing in the stall dismissed her original fear. Cautiously she peered into the stall to see her husband and Mrs. Colby crowded around the neighbor's mare Belle, who was in the process of becoming a mother.

"Mind if I watch, too?" Vanessa asked, leaning over Annie's shoulder.

"I don't think Belle would mind another observer," the doctor answered without looking away from his work.

"Vanessa, this is Mrs. Colby, and my husband, Mark," Annie said, making a feeble gesture toward etiquette.

Vanessa nodded at the short, bosomy neighbor and studied the back of Mark's head, his tousled brown hair tinted red in the light thrown from the kerosene lantern. "Pleased to meet you," she responded, her tone acknowledging the inappropriate circumstances for a more lengthy introduction.

Mark didn't answer. The mare's breathing was heavy. She needed his undivided attention.

"Would it be all right if I snapped a few photographs?" Vanessa whispered to Annie, unraveling her camera strap from around her neck.

"Just keep the flash out of the mare's eyes," Mark told her. "She's nervous enough."

The warning was unnecessary. She understood how offensive flash light could be, and since her purpose was always to capture her subjects in their natural attitude, she had learned to adjust her equipment rather than her environment. Unobtrusively she moved around the stall, careful to stay out of the doctor and the mare's way.

It would have been easy to shoot a hundred pictures in the time it took to deliver the foal, but she didn't want to disturb the horse or its attendants so she chose her angles prudently. Of the dozen pictures she took, not all were of the horse; rather, she caught the look of rapture on Danny's face as he sat spellbound observing the horse; the empathy in Annie's, as if she were going through the labor herself. She steadied her camera and focused in on Mark's intent expression, thinking he might enjoy having a document of the event, but from beyond the camera she saw his look of concern turn to worry.

"Mrs. Colby, I need you to hold Belle down," he directed. "I'm afraid the foal is breech, and Belle has to be calm if I'm to turn it around."

"Oh, Dr. Abrams—" Mrs. Colby started.

Vanessa watched the woman turn pale at the thought of participating in the delivery; the sight of the foal's leg protruding from the mare's womb made her close her eyes in a near faint before she hurried out of the barn.

"Annie?" he beseeched. "Can you help?"

Annie was already edging toward the door. The freak delivery made her sick to her stomach. "I'm afraid I can't, Mark. . . ." She steadied herself. "I'm going to make sure Mrs. Colby's all right." She grabbed Danny's hand and took him with her.

"I can help," Vanessa offered, dropping to her knees near the mare's head. Stroking the coarse hair of the chestnut mane, she spoke to the animal in a gentle, soothing tone, as she might comfort an upset baby. The horse shuddered beneath her hand. "Just tell me what to do."

"Keep her calm," the doctor instructed. "That's right. . . keep talking to her."

He reached up between the animal's legs and eased his hand over the swollen belly. "Come on, Belle." His voice was soft, coaxing. "Don't fight us. . . you'll be all right."

Vanessa stroked the mare's forehead, watching the frightened animal's eyes dilate beneath long, straight lashes. "Don't be scared," she whispered, lying down beside the animal, without a thought to her clothes, wrapping her arms around the horse's neck, hoping to communicate a calm through the warmth of her own body.

Belle exhaled a deep breath and closed her eyes, as if tired of her chore. Little spasms ran up and down her spine, as if she were twitching flies off her back. Her nostrils quivered.

"Keep her still —I think I've—"

Belle tried to bolt but Vanessa used all her weight to hold her down. A convulsion started in her womb and ran downward. No longer were her eyes closed, nor could Vanessa do anything other than restrain the sweat-soaked mare.

"I've got it turned round. Let's hope she has enough strength left to push it out."

"What should I do—?"

"Stand back," he answered. "This part's between the mare and her foal."

For what seemed like a long, long time the horse didn't move at all; then contractions shot through her like a comet through the sky. "Can't we do something to help?" It hurt her to see the animal in labor.

"I'll help if she can't make it on her own, but she's got-

44

ta do most of the pushing herself."

A sudden flush of blood filled Vanessa's cheeks at the sight of the foal's head crowning, and she sank down to watch Mark assist with its entrance.

"Slow—slow. Give us a strong, even push, Belle."

She wanted to do something—anything—to help. She felt totally useless kneeling there while the mother suffered. "Now again—" Mark crouched, extracting the newborn from its womb. "Atta girl."

Vanessa remembered her camera in time to focus on Mark lifting the slippery foal into his arms. She had missed the chance to photograph its dramatic entrance— her thoughts were full of the mother—but she wouldn't have exchanged the exhilaration of participating, not even for a good photograph. A second shot caught the gangly newborn standing, shakily, to be sure, on its four fence post skinny legs. The third shot caught it staggering forward, and the shot captured it trying to nestle its mother.

When she emerged from behind the lens, she peered directly at them, but they took no notice of her; they proceeded as intimately as if they were alone. At her side Mark, too, watched with an expression of awe on his face.

"I don't think there's anything more beautiful than a mother and her newborn," Vanessa reflected softly.

They watched the mare lick her foal clean, as if she had been bathing him all her life.

"She's a natural," he answered, laughing.

"Aren't all mothers?" she asked.

"That's the theory," he said, but he didn't sound convinced.

"Isn't that proof?" she paused, gesturing at the suckling foal. She had her own doubts—about her own maternal instincts—and she wanted to quiet them. "How can there be any doubt when you see them together?"

Mark nodded solemnly. "When I see animals relate, I don't have any doubts. But I spend most of my time delivering humans into a more complicated world, where basic responses are sometimes absent. . . ." He was thinking about the woman who had been too tense to breast-feed, so that the baby had to be put onto formula. . . . Annie had been tense, too. "Not every woman knows by instinct," he said. "I sometimes think I would have been happier as a veterinarian."

"For a minute I forgot that you weren't."

"This is the first time I've had the pleasure of such a delivery."

"You're kidding," she said. "You were so calm, I thought you might be bored."

"Never," he laughed, drying his hands on a rag hanging in the rear of the stall. "But even if I had delivered a foal every day for a year, I don't think it would cease to astonish me." He watched the foal nuzzle his mother's teat for nourishment. "Though it would have been exciting enough without the breech." He smiled at her, and even in the dimly lit barn she could see the gold flecks in his eyes: eyes that looked as wide and curious as Danny's.

"By the way, it's good to see you, after all this time." He held out his hand to grasp hers.

She laughed and the sound echoed throughout the old cedar building. "I feel like I really know you, but we hardly exchanged a word on the one occasion we met."

She recalled the frantic day at the hospital: Annie in labor, Mark distracted, the sight of a newborn baby son.

He nodded his head. "If I hadn't already felt that way, from all Annie's said about you, I'd feel it now. Funny how emergencies bring people close." He watched the foal suck from its mother, already an expert. "Come on, let's get Daniel. He shouldn't miss seeing this."

She followed him out of the barn. It was a still, clear night, the moon bright above the treetops. They crossed the expansive lawn up to the neighbor's house without talking, each filled with the vivid experience of the birth.

Annie and Danny were in the kitchen, drinking hot chocolate with Mrs. Colby. Both women looked calmer now.

"You are the proud—what? Owner of a beautiful little colt."

"Dr. Abrams, bless you. How's Belle?" asked the middle-aged woman.

"Glowing with pride. Come on and see her. Yes, you can come too, Daniel." He opened the door for her, and Danny ran to his side.

Seeing the boy in the presence of his father confirmed the similarity Vanessa had always imagined. Except for the blond silky hair he had inherited from Annie's side of the family, his other features had been passed on directly through Mark. The boy's dark, questioning eyes, one minute serious beyond his years, the next mischievous, were decidedly his father's. They shared the same strong brow line and ridged nose. Mark's full lips parted frequently in a smile, revealing a row of white, even teeth. Even an expression she had thought unique to Danny was instead an attempt to mimic his father's look of bemusement. She had remembered that Mark was taller than Annie, but that he surpassed her own five feet, ten inches pleased Vanessa, made her feel less imposing in their company.

Annie and Vanessa trailed after them back over the lawn, listening to the talk rising out of the darkness.

"I don't know how to thank, you," Mrs. Colby continued. "I felt just awful barging in on you, but I didn't know what else to do. I couldn't reach the vet."

"You did the right thing. A breech can kill both the mother and the unborn if you're not prepared to help."

Annie whispered to Vanessa, "I wish he wouldn't speak so candidly when Danny can hear."

Vanessa squeezed her friend's hand. "Oh, he's probably not even listening, and what he hears must float right over his head. I wouldn't worry."

Annie disagreed. "You think he's a baby still, but at five they not only hear everything, but most of it gets repeated. Last week he asked me what an orgasm was."

Vanessa stifled her laughter. "What did you tell him?"

Annie's indignation failed, and she giggled in spite of herself. "I told him I thought it was like a fuzzy feeling —a glow all over. Later I found out he was asking about an *organism,* something he'd picked up listening to Mark lecture a group of interns."

"Oh, look," Vanessa exclaimed. She pointed the flashlight into the barn, and there, resting side by side, were the happy twosome.

The foal clambered to his legs to receive his audience, but the mother didn't stir.

"I don't blame her for not moving," Annie sympathized.

"You can come close," Mark told his son, "but don't scare him. There—"

The foal licked the palm of his hand, and tried to suck on the boy's finger.

"Ick!" he said, pulling his hand away and wiping it on the leg of his corduroys. "Why did it do that?"

"He doesn't know who his mother is yet," Mark explained. "All he knows is that he's hungry."

The colt's legs folded beneath him, and he collapsed beside his mother and closed his eyes to sleep.

"That looks like a good idea," Mrs. Colby said, covering a yawn with the back of her hand.

"Which reminds me—come along, young man," Annie said firmly.

"Ah, Mom, 'Nessa just got here."

"Remember your promise. . ."

He nodded, hanging his head.

"Come on, let's *all* go home," Vanessa said, taking his hand and steering him out of the barn. At the door they stopped to look back at the nestling animals. "Looks like they would like some privacy."

***

"'Nessa, are you awake?"

She opened her eyes. Danny peered over the edge of the bed at her, his own eyes as bright as sunlight, at an hour when Vanessa was reluctant to wake.

"What time is it?" she asked sleepily. She and Annie had stayed up talking nearly till dawn. She felt as though she'd just closed her eyes.

Danny studied the hands of the clock before answering. "It's nine thirty, I think."

She rolled over onto her back. "Guess I should be getting up," she said, shielding her eyes from the faint morning light.

His eyes lit conspiratorially. "We can play with my puppets!"

"Is your mom up?" she asked, still foggy.

"No, not yet."

"Your dad?"

He shook his head negatively.

"Maybe I'll sleep a little longer," she said, glancing over at the clock beside her bed. "Honey, it's only a quarter to six."

His mouth twitched. "Guess I read the hands wrong." Disappointment clouded his eyes. "I don't have anyone to play with."

"Honey, it's too early to play, but— if you'll lie quietly"— she lifted the covers to invite him in—"you can get into bed and cuddle with me."

He scampered up over the edge of the high bed and dived under the covers. Snuggling into her arms, he squirmed to get comfortable against her warm body.

"Shhh," she reminded him.

The last thing she was aware of, as she drifted back into sleep, was his body beside hers, rigid with an attempt to lie still.

CHAPTER FIVE

"Have you thought about what kind of work you'll do in the city?" Mark asked.

Annie slid three strips of bacon onto the plate next to the cheese omelette. "She hasn't decided yet—"

Danny was pulling on her sleeve. "Mom?"

"Get into your seat and don't interrupt."

Vanessa put down her coffee cup and answered Mark's question. "Annie's right. I really haven't had time to do more than worry. I have a number of people to contact, and several offers for work. But for now, if I want to keep my sanity, I'm only looking ahead as far as finding a place to hang my clothes."

"That's a job in itself," Annie said.

She nodded, accepting a piece of toast from Annie. "Sit down, eat," she urged her friend. She hated to have Annie wait on her.

Annie returned to the stove and dished out a plate of eggs for herself. "I remember when I first moved north. Mark was sharing a one-room apartment with another resident at Columbia. I would have been lost if we'd had to look for a place."

"What did you do?" she asked, looking from one to the other.

Annie took her seat beside her son.

"We stayed with Philip."

"Who?"

"My brother," Mark answered, simply.

Annie elaborated. "He has an enormous apartment over-looking the Hudson, on Riverside Drive—"

Mark interjected, "Why, Phil is the perfect solution to Vanessa's problems." He sipped his coffee. "My brother has this huge apartment, and he's hardly ever in it. Phil's a consultant for Ives. Which means he spends most of his time traveling. He spends about one weekend a month in Manhattan."

"If that much," Annie added.

Vanessa was beginning to understand the idea. "I could always make myself scarce if he came home."

"You wouldn't have to worry. His apartment is so big he'd never know you were there, unless you happened to meet him in front of the refrigerator."

"With crime being what it is in the city, I'm sure he'd be grateful to have his apartment occupied," Annie contributed.

"It certainly would make my life easier if I didn't have to look for an apartment right away." She could stay in Mark's brother's apartment and, at her leisure, search for a place of her own. "Why, I'd be free to start worrying about work right away!"

"I'll call Phil. I'm sure he'll agree."

How relieved she felt as she finished her omelette. "What do you all do around here on Sundays?"

Danny answered first. "Sometimes we go swimming at the quarry, and sometimes we play softball in the Wehrle's field, and sometimes we fly kites at the schoolyard."

"I like to lie in the hammock with the *Times*," Mark

answered for himself.

"But he doesn't read," his son shrieked. "He lies there with his eyes closed, humming."

"Can't a man have a simple secret around here?"

"No!" Vanessa and Annie chorused their answer.

"Apparently not," he agreed, trying to look stern at his son.

"How do you spend your Sundays?" she asked Annie.

She pointed to Danny. "Sometimes we go swimming at the quarry and sometimes . . ."

"Don't forget to call Philip," she shouted at the hammock as they were on their way to the car. "Hurry, now," she said to her son. "I told Joshua we'd pick him up by noon."

"Who's Joshua?" Vanessa asked, fastening a seat belt over Danny's lap.

"My bestest friend," the boy reported.

"It's better to bring a friend along for him," Annie explained. "It will give us time to talk, and if I watch Joshua today, his mother might invite Danny over during the week."

"Clever idea."

"When it works."

They drove through the green hills and into an ash forest, Danny amusing his friend with "knock-knock" riddles. Before they could repeat the "Boo," "Boo Who?" "Why are you crying?" for a fourth time, Annie had turned off the highway, down a tire-track dirt road to the end of a path.

Danny and Joshua ran straight for the water while Vanessa helped Annie spread a blanket on the shore.

"This place is gorgeous!" she said, glancing across the water to a towering rock wall. Across the top of it a group of boys lined up to dive into the clear, deep water. The braver the boy, the more flamboyant the dive, she noticed. She watched a skinny adolescent take off backward and do a double flip before slicing the water with hardly a ripple. A second boy, several years younger and at least thirty pounds heavier, brought shouts of laughter from his peers as he held his knees to his chest and cannon-balled into the center of the pool.

Vanessa looked at Danny playing at the edge of the pond, his attention directed to the pebbles in his hand rather than the older boys across the water. They wouldn't have to worry about him today, or even next year, but before long he'd get up his nerve to ask, and she wondered how Annie would handle his request.

Vanessa glanced around at the rest of the pond. "I'd love to photograph the quarry some morning before the crowd sets in. It must be a magnificent light, reflecting off the rocks, against the water." She studied the tall reeds around the far bank, a murky grass sprouting at the edge of the water. "This certainly is beautiful country you live in."

Annie glanced around as she unbuttoned her blouse to reveal a navy blue bathing suit. "After six months of winter the warmth is a welcome change."

"Six months?"

"Well, actually, it's only five, but it feels much longer. We get our first snow sometime after Thanksgiving, and the ground doesn't thaw until late April. If you're locked inside day after day with a five-year-old who doesn't know how to amuse himself, it feels like an eternity."

Vanessa looked down to the water. Danny and Joshua were trying to float on their backs, but without much luck. Instead of putting their heads back into the water, they kept watching each other, and their feet sank to the bottom.

"I would think he'd keep *you* entertained."

Annie sighed deeply. "Oh, *I know* he's cute and everything, but I've been with him almost every day now for five—nearly six—years. That's a long time to stay amused."

Vanessa shrugged. "I don't know if I'd ever get bored," she speculated, watching her godson hold his friend's feet afloat.

"You would, I assure you," Annie told her with certainty. "A few days is very different from five years." Vanessa didn't look convinced, so Annie continued. "It takes twice as long to do the simplest thing with him trailing after me. And in the winter, forget it! When I need to go out, it's twenty minutes getting him dressed warmly enough, another twenty minutes to get the car started and out of the driveway, that is if Mark has remembered to have someone clear the snow. The roads are dangerous when they are icy, which makes me nervous for Danny's welfare. The salt they put on the roads ruins the soles of his boots, and there is no way to keep him from tramping snow into the house, or Mark either, for that matter. Last January I wanted to take a course at the college to finish my degree, but I couldn't find a baby-sitter because no one wants to risk the road out to the house when there is a bad storm."

"Sounds horrible. Why do you stay up here if you and Mark don't enjoy the winter? Couldn't he practice elsewhere?"

"I said *I* didn't like it. Mark thrives in the cold. He cuts wood for the stove, builds fires, snowmen. He loves to ski."

"That's how the Norwegians get through their long winters. Do you know how to ski?"

She shook her head. "The speed scares me, and I'm afraid I'll lose control. Maneuvering through a winter would be impossible if I were to break a leg." She shivered at the thought. "Last Christmas Mark bought Danny a toboggan—I thought I'd die for worry."

"Cross-country skiing is slow and fairly safe," Vanessa suggested, a little surprised by Annie's tone. She had always been cautious, but never so nervous. "It's more like walking through a winter landscape."

"I tried it once," she conceded. "Mark bought me the equipment a few years ago, but the wind was murder on my skin. If the sun was shining, I got sunburnt; if it was cold, my skin chapped: It's just easier to stay inside. I curl up on the couch with a book, if Danny will let me, and read."

"You always loved to read," she recalled. "That must be a luxury."

She thought a minute. "Funny, there was a time when I would have given anything for six months to sit with my books, but now, well, now even reading doesn't satisfy me, not with all the distractions I have. Even the bits of writing I've found time to do haven't inspired me. I guess I'm just not meant to like the winter."

"Well, no need to worry about it now," Vanessa instructed, taking a look at the lush green scenery surrounding them. "It isn't winter anymore. I've never seen a bluer sky, and the air is so sweet, I swear you could bottle it."

Annie followed her friend's gaze out over the pool of sparkling water. The sun had turned it from blue to silver, a spread of diamond crystals across the smooth surface. She could feel the sun's rays against her skin, but for some reason they didn't warm her, any more than the vibrant June colors dimmed her persistent vision of winter's barren white. Inside, she still felt cold, as frozen as the Arctic landscape that had kept her locked inside for months on end. Then, she had thought that spring would remedy her claustrophobia, that it would end the boredom and listlessness that accompanied winter. Yes, the spring was beautiful, she thought, but it had failed to renew her this year. Or the year before, she realized.

Was her complaint really with the seasons? Yet even as the question formed, she knew there was a deeper dissatisfaction festering in her life, and it was deep inside of her.

She had been waiting for freedom to come with the seasons. With alarm she understood that she had been letting time slip by while she had been growing more miserable every day. If she wanted things changed, it would have to be she who acted, she thought resolutely, but at the same time the idea frightened her. Was there anything she could do? Wasn't her role defined by her family? If she were to make a change, what would that mean to Mark? What would she do with Danny? He started school in the fall. . . would that make a real difference in the way she felt?

"I hadn't realized how late it had gotten," she said frantically, and stood up, gathering up her belongings as she glanced at her watch nervously. "I promised Mark I'd cook an early supper, so he'd have time to make a house call. Danny!" she called to her son. "Time to go home."

CHAPTER SIX

"Aw, let him have it." Mark winked at his wife.

"Yeah, be a sport," chimed Vanessa. They had been teasing Annie all through dinner. "If he gets a stomachache, at least he'll know why."

"All right," she said, and reluctantly took a piece of corn from the bowl and laid it beside the four empty cobs on her child's plate. "You all make me feel like Simon Legree," she added, and pushed away her plate.

"You did the right thing, honey," her husband answered, pushing his empty plate to one side, sated.

"Not only did you cook us a delicious meal," Vanessa said, wiping her lips with a napkin, "but you are a most accommodating hostess."

"Well, I just hope you all have room for dessert. I made a blueberry cobbler," she said proudly, then stopped. Her smile disappeared, to be replaced by a look of dread. "Oh, God, how could I have forgotten?"

"What is it, Ann?" Mark asked, bothered by her sudden upset.

"I forgot the ice cream!" Danny groaned, but Vanessa hurried to reassure her. "We don't need ice cream *and* cobbler."

Annie disagreed. "Without ice cream, a blueberry cobbler isn't any good," she insisted, shaking her head. "It's too dry. I made a trip into town especially for ice cream.

I'm getting absentminded."

"Senile," Mark teased.

Water filled her eyes, and a silence fell over the table. She was obviously too upset for the good-natured ribbing they had been giving her.

"No big deal," Vanessa told her. "I can walk into town and bring some back. I'd like to see what the town looks like anyway."

"I'll drive you in," Mark suggested. "I have to stop in on a patient," he said, standing from the table, "but that will only take a second."

"As long as you're going . . . maybe I should stay and help Annie with the dishes."

Annie waved her away. "You go with him, and make sure he doesn't linger any longer than he has to. With Mark, a bed check can turn into a major social event." With that the two went out the back door to where the car was parked.

She couldn't say why, but Vanessa felt an unexpected burst of energy as they drove through the tree lined street of Sherbroke. People recognized the car and waved. Mark pulled over to the side of the road to ask a man watering his lawn how he was doing after his hernia operation.

At the stop sign at the center of town an elderly lady walked over to thank him for the lecture he had given, "Ten Ways to Avoid Cardiac Arrest."

"She's the town Gray Panther," Mark explained. "She intimidates me into telling our senior citizens things *she says* they need to know."

"Do you know everybody in town?"

"Except for the ones who just moved here, and a few

recluses, I believe I do."

She had always felt a little awkward whenever people had recognized her father, but somehow this was different. The attention Mark received was personal: it went both ways. Fame brought another kind of recognition—from people who didn't know you, but only your reputation. Vanessa couldn't really say which was more impressive, but where Clemens had been greeted with awe, Mark was received with both respect and affection.

"I guess you might say that I'm a big fish in a little pond," Mark smiled.

"How do you measure those things when you're dealing with people?"

"That's true." Mark looked at her more closely. He was beginning to understand why his wife valued Vanessa so much as a friend. She had a way of speaking to the heart of a matter. "I had the opportunity to do my residency at Columbia Presbyterian. I could have become a Park Avenue doctor, complete with my own stockbroker, tennis club, and condominium."

"So, why didn't you?"

"Good question," he answered. "Doesn't sound so bad to most people, and maybe it isn't. But up here I see the people I care for on the street every day. I know their fathers and mothers, their sons and daughters. I have an opportunity to affect their lives in a hundred small ways, which would be impossible under other conditions."

"Don't you get tired of caring for so many people?"

"If I did, I'd be in the wrong profession, wouldn't I?"

"No. But you might be a Park Avenue doctor," She smiled.

"Just so." He was amused. "But I'd rather be up here

61

with the horses, instead of down there with the asses."

"Then you like it here?"

"More than that, Vanessa. It's home."

"And Annie?" She tried to voice something that was troubling her.

"She has a harder time.... I thought she'd be happy living in Vermont, but she has never settled in, really."

"She told me this afternoon that she doesn't like the winters much."

"No, they're hard on her. By February she's restless for spring. I hope to take a few weeks off next year. A trip to Florida will break up the monotony for her."

Vanessa nodded thoughtfully. "Danny starts school this fall, doesn't he?"

"He does," he answered proudly. "We'll go south during his Christmas vacation."

"That should make the winter less strenuous for Annie," Vanessa added.

'He's an active child, all right. Up until now he's required a great deal of her attention."

"But he's an absolute treasure—"

"I know." He looked at her appreciatively. "I feel the same way." He paused. "It hasn't been easy for her," he admitted, "but it is getting better. She wants to take courses next fall at the college in Bennington. I told her to hire someone to help with the housework. She needs to keep her mind active, develop some new friendships. I see things getting better for her."

He sounded more hopeful than assured, thought Vanessa. But she hoped he was right. In any case, one thing was sure: Vanessa had never run into any man as caring and open, as warm as he was. Annie might want more in her life—Vanessa couldn't argue with that—but she hoped her friend appreciated what a fine mate she had.

She thought about the men she had known, the college flirtations, the emotional con-men she had met as Clemens's daughter through the capitals of Europe. They had about as much depth as a mirror image.

"And you, Vanessa?"

"What?"

"Your life. How are you doing?"

She thought for a minute. It was difficult to fight back the urge to tell him, but she did. If she had spoken candidly, she would have told Mark that for the first time in her life she was at a crossroads. Terrified, without the certainty of a direction. Instead she heard herself telling him: "I'll settle in New York for a while, and try to set up a studio." She hadn't seriously considered the possibility until that moment. Her words surprised her but she didn't amend them.

"A studio on your own?"

He had put his hand on a nerve. She felt a fluttering in her stomach before repeating, "Yes, on my own."

"That sounds exciting."

"I'm sure it will be." She tried to sound unconcerned. "Once I've had a chance to catch my breath."

"I hope you'll consider our home yours, also. The fact that you're near means a great deal to Annie." He paused. "And to me, too."

"Thank you, Mark." She smiled. His dark, rugged looks seemed almost delicate just then.

They drove around a traffic circle past a row of white houses on one side, a white church about a hundred eighty degrees opposite that, and into the main street. Mark pulled the car up in front of the general store.

"The butter pecan," he whispered, "is out of this world."

It was a real country store, with penny candy, copper pots, storm lanterns, and the most exotic selection of ice cream Vanessa had ever encountered. They picked up a pint of Mark's coveted butter pecan, and another pint of what sounded indescribably good to Vanessa—banana-rocky-road-fudge-ripple—which, Mark informed her, was his son's favorite, too.

"We'll take the back road to the Griffiths'," said Mark, sliding behind the wheel of his blue Toyota. "I'm teaching their little girl how to give herself insulin shots."

"Ouch."

"She's as brave as she is sweet."

They continued straight through town, down a hill, around a wooded bend, to follow an aqueduct running above a river with a stone bed. The sky was a dusky rose behind them; ahead, a sheaf of deep purples, bright yellows, and thin ribbons of oranges arched behind the tree line.

"A nice place you live in, Doctor."

"I'm glad you like it."

A half mile farther on they made a right into a long field, then another right beyond a cow barn.

"The Griffiths are fine people," Mark told her. "Unfortunately Mr. Griffiths got laid off at the lumber mill this year, so things have been a little rough for them. You'd never hear a word of complaint. Great dignity, these Yankees."

"What will he do?"

64

"Mr. Griffiths? Oh, he'll do odd jobs, whatever he has to do until the mill starts hiring again. It happens like that up here."

They stopped in front of an old Colonial matchbox house that practically leaned on a huge maple tree. The front porch and window frames were badly in need of paint, but the grounds around the house were well kept. Even in the fading light she could see that the property extended far behind the house, sloping down into a forest.

"Doctor, come in, come in." A woman in her forties, with salt-and-pepper hair, called from the porch. The few lines on her face were deep, but her cheeks glowed like polished apples, and she wore a clean, starched apron around her ample middle.

"I hope we didn't take you away from your dinner."

"Oh, no. George and I were just watching the news. George!" she called, leading them down a hall, past the kitchen, into the living room.

"Doctor, hello. Mrs. . . . " a man with hair almost as gray as her father's stood up to greet them.

"Vanessa," she shook his hand.

"Please, have a seat," Mrs. Griffiths told them. "Nora's in her room. I'll get her for you, Doctor."

"That's all right. Point me in the right direction, and I'll find her."

Mark disappeared with Mr. Griffiths, and Mrs. Griffiths brought out a cup of tea and a plate of homemade cookies. Vanessa answered her questions, but quickly turned the inquiries back to her hostess. She wanted to know about the woman, and how she liked living in a small town.

"Well, dear, our news isn't as spectacular as it is in the big cities," she said, pointing to the newscaster's announcement of a bombing in London. "But up here you know everyone, so the local news is very interesting." They listened to the sounds of girlish laughter escaping from the distant bedroom, followed by Mark's voice saying something indistinguishable. "He's a blessing, the finest," she went on to tell her. "Why, I stopped worrying about my baby Nora when Dr. Abrams moved to Sherbroke."

By the time the weatherman was telling them that tomorrow would be clear and cool in the mid-seventies, Mark returned, holding the hand of his young patient.

Nora had black hair and chestnut eyes and was about eight years old. When Mark introduced her to Vanessa, the child met her gaze directly.

"How are you, Nora?" asked Vanessa, enjoying the girl's radiance.

"I'm good," she announced resolutely, "and I can give myself the shots now, can't I, Dr. Abrams?"

"She's a professional," he proudly reaffirmed. "Next patient I have to teach, I'm sending Nora in my place."

"Doctor, we really appreciate all you've done." Mrs. Griffiths took his hand rather than shook it.

"What do we owe you, Doc?" Her husband cautiously opened his wallet.

"Don't worry, I'll send you a bill."

"That's what you said the last time."

"It's on the cuff, George."

The man accepted the generosity without a crush to his pride. "When I return to work, I'll stop by."

"That sounds fine to me."

When they reached the front door, Nora jumped up and hugged Mark before he could leave, and again Vanessa was impressed by the genuine warmth he generated wherever he went.

Mark checked his watch when they were back in the car. "That didn't take too long. We should make it home by eight thirty."

"That little girl," whispered Vanessa, "was precious."

"Isn't she, though." Mark seemed pleased by Vanessa's appreciation of the child. "I think she's very special."

"I'd love to shoot her."

"What?"

She laughed. "Photograph her. You know, do a session with her."

Mark laughed nervously. "Perhaps that could be arranged. She seemed to like you."

"Doesn't she like everybody?"

"No, not everybody. But she wants to like everybody."

"Yes." Vanessa understood. "That's what's so moving about her." She thought about Danny. He was younger by several years, but the expressions on his face were already more guarded. Not that he didn't want to like everybody, but that it was more important for everybody to like him. He lacked Nora's confidence, and the thought of it hurt Vanessa deeply, almost as if the pain were her own; as if, at some time in her life, her confidence had been shaken in a similar way. What did he have to guard against?

* * *

"What took you guys so long?" Danny inquired.

67

"We had to see Nora. And why haven't you got your slippers on, young man?"

Danny, in Superman pajamas, disappeared into his room to find his slippers.

"Hope we're not too late," Mark said, coming up behind his wife and kissing the top of her head.

Annie slid out from under his touch, and moved to the counter where she had the desserts laid out. She opened the bag and removed the two containers of ice cream.

"Didn't you get any vanilla?" she asked, pure misery pouring out of her question.

"No, should we have?" Mark asked, puzzled.

Vanessa busied herself taking spoons from the drawer, unsure why her friend's voice was shaky.

"Blueberries taste terrible with this syrupy stuff," she said, "and it's *melted!*" Unable to contain her disappointment, she left the desserts and ran to her bedroom.

Danny appeared wearing his sneakers, the shoelaces untied and dragging. "I couldn't find my slippers," he explained, and looked from his father's stunned face to his godmother's pursed lips. "Where's Mommy?"

"She's gone to the bathroom," Vanessa lied. "Do you want your dessert now?"

It was a silly question. She held out the two containers of half-melted ice cream for him to choose from. He pointed to the swirl of chocolate and marshmallows. "Or"—he hesitated—"maybe I should have some of both."

She put a little of each kind into the two bowls of cobbler and sent Mark and his son to the den while she went to find Annie. "Are you okay?" she asked finding her friend examining her face in the bathroom mirror.

She shook her head, continuing to study herself. "I'm

so ashamed. I invited you up for some peace and quiet, and now all my troubles spill out."

"It's all right," responded Vanessa. "You don't have to hide from me. Maybe I can help."

"Why am I upset by such silly things?"

A thought occurred to Vanessa. "Annie, could you be pregnant?"

Annie shook her head. "I'm due to start my monthly."

Vanessa looked at her sadly. The circles under Annie's eyes were deep, the skin around her mouth blemished, her hair lacked luster, and there was no trace of the joy that Vanessa had always envied in her. "I just wish you were happy," she said softly, putting her arms around her friend's shoulders. For a minute they held the embrace, Vanessa swaying slightly, almost rocking. "Tell me what's wrong," she encouraged.

Annie forced a weak smile. "I wish I knew. . . . I had such high hopes that I'd feel better as soon as you came to visit, but instead I only remember that I used to be a happier person."

"And you will be, again."

"Promise?" Annie asked skeptically.

Vanessa laughed. "Of course, didn't I just promise you?"

Annie smiled faintly.

"That's better," Vanessa prompted. "Now come and have some dessert. My very best friend made it, and it's sure to be delicious."

"I'll even have some of that wretched-looking ice cream."

Mark carried Danny piggyback to bed. When he returned to the den, Annie was building a fire in the woodstove, and Vanessa had finished her dessert and was relaxed on the sofa, examining a book of photographs by Rolof Benny called *Ruins of the Ancient World*.

"A little cognac before bed?" suggested Mark. The problem, whatever it had been, seemed past now. He could talk to Annie about it later. He saw no reason to spoil any more of the evening.

"I could use a splash," Vanessa said, and Annie agreed. He went to the sideboard, filled three snifters with Martell's, and passed them to the women.

"To a lovely home," Vanessa toasted them, "and the special people in it."

"To the return of my friend." Annie raised her glass, hoping to convey her deep feeling with the gesture.

"Welcome," Mark added simply, sipping the warm amber liquid.

Vanessa inhaled the vapors, relieved to see Annie's face start to relax. Even if the tightness around the mouth hadn't disappeared entirely, at least the terror in her eyes had quieted, and once again she saw the girl she had always loved and admired.

She watched a smile lighten at something Mark said. Taking a seat beside him, Annie let her hand rest on his shoulder, and Mark looked easier, too. This was how Vanessa had pictured her friend's marriage: warm and caring; close, in front of a glowing fire, in the comfort of a beautiful home. Suddenly Vanessa felt out of place, as though she didn't belong here at all. Her urge to flee was so intense that she all but forced herself to remain seated until the liquor was gone from her glass, before she could casually make an excuse to leave.

"I'm awfully tired," she said, putting her glass down

and covering a feigned yawn with the back of her hand.

"One last swallow to help you sleep?" Mark asked, already on his feet.

She held up her hand to discourage him. "I don't think I'll have any trouble sleeping tonight. I crossed the Atlantic by ship, but I feel as if I've got jet lag."

"Danny woke you this morning, didn't he?" Annie smiled, thinking she understood. "I should go to bed, too," she added, and gave her husband a nudge in the ribs. Feel like coming to bed?" she asked.

"That's the best offer I've had all day," he teased. "I'll be right in," he told Annie, finishing the last drop in his glass.

"Good night, Mark," Vanessa said, rising and extending her hand. Turning to Annie, she kissed her friend's downy cheek. "Sleep well," she added, before turning to go from the room. At the doorway she paused. "See you in the morning," she added, as if to postpone the exit she had been so impatient to make.

Mark closed the doors to the woodstove and looked up. "Yes, see you tomorrow, Vanessa."

In her room she undressed and got into bed. Turning out the lights, she tried to force herself to sleep, but the command didn't last more than a few minutes. Lying awake in the dark, she became aware of a whisper emanating from the bedroom across the hall. A trickle of laughter, like a small stream of water down a rock, ran through her wakefulness, and made her unbearably lonely. She imagined them in bed together, touching . . . embracing . . . a tenderness turning passionate. She wished now that she had accepted that last glass of brandy. She needed something to cloud her mind, to dull her emotions.

A strain of resentment sprang out of her loneliness. She had no doubt that Annie had a demanding life, but she also had rewards: to be held close by such a man was worth a great deal. Her friend was, in fact, a most fortunate woman, and she didn't seem to appreciate it. If she, Vanessa, had been raised differently, if she'd had a more normal childhood, perhaps she might have shared her life with such a man, been a mother to a child like Danny.

That was not her luck. She might find refuge here for a while, but she'd have to be careful not to let her fantasies roam in a direction she couldn't follow. She had her own life to live, and soon she'd have to start making decisions about the direction she wanted it to go.

Her thoughts were interrupted once again by muffled voices and a culmination of activity. In another few minutes the voices ceased, and the only sounds were the creaking of an old house contracting on an unseasonably cool summer's night: the occasional gurgle in the plumbing, the groan of the porch swing, the wind against the windowpanes. She shifted under the covers, wishing she could lose her thoughts to dreams. *They* are fast asleep, she thought, and pictured them content and curled in each other's arms, like two fitted parts of a puzzle.

But where did she fit in?

CHAPTER SEVEN

Vanessa woke with a start from a dream that had unnerved her. Though she shook her head to dislodge it, the dream spilled into her consciousness like white morning light pouring through the open window. It wasn't cold, but she shivered beneath the quilts, feeling inappropriately dark and haunted in the midst of the sunlit guest room.

The details of the dream—or nightmare, actually—were vivid. Danny had been sitting on her lap, whispering something in her ear. She whispered back, "I love you, too," but when she turned to kiss and hug him, she found herself holding Mark. And the kiss he gave her wasn't sweet or innocent. Nor was her response. Their embrace was fierce, albeit brief, before a censor—a voice rebuking her—broke them apart. Vanessa pushed Mark away, tore herself from him, and ran to find Annie, to beg forgiveness. Breaking out of her dream, finding herself in her best friend's home, she felt sick. She wanted to run away. Disappear. Hide before Annie discovered her disloyalty.

Vanessa leaped out of bed, disgusted with herself, but once on her feet she reacted more calmly. Yes, she felt guilty, she thought, wrapping herself in her bathrobe. But it was only a dream. She hadn't actually stolen Annie's husband from her. In truth she hadn't done anything at all, other than flirt with him in her imagination. She wasn't going to punish herself long over that: she wasn't a puritan, after all. If she found herself acting out her fantasies, *then* she would worry. For now all she had to do was make sure her nighttime dreams didn't translate into daytime realities.

She was glad she didn't run into anyone on her way to the bathroom. By the time she stepped out of the shower, the lecture she had been giving herself was beginning to sink in. Okay, she'd had a bad dream. Probably meant she should be a little less playful with Danny, now that he was almost six. And if she found herself dreaming of Mark, well, he was a handsome man, and she was glad for Annie. It might be a little peculiar for her to wonder what she'd feel like in Annie's place, but hadn't they been playing that game for as long as they had known each other? That was a basic ingredient of their friendship. Annie had always had what Vanessa wanted, and vice versa. Not that either of them would have actually traded, if that had been possible, but to dream . . . that filled out their lives. Vanessa might never marry. It might not be in the cards for her. She wasn't going to dispute fate, but she still could have her dreams.

Grabbing a T-shirt from her suitcase, she threw it over her head and stepped into a pair of jeans. Pulling up the tight-fitting denim, she buttoned them before leaning out the window to check the weather. The sun was already hot, and there was no breeze. The newscaster had been wrong. Just as quickly as she had dressed, she exchanged her jeans for a pair of khaki shorts. Before she left the room, she ran a brush through her thick hair, and pulling it back with an elastic, she let it hang long in a ponytail.

Annie had left a note in the kitchen. She was out shopping. Would be back in an hour. Breakfast was in the refrigerator and on the stove. Annie didn't need to tell her to make herself at home. Vanessa knew that was what she was expected to do. Really the only way a long visit could be successful was if one made oneself part of the family.

She heated coffee and spooned wedges of melon into a smaller bowl while the pancake batter cooked on the grill. Juicy, plump cranberries protruded out of the bubbling dough. She wondered if Danny had gone into town with Annie, and a tremor of guilt surfaced when she thought that she might be left at home alone with Mark. What would she say to him? How could she face him? He wasn't a mind reader, she reminded herself. Just because she had dreamed of him, didn't mean he'd had a similar dream of her. Besides, it was Monday, she remembered, and Mark was most likely in his office already.

Relaxed enough to chastise herself for senseless worry, she realized she was responding to imaginary problems. Yet even as she excused herself she knew that beneath her commonsense reasoning there were reasons to fret. Her dream continued to plague her, and the emotions it had stirred released new bouts of shame. She fluctuated between remorse and absolution until the sound of Danny's voice booming from out of doors drew her attention away from herself. Thank God for little distractions, she thought, as she carried her coffee into the sunlight. Danny spotted her from across the yard. "Come quick," he called to her, his voice hoarse trying to carry a whisper across the great distance. "Look what I found."

"What is it?" Vanessa asked quietly, bending down to sit with him in his hideaway beneath the sycamore tree.

Danny put his finger to his lips, warning her to be quiet; then, in the loudest whisper she had ever heard, he told her it was a dinosaur.

"A dinosaur?" her eyes widened as big as his own.

"That's right. I forget the kind of dinosaur, but I have a book in my room with all kinds of pictures. And my dad told me that lizards were tiny dinosaurs."

She nodded, amused.

"Did you know dinosaurs lived before there were cities?"

"They lived a long time ago," she answered. "Did you know that dinosaurs weren't very smart?"

He nodded enthusiastically. "Their brains were the size of peas," he reported. "That's why they shrunk. Now they are smart for their size." He scrunched his mouth, thinking. "This one is a *Tyrannosaurus rex,* I think."

"He's a beauty," she said, reaching forward to stroke the twin-striped length of its body.

Danny grabbed her arm. "Don't, you'll scare him away."

"It's okay," she promised. "He won't mind, if I'm gentle. Watch," she said, running an index finger under the lizard's belly, from his head to the tail, repeating the gesture.

Danny's eyes bulged, but the lizard's eyes were closed, its breathing quickened perceptibly. "He's in a kind of trance," she told him. "You can stroke him if you want."

He reached forward. "Gently," she reminded him.

The lizard opened his eyes and watched the boy stealthily, but seemed amenable to his attempts at gentleness. It was Danny who was nervous.

Vanessa lifted the lizard slowly into her hand, and laid it on her shoulder. "Now pat him," she coached again.

When he was holding the lizard himself, Danny suggested they show his dad. He kept his hand on the lizard's back as they crossed the yard.

"Isn't your father at the office?" she asked him.

"No," he answered, pulling open the side porch door and leading the way through the den. "He doesn't have to work until after lunch today."

Vanessa realized they were going to his study. Of course Annie wouldn't have left her son unattended. "Are you sure we are allowed to disturb him?" she worried, not entirely anxious to confront him just yet.

"Sure," he said, opening the door without knocking. "He says to come find him if anything important happens."

Mark stood to greet his two visitors. Catching her eye, he gave her a shy smile. "What's up, Daniel?"

"I found a reptile," he said proudly, "and 'Nessa taught me how to tame him." He drew his hand back from his shoulder to reveal the dazed lizard.

Mark paid his proper respects, though Vanessa deduced from the stack of material on the desk that he had been busy. She glanced around the room while Danny talked. It had the comfortable clutter of opened books and work in progress. Unlike the rest of the house, which benefited from Annie's sense of order, the furniture in Mark's study looked well-worn for comfort. On the other hand, instead of the casual clothes he'd worn all weekend—the faded navy-blue Harvard sweatshirt and grass-stained jeans—Mark now wore a buttoned-down Oxford shirt and dark trousers, the crease recently pressed. When she looked up at his face she thought she saw him blush, as Danny showed him how to stroke the lizard's back.

"He's a handsome specimen, there's no doubt. Where did you find him?"

He didn't seem to mind the interruption, Vanessa noticed. Rather, he seemed to encourage Danny to tell him. Vanessa wondered if he actually liked lizards. She watched the light shine in Danny's eyes as he showed his father again how to stroke the lizard into a trance, engraving the method into his young memory while he spoke.

"That sounds like your mother's car," Mark told him.

"Let's show her your pet?" Vanessa suggested.

Danny clenched his teeth, "No, she doesn't like lizards," he said worriedly. "I'm not s'pose to bring them inside the house, either."

"Then hurry out with it," his father prompted. Danny grabbed the stunned animal in both hands and ran toward the kitchen. "Take the side door," Mark called after him. Shrugging, he added to Vanessa, "No reason to upset her."

Vanessa nodded in agreement. At the door she turned to ask, "Are you interested in lizards because you like them, or because you are being a good father?"

He covered his surprise at her direct question with a smile. "A bit of both, I guess. *I do* happen to like lizards, but even more, I like my son. I guess I'm interested in what interests him."

She wondered about his answer on her way to the kitchen. Why had *she* been interested in the little animal when she had never cared—liked or disliked—lizards before? Being with Danny let her enjoy pleasures simply, on his level, and that felt purely good.

Mark meant something different, she thought. She could picture him as a boy, capturing lizards, making them his pets. Maybe that was what made him a good father, remembering his own boyhood pleasures.

In the kitchen she found Annie standing in front of the counter, staring into the grocery sacks.

"Need help unpacking?" Vanessa asked, not sure how to address the pained expression on her friend's face.

"That's okay," she said, without looking up.

"Is anything wrong?" she asked, taking a seat beside her, waiting for her friend to speak, though she herself didn't really feel like listening to a round of complaints just then. She was feeling temporarily overwhelmed by the pressures of her own life. "You've been gone a long time."

"I know," Annie said, pulling herself up out of her chair and unpacking a box of Lipton tea from the top. "There was a crowd at the supermarket." Her voice was flat, without energy, like a recorded message. "Mondays aren't usually busy, but I had to wait in line forever, it seemed, in both stores I went to." She was moving around the room, putting each item in its proper place. She swung open the refrigerator door and began stocking vegetables in the bin. "When I got to the parking lot, I found I had locked my keys in the car." She shook her head miserably. "I haven't done that since I was in college, and nervous about final exams."

"What did you do?"

"At first I didn't care much. We keep a spare key in a holder beneath the fender. Mark has a history of locking keys into the car when he's gone out on an emergency," she explained.

"I can imagine," she sympathized.

"Anyway, I fumbled around under the fender, but when I brought the holder out, the key wasn't in it. I was so mad, I wanted to dump all the groceries in the parking lot and walk away. I figured Mark must have forgotten to put it back. Or Danny had found it playing. I was ready to kill them both." She stopped fidgeting with the eggs. "Until I found I had the spare key in the bottom of my purse."

"Well, at least you found it." Something about the nature of Annie's complaint grated on Vanessa's nerves.

Annie shook her head dejectedly. "I didn't realize I had the key until *after* someone helped me break into the car with a coat hanger."

Vanessa studied her friend's face while she talked, but in fact, the words didn't matter, the face said it all. The mouth that could always turn quickly into a smile was now drawn with unarticulated anger. Her eyes looked worn, vaguely out of focus. "Annie," Vanessa interrupted, feeling guilty about wanting to dismiss her friend's complaints as trivial. "Tell me what's wrong. What's really bothering you?"

"I just feel so stupid right now."

"About the keys?" she asked, making the incident sound insignificant. "Can't you let yourself make a mistake?"

80

"It's not just the keys," she said, and the harshness in her face changed into sadness. "It's everything."

"Tell me," Vanessa urged, taking Annie's hand and leading her to the table.

She blinked several times in rapid succession and her eyes glistened, but no tears fell. "I don't know what to say. She let herself be guided back into the chair and Vanessa sat down beside her.

"What's happened?"

"I'm going crazy, Vanessa."

"Tell me."

Annie took a deep breath and started talking, her voice low and unsteady. "I was driving home from the store, down a road I've traveled hundreds of times, and I made a wrong turn."

"So?"

"I drove for several miles before I realized I had turned the wrong way." She burst into tears.

Vanessa patted her hand. "But that's no big deal—"

"I was almost to the highway before I knew what I'd done." She looked at her friend beseechingly. "And you know what?"

"What?" She waited.

"Even after I knew, I didn't turn around. I just kept on going. I didn't care whether I went to New York or Montreal. The point is"—she sniffed—"I just didn't want to come home."

CHAPTER
EIGHT

Tuesday was overcast; a heavy dew lay on the ground. The Toyota stalled when Mark stopped at the signal north of Main Street. He waved at Mr. Masters as the postman started his rounds. The general store was open already, and Mrs. Crocker, her key in the door of the pharmacy, waved back as he drove past.

Mark had worked hard to fit into the community, to feel as though he belonged, but it was as much a compliment to the natives of Sherbroke as to urban expatriates like himself that they accepted him as one of their own. As Daniel grew older, made friends in school, he'd be accepted as thoroughly as if he'd been born in Vermont. He hoped Annie, too, would find a niche in Sherbroke's community, eventually. At Pearl Street he made a left and pulled into the driveway of a white wooden house.

"Good morning, Dr. Mark," his secretary said, taking the coffee from the burner.

"Morning, Jane," he greeted her warmly as he walked past the desk, picked up his mail, and disappeared into his inner office. As doctors' offices went, it was a cheery space, more evocative of a study than an examining room. Behind his desk, light came through a bank of windows overlooking a backyard expanse of lawn. There was an imposing leather couch along one wall and medical books lined the others. Flowers crowded the window ledges and ferns in hanging ceramic pots cascaded down like light from the ceiling.

The examining table and the patients' bathroom adjoined the office. His instruments, also, were in the adjacent room. He preferred it that way. So did his patients, many of whom were youngsters, and easily frightened by the sight of a doctor's tools.

"Your coffee, Dr. Mark."

Jane pulled up a chair in front of his desk, spread her white uniform over her opaque-stockinged knees, and opened the appointment book. She waited until he had taken several sips of his coffee before reading off the schedule of morning appointments. This list did not include those who walked in unexpectedly, or the emergencies. Last week he had practically sewn on Charlie Nichols's index finger. The man's hand had slipped on a lathe, and he should have gone directly to Sherbroke's emergency room, but Mark's reputation was such that the injured workman would rather come to his office.

"Busy, but routine," he muttered, as Jane stacked the patients' files in order of their respective appointments on a far table.

"After your hospital rounds Mrs. Marsden will be in to get the results of her CT Scan. She couldn't come in this morning. "

"You know," he confided to his capable nurse, "I've studied her scan from every angle, and I can't find a thing wrong with her. It's very puzzling."

"Maybe it's all in her head," she suggested.

"Possibly," he mused. "Back pains and fevers of unknown origin certainly can be psychogenic, but I just don't believe that Mrs. Marsden is the type."

Mark slipped into his white coat. It was his one concession to medical formality. For the rest, his skills spoke for themselves. As a country doctor he knew the ins and outs of general practice far better than city doctors, most of whom chose to specialize. Mark could do everything from setting a bone to all but the most sophisticated of surgical procedures. Moreover, he prided himself on keeping up with the latest developments in internal medicine. If he had stayed in Manhattan, of course he might have made an affluent life for himself and his family by examining only ears, or eyes, or even kneecaps; but he would have been bored to death. He liked people and wanted to heal any part that ailed, not only the part that brought him the greatest income.

By eleven he had seen two children with inflamed tonsils, lanced an infected toe, and diagnosed a case of hives. A teenage girl he had known since her grade-school days received a tactful lecture on the wisdom of birth control, and how to guard against further cases of herpes. Once she got over her embarrassment, the girl thanked him profusely, telling him that if it weren't for him she didn't know what she would have done. Certainly, the hospital would have informed her parents, and she wouldn't have had that happen for anything. Mark suggested she try to discuss her feelings with her mother, or her pastor, but he knew enough about the world not to frighten her off, and invited her to come back if she couldn't find someone to talk to. After she left, he considered how difficult it must be for girls of that age, caught between their adult drives and the emotional needs of adolescence. But, then, life had a cornucopia of difficulties at all stages. Leaving childhood was just the first hurdle.

He was at Sherbroke Hospital by eleven thirty. On the second floor he picked up Mrs. Bidley's chart and found the octogenarian in room 211, sitting up in bed, her nose buried in an historical romance set on the Spanish Main.

"Hello, Dr. Abrams." She raised her snowy head.

"Good morning, Mrs. Bidley."

"Morning?" Her face broke into an intricate network of cobwebs when she smiled. "They woke me at six o'clock today. *That's* the morning. This is late afternoon."

"How does the hip feel?"

"Better than the other one. I made it as far as the desk in my walker."

"I'd call that progress."

"By next week I'll be jogging."

"Or jumping rope."

"I'm a tough old bird, Doctor."

"Indeed you are, Margaret." He took her by the hand and met her eye.

"You know, I had a dream last night," she told him, her ancient voice cracking. "My husband and my oldest son were standing in a dark hallway. My husband, Lou, said, 'we've been waiting for you, Margaret.' And I said, 'Lou, I'll be along soon enough, but I guess I'm just not ready yet.' "

Her head quivered as she stared at Mark.

"I don't believe there's a power in the world that could rush you into anything, Margaret." He leaned over and gave her a very unprofessional kiss on the forehead. "For selfish reasons, I'd like to keep you from Lou a little while longer."

He returned the chart to the nurse at the desk, and had started for the stairs, when he heard his name being paged over the public address. *"Dr. Abrams wanted in Emergency. Stat, Dr. Abrams, you're wanted in the Emergency Room."*

He hurried down the stairs, through a long tiled corridor, and through a swinging door just as a stretcher was rolled off the ambulance.

Dr. Glover, the young resident in charge of emergency, was waiting for him. "I'm glad you're here, Doctor." He put his hand on Mark's shoulder. "I've got an acute AP waiting for me in Surgery, and this just came in."

"What is it?" he asked as they approached the paramedics beside the stretcher. Mark's pulse started racing when he recognized Mr. Masters, the postman.

"Quick!" Mark yelled. "Wheel him into an operating room. I want blood . . . do we know his type yet? Nurse, an IV, quickly!"

"He's in shock, Doctor," one of the paramedics said as they rushed the unconscious man to the operating room.

"I can see that!" he said impatiently. "Nurse," he called to the young woman running beside them, "prepare fifty cc's of insulin."

The nurse nodded and hurried away.

"Do you know what happened?" Mark asked one of the attendants as they raced down the corridor.

"Mr. Masters was in his jeep, delivering the mail. A truck ran a stop sign and crashed into the jeep head on." Mark groaned, scrubbing his hands before pulling on sterilized gloves.

"The driver of the truck was unhurt—a Bennington

man—but they had to pry Mr. Masters out from under a crushed dashboard."

The postman was a mess. Even after they'd administered the insulin, his pulse rate began to flag.

"Blood pressure is falling," called out a technician.

"Heart rate, Doctor. We're losing the heartbeat."

Mark tried everything. At last, he administered a series of electric shocks, but they failed to revive the dying man. The damage was beyond repair. In addition to everything else, the postman had a ruptured spleen.

Mark walked out of the operating room, removed his mask and smock, and threw them in a laundry bin. In the dressing room he leaned his head against a locker. It was the same each time one of his patients died. Who did he think he was, to play God, to assume the power of life and death, only to be found helpless, wanting?

Mark forced himself into his jacket and out to his car. Was it this morning that he had waved at Mr. Masters? If only he had known, had been able to tell the postman not to go out today, to leave the mail undelivered. Certainly everyone would have foregone their mail for the day. That wasn't too great a price for the life of a man.

You are a fool, said a voice inside of him, and he drove the rest of the way to his office numb to his feelings.

Jane was out to lunch when he returned. Mark went directly into his office, opened the bottom drawer of his file cabinet, and poured three fingers of Jack Daniel's into a paper cup. It felt warm going down, and he needed something to fill the dreadful, resounding void. Another three fingers would numb his need to cry out, would melt the lump of sadness in his throat, but he hesitated: he had patients coming in this afternoon—nothing he couldn't handle with his eyes closed—but what if another emergency cropped up? He'd never stop blaming himself if something went wrong. The phone rang, and before he answered it, he returned the bottle to the drawer.

"Mark?" It was Annie. "Why didn't Jane answer the phone?"

"She's out to lunch still."

"Oh." She digested the news before continuing. "Listen, I told Mr. Gruen at the bank we'd be in today with last month's mortgage payment, but you forgot to take it this morning."

"Oh."

There was a pause on the other end of the line. "I've got the check right here, in an envelope. Can you pick it up?"

"No," he told her, "I'm alone in the office. Can't you bring it in?"

There was another silence. "With all I have to do today? I haven't begun the laundry, and we have no clean sheets. I've got to cook dinner, and find something to entertain Danny for the afternoon. Where do I have a spare minute?"

"I'm sorry, Annie, I just can't leave the office before three o'clock, and by the time my patients are gone, the bank will just about be closing."

"Can't you send Jane, when she gets back?"

"No, Ann. She's not our personal secretary. The mortgage payment will have to wait until tomorrow."

"I told Mr. Gruen I'd have it to him this afternoon. We're already two weeks late."

"Ann, I have patients waiting."

"Then, tend to your precious patients!"

He pulled the phone away from his ear before it hit the cradle on the other end, but he didn't feel anything approaching remorse. Her dissatisfaction was like a continuous ultra-frequency sound, almost inaudible, yet taking a measurable toll on his nervous system. He just couldn't deal with anything more today, and if that made him a failure, well, that's precisely how he felt already. He considered taking that second shot of Jack Daniel's, then thought better of it.

"Dr. Mark." Jane peeked into the room. "Mrs. Marsden is here."

"Send her in."

A dignified woman in her early fifties, Mrs. Marsden was a lady to the Manor born, and carried herself accordingly. Her husband had been the president of Marsden Electronics, an international corporation of which his wife was now the major stockholder. Her long, frosted hair hung down to her shoulders in thin, dry strands. Her fine cheekbones were so prominent that her face was almost skeletal. And she had a malaise that defied diagnosis, in addition to the fact that she was being eaten up by some ineffable sadness that Mark couldn't define. In spite of which, she maintained the dignity and carriage of a lady.

"How are the back pains, Mrs. Marsden?"

"The Percodan helps, Doctor. But I can still feel my lower back. And the fevers."

"I've studied the CT Scan, been over them with a fine-tooth comb, and I can't find anything, Mrs. Marsden. That doesn't mean there isn't something there, I just can't locate it."

"I see." She allowed herself a moment of thoughtfulness. "What do we do next?"

"I've called a colleague at Johns Hopkins. They have a special unit geared to deal with the diagnosis of fevers of unknown origin. How would you feel about spending a week in Baltimore?"

"I see no reason why I shouldn't."

"Good. Then I'll make the arrangements with Dr. Hartley."

"And if they don't come up with anything?"

"We'll cross that bridge when we come to it. They've had some past success with this kind of problem. Let's give them a chance."

"Thank you, Doctor. I'll await your call." Mrs. Marsden rose and extended her hand. "You know, you're a terribly patient man."

"How so, Mrs. Marsden?"

"Another doctor would have dismissed me as a neurotic, recommended I see a psychiatrist, or abandoned the whole case out of sheer frustration."

"Just because we have difficulty finding the cause doesn't mean it isn't there. I believe it is, and, what's more, I have every reason to believe we'll find it."

"Thank you, Doctor ".

He saw her eyes glaze over. After a minute he escorted her to the door.

He was relieved to see there was no one else waiting in the outer office. Returning to his desk, he put his head on his arms and at once fell into a deep, untroubled sleep.

* * *

The next thing he knew was the pressure of a hand

91

shaking him from his shoulder. When he opened his eyes, he found himself staring into the cocoa-brown eyes of his son.

"Danny, what are you—?"

"Hi, Dad. Did you have a good nap?"

"Yes, but—" He raised his head and saw Vanessa standing at the side of his desk.

"We decided to walk into town," she said. "Annie asked me to give this to you." She put a white sealed envelope down in front of him.

"You didn't have to go to all that trouble," he said, combing his fingers through his tousled hair, and hoping he didn't look too disheveled.

"No trouble," she assured him. "It gave us an excuse to take a walk."

"Terrific." Mark felt his spirits rise. He glanced at his watch. "Do you feel like a walk to the bank?" he asked, removing his white coat and tucking his shirt securely into his trousers. There was just enough time to get there, if they hurried. "Afterward we could stop for an ice-cream sundae at the drugstore."

"With bananas and sprinkles?" Danny asked excitedly. Mark nodded.

"I can't think of anything I'd rather do," Vanessa agreed.

They stopped in at the bank where a tall, bald, funereal man accepted the mortgage payment with the smile of an undertaker. At the drugstore counter the two adults sipped cherry phosphates while the child consumed a mammoth banana split in a matter of minutes. Back at the office Vanessa and Danny continued on their walk. Mark stood staring at traffic long after they had disappeared hand in hand down the street. What could he do to reroute his burgeoning feelings for this dark-haired beauty? Surely there was a way to accept her friendship without upsetting the precarious balance of his marriage.

"Hello, Phil?"

"Yes, is that you, Mark?" The voice was distinct in spite of the echo of an overseas connection.

"Yes—your secretary told me where I might reach you."

It was always a strain talking to his older brother. A successful consultant to the international corporate giants, Philip lived for money the way certain mathematicians lived for the equation that expressed some physical principle that couldn't be conveyed in words.

"You just caught me.... I leave Tokyo for Abu Dhabi in an hour. How are you, Mark?"

"Do you really want to know?"

"Sure"

"Lousy. I lost a patient this morning on the table."

"I'm sorry to hear that."

He believed his brother was, although his voice was as dry, emotionless as a bailiff's. Not that he begrudged Philip his way of life. Simply, he didn't understand it. Instead of emotions, his brother had a ledger in which he entered credits and debits. But Philip meant well. If there was something Mark needed that his brother could provide, there was no question that it would be forthcoming.

"Listen, Phil, I have a favor to ask."

"What is it?"

93

"Is your apartment in Manhattan going to be vacant for the next couple of months?"

"I don't think I'll be back until December, and then only for a week or so. Why do you ask?"

"Because there's a young woman staying with us, a friend of Annie's, who needs a place to live for a while. Her name is Vanessa Ansel."

"Any relation to the portrait photographer?"

"She's his daughter. And she'll water your plants, make sure no one breaks in, and record all your messages."

"I have an answering service." Philip paused to consider the proposition before agreeing. "If you say she's reliable, Mark, she can use the apartment. How long does she intend to stay?"

"Until she finds a place of her own, I guess."

"That could take months." He hesitated. He wouldn't mind the additional security. "Well, tell her she can use it for the rest of the year. I'll arrange to leave keys and instructions with the doorman."

"Thank you, bro'."

"By the way, Mark. I meant to phone you anyway." His brother's voice assumed a businesslike tone. "I got a bill from the cemetery yesterday. I sent them a check for two hundred dollars for the planting of yews around Mom and Dad's plot."

"I'll have a check in the mail to you tomorrow."

"Good, Mark. I'll talk to you when I return from Abu Dhabi,"

"Thanks, Phil."

"No problem. Don't forget that check."

In his Toyota, driving north on Route 6, Mark pictured his brother: tall, gaunt, almost bald, wearing a conservative, blue, three-piece suit. In Philip's world the books, had to balance. No matter how wealthy he became, and he must be worth a fortune, he expected Mark to absorb his half of the cemetery bill. It wasn't that Phil was ungenerous; rather, it was a question of balancing the ledger. What a convenience it must be to have the world reduced to such a reasonable set of principles. It was different in his world. Mr. Masters, who had been this morning, was now no more. How did you make the books balance on that one?

Suddenly he thought of Danny, saw the child's eager face over an ice-cream sundae, looking up at Vanessa as they'd bade him farewell at his office. He saw Vanessa's expression—kind and concerned when she'd leaned close to him and whispered, "I smell bourbon."

"It's been that kind of day," he had told her, and she had understood. She was becoming his friend as well as his wife's, and with all the people he had to comfort, he needed a friend, badly.

What a difference her compassion made! It helped to justify the figures where nothing else did. It didn't undo anything, but it softened the irrevocable, distributed the inevitable—made the grim reality that much more digestible for being shared.

If that was so, he thought as he pulled into the driveway, why was he so reluctant to return home?

CHAPTER NINE

"If you want to take pictures, you're welcome to come along with us," Mark offered, packing the gear into the trunk of the car.

"I'll show you how to fish," Danny volunteered, poking his head out of the front-seat window.

Mark raised his brows in question. "If you think you *might* like to fish, I can bring an extra reel." He tried to gauge the ambiguity of her response. "Or, there are plenty of spots on the river where no one will distract you."

She looked uneasily back at the house. "I'd like to go, but I feel like I should stay here with Annie."

"Well, maybe you can persuade her to come along."

"I—I can try—" she stammered. "Maybe we can both enjoy a day on the river."

Quickly she strode back across the yard and into the house, locating Annie in the bedroom, changing her blouse.

"Hi, what's up?"

"It's such a beautiful day, I thought I might take some pictures. Mark suggested we come along to the river. Does that sound like fun to you?" Annie grimaced. "You'd probably like it more than I. All I see are the snakes in the water and the swarm of bugs in front of my face. But go along with them, if you want."

Vanessa felt torn at the prospect of leaving Annie behind. "What are you going to do?" she asked awkwardly.

"Oh, don't worry about me. A friend and I are going to the park. William Standard is in town for a poetry reading, and I've been looking forward to hearing him for months. I'm going to write a follow-up article on him for the local paper." She looked thoughtfully into her friend's eyes. "You're welcome to come along if you like, but don't feel obliged."

Vanessa didn't think she could sit still through a reading. She had so much excess energy, if she didn't work it off, she'd explode. "Sure you won't feel abandoned?" she asked her friend.

Annie didn't let a trace of her disappointment show. She took out a pearl knit white cardigan and wrapped it over her shoulders. "Of course not. I'm sure you'll love the river."

The horn sounded from the driveway. "All right, then." She hugged her friend quickly. "See you later—"

The ride south to the river was twice as long as the trip to the quarry. The scenery was different, too. Steep hills bordered the two-lane road on either side, and patches of pine trees gave way to reveal impressive black granite. At the road's summit, water cascaded over a rock, cutting a path in the stone as it passed. At the top of the waterfall Vanessa could see ice formations still, but in another few days, if the sun continued to shine, they would all be melted; the waterfalls would vanish until next spring. In some parts of the world, where the seasons never changed much, one lost an appreciation of nature's mutability. If Vanessa hadn't come along today, if she had instead gone with Annie into town—she would have missed seeing an event that wouldn't repeat itself for another year. The mystery of nature moved her, and she couldn't wait until they reached the river.

Mark filled Danny's arms with fishing gear and handed Vanessa a bag to carry. He gathered up the rest of the equipment before leading them down to a narrow river.

"We make camp here," he said, laying their supplies on a dry bed of dull white stones. "But feel free to explore upstream. There's a lovely pool around the next bend."

"But don't swim," Danny warned her. "You'll scare away the fish."

She removed her shoes and touched a bare toe to the transparent water. "Brrr! I doubt I'll wade any deeper than here," she said, drawing a line at her ankles.

Danny sat on the rock-strewn bank, pulling his rubber boots high up over his hips. Clearly they were meant to be worn by an older child; they looked more like clown pants when he hooked them to braces and suspended them from his shoulders, but he didn't seem to notice they didn't quite fit, he was so busy preparing his line.

"Mind if I just sit and watch?" she asked, the heat from the rocks feeling good on her cold feet. She could wander around later, but right now precious material was slipping by unrecorded.

Mark looked up from his reel. "Whatever you feel like doing . . ." he said, returning his attention to a multicolored assortment of flies.

The light was more complimentary on the other side of the bank, but she didn't think it tactful to ask them to move for the sake of better photographs. Instead she changed from the wide-angle lens she had anticipated using and mounted the telephoto. Glancing around, she wished she'd brought her other lens. Later she could switch back. She had a feeling she wouldn't lack subject matter the setting was so captivating. But for right now her choice of subject matter was a familiar one: the curious and ever-changing expressions of her favorite boy.

By the time she had captured a dozen poses, he had moved into the water, his concentration focused on the lesson of the day. She caught the determined stance, as well as the look of wonder whenever he hit the target. Then his father brought in his first fish of the day, a foot-long trout, and she snapped a series of pictures, documenting the spirit of the fight. Even if Annie couldn't be here, she thought to herself, at least she could see what she was missing.

The three of them came together to examine the fish. Mark held it in the palm of his large, capable hand, his thumb positioned over its fin so it wouldn't flip back into the water. "It's a rainbow," he said, using his other hand to point out the interesting markings.

The fish's color fading in the sun saddened Vanessa, but she didn't say anything. She watched its struggle abate, and was glad when it ceased to fight. She knew that nature balanced itself in peculiar ways, but that didn't make her feel any less guilty.

"I think I'll wander upstream," she said, picking up her camera bag and slinging it over her shoulder.

Danny hardly heard her; his attention was back to catching a fish the size of his father's. Mark dropped the trout in a bucket of standing water, looked up at her, and nodded his head. "If you get lost, or need anything, just holler."

She smiled. If she could find her way through the Black Forest and drive without incident through the streets of Rome, she shouldn't have any difficulty maneuvering a curve in a river.

The pool Mark had mentioned was farther than she had thought: she walked for ten minutes before she found it, and even then, it wasn't large, or very deep. Surrounded by overhanging trees, the water was calm, and as clear as glass. Dragonflies chased each other across the diameter; their reflections skimmed the surface of the water. One alighted, and from beneath it a minute ripple expanded outward. A second insect started another set of circles, and they were off again; the pond settled before another group of tiny inhabitants appeared.

Vanessa crouched at the side of the pool, watching, too absorbed even to photograph. On the one hand she felt the serenity of being alone. On the other she realized she was one of the hundreds of creatures occupying this space in nature. The idea made her laugh. It was just like living in Manhattan. Another single girl, come to the big city to make her fortune and a name for herself.

Though she had tried to put her father out of her thoughts, she hadn't succeeded. Vanessa was still angry. He had hurt her deeply, and she knew it would take more than a trip to the country to heal her. What she needed was a time machine that would zap her forward, to the place where she'd be able to see why everything had happened for the best.

Vanessa watched a leaf drop from a tree overhead, then drift for a moment before landing on the water, to be swept along by the pull of the current. Soon she'd be in New York, and ready or not, she'd be making decisions. Or, she thought, watching the leaf disappear around a bend, choices would be made for her.

Out here, in the presence of nature, it was hard to deny that she was subject to a force more powerful than herself; and having relinquished the control, she leaned back against the eroded grass riverbank and again took notice of just how spectacular was the beauty surrounding her. For a minute she, like Annie, had mistaken spring for winter. No, she was wrong to let her emotions cloud a sunny future. Hadn't people clamored after her in New York? Hadn't Rick wanted to send her on another assignment? Sure, she was her father's daughter, but that didn't diminish her worth.

Since their split she had felt obliged to compare herself to her father, but now she saw how self-deprecating that kind of thinking was. *Of course* Clemens was more established than she. He'd been at it thirty years longer. At her age he had been knocking on doors that shut him out more often than invited him in. Yes, she still had to make a decision about direction, but at least she had offers.

Vanessa glanced around her and wondered at the calming effect the river had on her, as if worry were too slipshod to be brought into nature's sanctuary. She'd make her decisions soon enough. A few more days in a setting like this and she might even make the right choice.

A twig snapped and Vanessa looked across the pond to spot a deer approaching. It spied her at the same instant and for a moment they locked eyes, before Vanessa angled her camera and the animal shied back into the foliage.

A tree fallen across the water a few yards upstream provided a crossing to the other side, if she were careful, she thought. Securing her camera across her back, she edged along the trunk, rising up on all fours when a limb blocked her path. One bare foot touched the water, and while it was uncomfortably cold, she was never in danger of falling farther than a few feet.

Near the other bank she got caught in the bough's dense top. As she lowered her camera safely onto dry land, her shirt got snagged on a branch, and she had to twist around to untangle it. Her foot slipped on the trunk, and she fell out of the arms of the tree and into the cold shallow water at the edge of the river.

Her first groan was addressed to the sudden cold, her second to the discomfort surging through her back. The water hurried past her, covering her legs and stomach, partially submerging her breasts and one shoulder. Although it was very cold, it failed to numb her to the hard rock bottom she lay on, or the now-throbbing agony in her back. She tried to sit up, but the pain kept her from moving, and she had no choice but to call down the river for help.

First, she worried that they wouldn't be able to hear her, and she called again, causing a spasm of pain in her ribs.

They would find her . . . she'd be out of the freezing water in another few seconds . . . the aching would be eased . . . she kept repeating to herself, hoping that would make it come true. She hardly worried that she was hurt; she was more embarrassed to be found lying wet and helpless at the edge of the water.

Vanessa managed to pull her wet T-shirt down to cover her bare midriff before they reached her, and tried to smile through her awkwardness. "Just lie still," Mark instructed calmly, kneeling beside her in the water, and quickly studying the position of her body. "What hurts?" he asked, putting his hand behind her neck so she wouldn't have to strain to keep her head out of the water.

"Other than the cold water?" she asked.

He grinned at her attempted good cheer, but his eyes continued to show worry. "Just pretend it's thirty degrees warmer than it is."

"That would make it about thirty-two degrees, right?" She tried to shift her weight off a sharp rock.

"That's right," he encouraged her. "And pretend you're lying on down feathers, while you're at it. Now, tell me, what hurts?"

She started to tell him it was only her back, but a pain shot down her leg and interrupted her.

He understood from the grimace on her face. "I'm going to try to lift you...." It was risky, he knew, but he couldn't let her lie in bone-chilling water. If there was too much pain he'd let her back down, but he had to try. "Can you put your arm around my neck?"

She lifted her arm and wrapped it around his neck. Her hand on his shoulder tightened when he raised her into his arms and held her close to his chest, and carried her to a grassy spot a few feet from the embankment. Ferns crushed beneath them when he knelt to lay her down. The pain returned as she loosened her hand from his shoulder.

"Danny—"

The boy was beside him in an instant.

"I want you to run back to the car, and bring me my bag, and the blanket that's in the trunk."

The boy nodded. "You'll have to press this button to open the lock. Can you do that?"

He nodded again, solemn in the face of emergency. Mark pulled a ring of keys out of his pocket. "It's this one," he said, holding one among many.

Danny started to leave, but his father held him back.

"Now, mind where you step, but hurry." Mark watched his son scurry along the riverbank for a minute before returning to his patient.

"You'll be all right," he said, stripping off his T-shirt and using it to dry her face and arms.

She nodded. "I'm more stunned than hurt, but I think I sprained my back when I fell."

"Maybe," he considered. "Or you might just have a bad bruise—you landed hard on a pile of rocks."

She tried to move. Her back hurt still, and in addition new pains were beginning in her shoulder and neck.

"Lie quietly," he told her, putting his balled-up T-shirt under her head for a pillow. With his hand he pushed back the wet strands of hair from her face, then brushed the soft, cool skin on her cheek.

Her arms were chilled, the little hairs standing up on goose bumps.

"I wish I had a way to warm you," he said, frustrated. He looked up to locate the sun's position, but the trees overhead shaded them. Her shivering chilled him. The sight of her black hair pulled back from her face showed a vulnerability he hadn't seen before. Her eyes were— darker than blue—almost violet—and scared, he thought. He laid his hand on her arm, and the contrast between the warmth radiating from him to her cold skin caused him to take her into his arms and press her near to him for warmth.

"I'm actually shaking," she said nervously, unable to stop herself. "I'm so cold."

He held her closer, wrapping his hands around her back and pressing directly against her skin instead of her wet shirt. "Can you put your arms around me?" he asked, thinking any extra contact would warm her. Pressing his lips to her forehead, he did what he could to comfort her. He touched his mouth to her eyes, but even when he held his cheek to hers, her teeth continued to chatter, and her body shook.

Her defenselessness made him feel helpless . . . if only he could make everything better for her. "Vanessa," he whispered.

She looked up at him with frightened eyes, her lips parted, as if she wanted to speak.

"Vanessa," he repeated, then realized it was he who was trembling, and before he realized it, their lips touched tentatively. . . . Neither closed their eyes: she watched him as closely as he watched her, and when a shiver coursed through her body, he brought her closer still, his tongue warming her mouth, her lips feverishly seeking his. Her hands touched the muscles across his shoulders and he returned the caress over the soft damp down on her back.

"Vanessa," he whispered urgently into the mass of black hair. "This is crazy, but—" He faltered. What exactly did he want to say to her? What was the intense feeling surging inside of him? Sure, he was reacting to her beauty, there was no fighting it, but it was some-thing deeper than that. Truly, he wanted to warm her.

"Vanessa—" he tried to speak again. Even if it sound-ed incredible, he had to tell her how he felt. She would understand. "I—"

Quickly she covered his mouth with her hand. "No, Mark, there's no need to speak. It wasn't your fault, any more than it was mine. It just happened. And no one ev-er needs to know."

The light faded in his eyes. She hadn't understood. "Vanessa," he beseeched. "I don't want to apologize. Or pretend it didn't happen. I want—"

"You want your wife to know what a louse her best friend is?" she demanded. "Or, what a faithless husband she has?"

"No, that's not true. I—"

"Or your son," she continued, refusing to let him talk. She pushed him away from her as she heard Danny's footsteps in the distance. "Do you want him to know about us, too?" Her eyes flashed warningly. "You are never to mention this to anyone. We are going to forget it ever happened."

"I can't, Vanessa. That's not the truth of my feelings for you." He looked back to see his son round the bend, hurrying toward them, his hands full of first-aid provi-sions. "Even for him, I can't lie about this."

"I can," she answered firmly. "If only for him."

CHAPTER TEN

Vanessa woke the next morning scratching her arms. Getting out of bed, she was reminded of yesterday's pain, which was, fortunately, a mere shadow of what it had been. But it wasn't until she removed her robe in the bathroom that she saw the fine tapestry of rash spread over her back, arms, and shoulders.

"Poison ivy," she said aloud to the image in the mirror, identifying the design that covered her. Just what I needed, she thought, in addition to everything else.

By *everything else* she meant the confusion of guilt and desire she felt when she recalled Mark's kiss. It was as though the softness of his lips held nourishment she desperately needed. It would have been easier for a starving wretch to walk away from a table full of food than it had been for her to push herself away from Mark.

Sure, it could have happened to anyone. They were both adults and understood that these things occurred. As much as she wanted to believe in the exclusivity of desire and the sanctity of the marriage vows (and Vanessa did believe in both of those things), accommodations had to be made. There was no harm done. This morning they would continue their lives as usual, as if it had never happened.

Fool! Vanessa stared at herself in the bathroom mirror, her argument dissolving before her very eyes. It didn't happen to anyone. It had happened to you, and with your best friend's husband. Furthermore, there wasn't the remotest chance that she could continue her life as if the kiss had never occurred. It was as though she had forced the realization of her dream. It had been an omen, and she should have heeded it more closely. Every time she looked at Annie now, she would feel the weight of her betrayal, and when she looked at Mark she would be forced to confront her desire. She wanted him and she hated herself for her feelings. But the most difficult visage of all was that of the child: Danny would always be there to remind her of the fragility and infinite importance of her two friends' union. She, Annie, and Mark were adults, they could take care of themselves. But Danny was helpless. He depended on them to make his world secure, and no matter how intensely she felt drawn to Mark, it couldn't compare to Danny's need.

Vanessa decided against a shower. She recalled from her own woodland adolescence that one of the remedies for the rash was to wash with brown soap, scrubbing thoroughly so as to break the blisters and make sure the poison was washed away, lest it spread. Yet for the moment she wasn't up to it. She deserved to suffer. If it spread to the rest of her body, so what? Maybe she'd be scarred. In her slippers she padded back into her room to dress. On her way to the kitchen she heard the sounds of Annie cooking breakfast.

"Vanessa . . ." Mark intercepted her at the door to his study. "I need to talk to you." His voice was a guilty whisper.

"Mark, please—" was all she could respond, more to the imploring look in his eyes than to his simple request.

"I've got to talk to you."

"Let it be, Mark." She turned and walked away.

After watching her disappear down the hall, he stepped out of the room and silently closed the door behind him.

"Mama's making gas-house eggs, 'Nessa," said Danny, cutting into a slice of melon.

"Come and eat them before they're cold," Annie prompted.

Vanessa slid into her seat at the table. "What are gas-house eggs?"

Annie served her two from the cast iron skillet.

"Oh, sure, we used to call 'em bull's-eyes."

"There you are," Annie greeted her husband. "I was wondering when you'd get hungry."

"I was looking for some calamine lotion for Vanessa," he said, holding out the bottle of pink liquid. "If she itches half as much as I do, she needs it."

"The Poison Ivy Kids," Annie quipped. She looked like a Gibson girl this morning, her hair piled up on top of her head. "Where I come from, when a man and a woman emerge from the woods with poison ivy, there's always a bit of speculation." She laughed. "If he," pointing at her son, "weren't covered with it, too, I might begin to worry."

"What's spec . . . a . . . lation, Mommy?"

"It's what young boys do at breakfast time," she said, gathering her son in her arms, much to his delight. "Come on, you two, eat your breakfast."

Vanessa kept her eyes on the pink splotches of medicine on Danny's arms. She didn't trust herself to look at Mark, and she didn't want to give him a chance to look

111

at her with those imploring eyes. Annie's jibe had been couched in good humor, but all it would take was for her to see the desperate look on her husband's face, and she would know.

The eggs basted to slices of bread were delicious, but Vanessa had to force them down. She listened to the easy conversation, but couldn't participate, except to agree with or smile at whatever was being said. She perceived them as a unit, a family, and herself as an interloper. She had entered the house as a friend to Annie, but the way things had turned out, she'd spent less time with her old friend than with Mark and Danny. It was clear that Annie was distressed, and Vanessa had been no help at all. Moreover, she had given the demands of her own life hardly any attention. What did she think she was doing here? Distracting herself from her own problems by creating chaos for others? Suddenly she made a decision.

"I think I should return to New York today."

Mark's jaw dropped. "So soon?" he asked, scratching a red spot on his hand. "What about your back?"

"I can hardly feel it today," she lied. "It's just bruised."

"But you just got here," Annie protested, her brow knit to form three deep ridges in the middle of her forehead.

"You said we were going to hunt for mushrooms tomorrow," argued Danny.

That they all wanted her to stay didn't make her feel any better. Perhaps if Mark hadn't kissed her, and if she didn't want to be kissed by him again, she would have been persuaded to stay. A few days either side of her career wouldn't have made that much of a difference, but now she was afraid to be alone with him, and the tension created by the need to censor her feelings would quickly be detected by her sensitive friend.

"You've all been lovely." She looked at Annie and Daniel. "But I've got to face the problem of making a life for myself."

"I don't want you to go," Annie grieved, on the verge of tears. "We haven't even really talked."

"I'm not going far." She gathered Annie's hands in hers to reassure her. "I'll be right there in Manhattan. You can come down to spend time with me."

"You mean it, about visiting you?" Annie was tentative.

"Of course I do."

"That might be nice," she considered. "All right, then, I'll let you go."

There was relieved laughter from her old friend, but not from Danny, who glared at her uncharitably, or from Mark, who stared at his empty plate.

Vanessa tried to distract him. "Do you know what time the trains leave Albany?"

"I'll check." Mark rose, opened a drawer at the far end of the kitchen, and returned with a train schedule.

"You could make the two fifteen." His voice was flat. "Or if you are impatient, you could probably catch the eleven forty-five."

"I can take a cab down," volunteered Vanessa.

"We wouldn't hear of it," protested Annie.

"But I don't want to spoil your day, or keep you from work."

"It's Sunday," Mark reminded her. "I just have hospital rounds. I can make them on the way home."

113

"Well, then." Vanessa pushed herself away from the table. "I guess I'll get ready."

"Need any help?" Mark inquired.

"That's all right. Danny will help me pack."

She was relieved when the child accompanied her to her room. It seemed the only way to avoid an embarrassing confrontation. As it was, Mark walked back and forth in the hallway, glancing in to see if she was alone. But she kept Danny close, showing him how to fold clothes so that they wouldn't wrinkle.

"One day I'll be a great packer," bragged the towhead.

"All it takes is practice," she responded, recalling that at his age she had, in fact, been a great packer. It was a skill her gypsy life had taught her. By the time she was ten, she could gather her things from a hotel room and be ready to leave in minutes.

"And after I become a great packer, will you take me with you, sometime, 'Nessa?"

"I'd love to, Danny." She hated to leave him now. "Sometime we will take a trip together."

"Promise?"

She nodded. "I promise."

CHAPTER ELEVEN

"The train is bound to be late," Annie predicted in a hushed voice from the back seat of the car. Gently she shifted her son, who lay asleep across her lap. "There's no need to hurry, dear."

"You're right," Mark conceded, but continued his speed until he turned off the highway and into city traffic.

"The one time I was late to the station," Vanessa contributed from the front seat, "the train was on time. A miracle, I'll admit," she said lightly, "but nonetheless true." She glanced at her wristwatch, and then sideways at Mark. "We still have fifteen minutes to get there." Did all this chitchat mask her tension?

Danny's head popped up from his mother's lap. "It's still not too late," he whispered conspiratorially, tugging on his father's sleeve.

"Too late?" Mark didn't understand. "For the train?" Before Annie could stop him, and in spite of her attempt to grab hold of his sprawling legs, he clambered over the seat and landed in Vanessa's lap.

"No," Danny said, slightly annoyed at having to explain his plan. "We still have time to *kidnap* her." His solemn expression bespoke the seriousness of his plea.

No one dared to laugh.

"I wish we could force her to stay," Annie agreed.

115

Pulling the car into the parking lot, Mark abruptly cut the motor.

At the sight of the train station Danny insisted, "I don't want 'Nessa to go!"

Mark jumped out of the car and busied himself with Vanessa's luggage. It was one thing for his five-year-old son to lose control, but Vanessa could be spared seeing any more of his emotions, and Annie didn't need to know how much he regretted the departure.

"Hey, Dr. Abrams! How's it going?" A black teenager crossed the parking lot to greet Mark.

"Hello, Raymond. How's your knee?"

"Ace, thanks to you!" The boy did a high-kick to demonstrate the extent of his recovery.

Mark winced. "Better take it easy for a few more days," he called after the boy. All he needed today was an emergency surgery. He found himself rehearsing what he wanted to tell Vanessa without knowing in fact if he'd have the opportunity, or the courage, to speak.

"Wasn't that Muriel Evans's son?" Annie asked. "What's he doing in Albany?" But Mark didn't seem to hear her. His thoughts were elsewhere. Probably back home with his patients, she thought. But then, she couldn't expect him to feel as she did about Vanessa's departure. He was probably relieved to have the house free of company. Inside the car Danny demanded to know why she was leaving.

"Because I have to work," she started to explain again.

"You can have *my* money," he said, shoving his hand deep into the pocket of his corduroys, bringing up three coins and other assorted treasures.

"I need to see the people who will buy my pictures," she said, but her reasons didn't sound very convincing, even to her. How could she explain to the child that she loved his father more than she should?

"I don't like you anymore," he said abruptly to Vanessa.

Annie opened the car door to hear, "Daniel!"

Mark softened his wife's reprimand with a hand to his son's shoulder. "Come on, Danny. Let's go see if that train is ever going to arrive."

Vanessa and Annie stared after them as the two crossed the lot and disappeared into the stone-brick terminal.

"I guess I'm not the only one who's going to miss you," Annie admitted sadly. "I hate to see you go."

"I'll be fine," Vanessa promised, speaking from a confidence she didn't feel. "Once I get settled. I am so grateful to Mark's brother for letting me stay in his apartment."

"I'm not worried about *you,*" Annie corrected, laughing through the tears that glistened in her blue eyes. "I wish I were going with you—or instead of you."

Vanessa handed her camera and her rail ticket to Annie. "I hope you enjoy the city"

But Annie declined without grasping the irony of Vanessa's gesture. "I feel so silly," Annie confessed, trying to control her tears. "But it's like the most important part of my life is about to disappear down the tracks."

"You aren't silly . . . or sentimental," she assured her. "But remember, I'm only four and a half hours by train. We haven't lived that near to each other in years." She squeezed Annie's hand. "We'll be all right, both of us," she said, and hoped it was true.

Danny ran ahead of Mark toward the car, his sneakers smacking loud against the pavement. "Look what Dad bought me!" he shouted, rushing into Vanessa's arms, proud to share his pack of cinnamon gum. "And we're coming to visit *you* sometime," he told her happily.

Suddenly the world seemed a little less unfair . . . the prospects of beginning a new life looked less bleak. Who knew, maybe she would even meet someone . . . someone who would give her a son like Danny . . . someone of her own, someone free to love her.

"Goodness, here's the train," Annie announced. The three adults shared a look of astonishment, trying not to look past the unusual punctuality to the imminent departure. "Miracles do happen," she conceded wistfully.

The sound of the train's shrill whistle stirred the crowd of expectant travelers on the platform into action. They reached for their tickets, shifted their luggage a half-step nearer to the tracks.

Danny's eyes lit at the sight of the locomotive barreling into the station. "Please," he begged. "Can't I go with you?"

Vanessa pressed her lips against her little friend's flushed cheek. "Soon," she murmured. It was all the comfort she had to give. Annie clung to her friend for a tearful moment and then led the weeping boy back to the car.

Mark hoisted her suitcase onto the train.

"I wish you weren't going, Vanessa," he said tenderly. "I feel as though I've forced you away." He wanted to say more, but she had made it clear it was too dangerous emotionally.

She lay her hand upon his arm. "There's no easy way to say good-bye."

He smiled ruefully. "Sometimes it takes forever to say good-bye." There was no more stalling. As casually as if she were leaving for a day trip instead of embarking on an uncharted journey out of his life, he turned, and walked back to his family.

"Good-bye," she called feebly, but her words were lost beneath the sound of the wheels on the tracks.

***

First the train window was a transparency. Through it Vanessa watched the New England landscape become rich bands of greens and browns, of telephone wires and poles. However, by the time the train had pulled out of Hudson, it had become an opaque screen on which the events of the last week replayed themselves time and time again. It felt as if she were transporting illicit cargo across state lines.

She saw Mark pick her up in his arms, soaking wet, watched as he bent over her, stroked her head, brushed his lips against hers. As a youngster at the movies she had sat beside her father and pretended to cover her eyes during the mushy scenes. In part she did it as a game to amuse Ansel, who had always poked fun at displays of affection, as if they were routines worked out for the amusement of others. But really, when she thought about it, she had been as embarrassed by her father's response to romantic scenes as by the scenes themselves. In fact she'd always peeked through her fingers to witness the kiss, the passionate embrace. When Mark's lips had touched hers, it was as if she had banished the lingering hesitations she'd continued to feel whenever she was on the brink of tenderness. She'd been surprised to find she was no longer the little girl watching the woman. She had become that woman herself, from the inside. All those fairytales—Snow White, Cinderella, Sleeping Beauty—they were stories of transformation, attempts to describe to a youngster that most magical of all transformations, whereby love gives birth to the adult out of the child.

'The child is the father of the man,' Wordsworth had said. Well, she was also the mother of the woman.

She could see the child in Mark, too. When she hadn't been too frightened to peer into his dark eyes she had glimpsed the boy, almost as though she had known him at twelve, fourteen, eighteen, as a young graduate from medical school. This new feeling of familiarity might have been wonderful if it were not for the impossible context. Annie was her best friend!

But Annie was not the girl she had once known. Of course she could still see the child in Annie, the girl she had shared some of the happiest days of her young life with, but that girl was buried beneath so many layers of confusion: the pain that knit her brow gave Annie a distracted air, made her appear, at moments, like a stranger to Vanessa.

Vanessa tried to stop the flow of thought, but her feelings were as unrelenting as the sound of the train on the tracks. She felt a deep wrenching at the center of her being, as though she'd been torn, had wrenched herself away from a physical connection. What was all the more disturbing was that she couldn't say if this connection had been with Mark or Annie; or by what strange emotional logic her life had become a cipher for theirs. And at the same time, amid all the confusion, she felt irresistibly drawn to the man. If only she could transfer these assets. If only the emotions were negotiable, like money; then she would cash in her newfound wealth and invest it in something safe, secure. Something with a future.

CHAPTER
TWELVE

Under the red glow of the developing light, Vanessa could see the beautiful facade of the Bouwerie Lane Theatre taking shape on the paper. It was a magnificent building, with ornate cornices and a graded staircase to a door with stone columns. It stood on the corner of Great Jones Street, three stories, with that angled, foreshortened line that linked it in time and sensibility to the Flatiron Building. In the week she'd been back in New York she had photographed it twice. The second time she had captured it at a good angle, under an afternoon sun that made the shadows on its facade dance with a life of their own. Watching the forms emerge never ceased to be an amazing experience for Vanessa. It was part of the reason she continued to use a film camera for her professional work instead of a more immediate digital. The image grew from nothing and became the ghost of itself before entering fully into a two-dimensional reality.

Is that the way wishes and dreams worked? Vanessa wondered. And thoughts? Ideas that worked their way out of the prodigious minds of the race to become works of art, the electric light, the Bouwerie Lane Theatre? The telephone? It was ringing. Always at the wrong time. Quickly she took the print out of the developer and left it to soak in the stop bath.

"Vanessa?"

"Hi, Rick."

"Where have you been all day?"

"Trying to get some work done."

"Me, too." His voice sounded rushed. "I've got in front of me a headache of an article about a flooded canyon in Utah that has to be finished by tomorrow morning, and I haven't been able to get a handle on where to cut it yet."

"You will."

"I'm glad someone has faith in me. Listen, are we still on for dinner tonight?"

"Oh, did we—"

"Don't tell me you've forgotten."

"I'm sorry, Rick." She turned to glance at the half-opened door of her darkroom. "Will you hold on for a second?" Without waiting for an answer she went into the room, took the print out of the tray and hung it up on a wire by clothespins to dry before returning to the phone. "I've been so frantic here, Rick, I'm afraid I did forget."

"I really do want to talk with you. Can you make it?"

"I could," she sighed, "if you don't mind a third party. A friend of mine is coming into town this afternoon."

"Male or female?"

"Your favorite flavor."

"In that case it would be a pleasure." His voice assumed its most charming register at the prospect of meeting a new woman.

"Sometimes I can hear your words melt in your mouth," she kidded him.

"But not in my hand."

"Okay, Rick. You're on. I have to finish up now.

Where shall we meet?"

"Il Cortile, at eight."

"Perfect. Annie will love it."

Hanging the phone up, she thought the evening might work out fine after all. When Annie had sprung her surprise visit on Vanessa at eight that morning, it was like an earthquake: the structure of the photographer's busy schedule seemed to lie in ruins at her feet. But now it appeared things had dovetailed nicely. Annie would abbreviate the business discussion Rick had in mind. Rick, on the other hand, would shield Vanessa against some of the awkwardness she felt at the thought of being in Annie's presence. During the week since she'd returned from Vermont, she'd had to struggle with herself at length to banish her recollections of Mark.

Her strategy had been to stay busy. She had transformed a wing of Philip Abrams's luxurious apartment into a working photographic studio, had set up a full schedule of appointments for portraits and high-fashion jobs to bring in the money she'd need to live in New York. She had even found time to do some work on her photographic essay on the Bowery. In addition she'd succeeded in keeping Rick on the line about the assignment he'd offered her, stalling for a few more days. She didn't particularly want to leave the city now that she had set herself up and been received with a certain amount of enthusiasm by the professionals in her world. But Mark's presence haunted her, made her emotions swing out of control whenever the image of his face occurred to her, as it did hourly. If she couldn't banish him from her life, if the draw was too powerful for her to resist, then she might be forced to leave New York, at least for a little while.

Generally, things had been going fairly well, and she was beginning to relax, until Annie had called with the announcement of her arrival in New York that afternoon.

Vanessa went back into the darkroom. She looked at the next few frames of film under the enlarger, but her mind wandered. She might as well face it: she felt positively guilty about her feelings toward her best friend's husband. She would just have to handle it. There would be no confessions at Annie's expense. Vanessa had to contain her own experience, keep her own counsel.

It was enough to try the patience of a saint. Even the excitement of her new life hadn't erased her memory of Mark. Right here, looking at the image of the Bowery's old Salvation Army Mission, with its arresting stained glass window, she was once again by a country stream, gazing directly into his eyes. Yesterday, while photographing a spectacular sunset behind the Jersey Palisades, she had felt herself being carried up that grassy slope toward the car in his arms. . . . It was as if the shutter behind her eyes opened for a moment to record the scene, then snapped shut. At first those fugitive moments left her feeling she was losing control of her own mind. But after the first week she merely accepted those moments into her routine, allowing herself those random glimpses of an intimacy in which she began to take a guilty pleasure. She couldn't censor her imagination; she might as well enjoy it.

But now, with Annie coming, she felt out of control once more. It was as if she were as transparent as a glassine envelope, and her friend could gaze through it at will, to discover Vanessa's dreadful secret. She wandered out onto the terrace. It was a balmy afternoon. The sun rode high atop the Palisades, bright at the end of its workday. The Goodyear blimp pivoted on an invisible axis; small planes and helicopter traffic over the river gave Vanessa a prophetic vision of future traffic jams. Why, even the sky was chaotic. Even the moon had been trespassed.

She turned, walked past the open chaise lounges and the potted arborvitae back into the apartment.

The doorman rang to announce that Mrs. Abrams was on her way up, and Vanessa hastened to the bathroom mirror to prepare her face. When the elevator stopped at her floor, she was standing at the open door waiting for her friend.

"'Nessa," cried Annie as they embraced. "It's so good to see you."

"Annie." She held her friend at arm's length and was surprised to see her expression transformed from the one she remembered in Vermont. "You look wonderful."

And, indeed, she did. Could her blond hair have grown out to give the lines of her face a softer look? Or was it the way she wore it, falling loosely to her shoulders? In any event she was radiant. "You look transformed!"

"The prospect of a weekend without any responsibilities" Annie was almost breathless. "And time in New York, with my very best friend."

"I only wish I didn't have so much work to do this weekend." Vanessa picked up the small valise her friend had dropped in the hall and carried it inside. "In fact, I have to be downtown in an hour," she hurried on before

Annie could start feeling disappointed. "You're invited to come along. I'm meeting my editor from *Time* magazine, but we won't talk business all night." She considered. "Or if you'd prefer, you can stay here and relax. . . . I don't think I'll be out late."

"I'd love to come along, if I won't be in your way. I don't want to miss a minute of Manhattan."

"Well, there's plenty to see and do. I just wish I had more time free to show you around."

"Oh, Vanessa." Annie held her friend's hands for a moment as her eyes filled. "I can't tell you how good it feels just to be here. I know this was on the spur of the moment—"

"Shush. Go on now." Vanessa couldn't tell what emotion lay behind Annie's eyes, but suspected it wasn't a simple one. "After dinner we can talk."

Annie's mood shifted once again. She was suddenly elated. "I don't have to be back in Vermont until Tuesday," she sang, dancing her way into the living room. "And what a palace to escape to."

Vanessa glanced appreciatively around the huge, sparsely furnished modern living room, still impressed each time she looked at her surroundings. "Philip has been most generous," she confided. "The first day I arrived, he called to make sure I could find everything I needed. He knew I was a photographer, and said he wouldn't mind if I converted the laundry room into a darkroom." She shook her head, unaccustomed to such kindness.

"Do you think you will?"

"Come, look at what I've done."

She led her friend from the living room, through a

formal dining room, through a classic white-on-white kitchen, and into a dimly lighted anteroom. Vanessa switched on the overhead light, and Annie found herself in a small but efficiently organized darkroom. A wide counter balanced over one side of the washbasin, and an enlarger sat on top; three trays lay side by side along the counter, and overhead was a shelf stocked with packages of paper, bottles of chemicals, and an assortment of utensils.

"Aren't you ever tempted to use a digital camera?"

"I do—all the time, but for professional work, digital can't equal film."

"It's all so wonderful." A momentary shadow hovered in Annie's eyes. "It's so cozy and —I envy your freedom."

"I think it's a matter of the grass looking greener," Vanessa suggested, and was glad to see the shadow vanish like a dark cloud swept away by a gust of wind.

Annie picked up an enlargement of a family portrait. The costumes bespoke great wealth and tradition of a kind one didn't encounter in the States. Beneath it, dramatic because of the contrast, two Indonesian children sat huddled in a doorway, staring out of the photograph with huge, hungry eyes. "Your work is so powerful, it sometimes hurts to look at it."

"Come on," Vanessa coaxed, smiling. "I'll show you the new stuff later."

Annie hesitated, touched her friend's arm as if to slow the driving pace. "Vanessa, will you have time to look at the newspaper clippings I brought down? I was hoping you might advise me—there must be something I can do with my writing."

"I'd love to, but right now we've got to hurry if we

want to meet Rick on time." She would rather have stayed home with Annie, but her relationship with Rick would suffer if she kept him waiting.

"Do I have five minutes to freshen up?"

"Sure," Vanessa answered. "I'll put your things in Philip's room." She opened a door and turned on the light. "You can use this bathroom. And I can bring the television back in for you. I don't watch it."

"Neither do I. I've brought several books with me. My God! I might even have time to write two consecutive thoughts in my journal without interruption!"

Vanessa waited on the terrace, watching the sun drop lower in the sky until the top of the Palisades glowed orange and red in the changing light. How many sunsets had she seen in her travels? It was always the same sun, always the same eyes through which she looked. Only the backdrop changed from country to country.

She watched the blue of the Hudson darken, then glisten silver as a cloud passed over the sun. Maybe *she* had changed? Certainly she didn't feel the same looking out over the water as she did in, say, Copenhagen, when her thoughts had been racing ahead to the next sunset she'd see, to the thrill of the unknown. The glamor of her former life felt empty in retrospect. Could her father have known? Could he, in truth, have been acting on her behalf when he left her behind? Today she thought she saw his point. For the first time she considered that what was right for him wasn't necessarily fulfilling for her. Maybe she wasn't a failure after all. Maybe she had other avenues to explore, hers, but not his. Maybe her decision to stay in one place wasn't cowardice.

For the last week she'd been enthralled by the subtle

changes she'd seen from the terrace, the minute varia-
tions in color and texture she'd noticed against the familiar landscape. There was so much more for her to discover in this one vista, and somewhere she knew she'd feel
cheated from a deeper understanding if she moved away
from it now. Adventure still appealed to her, that was
indisputable, but she could no longer mistake it for intimacy. She longed to know something completely, if only
a landscape.

"I'm ready." Annie slid open the heavy glass door. "Do
I look all right?"

Vanessa glanced down at the simple yellow dress, the
open-toed heels, then back at the pretty face. "Perfect."

Vanessa and Annie made their way past the crowded
pedestrian traffic on Mulberry Street, toward the imposing facade of wood and plate glass. Potted evergreens
were stationed in front at regular intervals, like soldiers
standing guard.

"Look at those cars!" Annie stared wide-eyed at two
stretch limousines, a black and silver model. "Who do
you think owns those?"

"That's a loaded question in Little Italy," Vanessa responded, taking Annie by the arm and hustling her inside.

"I know, I saw *The Godfather.*" She stopped before she
could utter another sound and gazed around her.

"It's gorgeous, isn't it?"

Il Cortile was a structure combining elements of the
old and the new world in a way that arrested the eye.
The floors were all imported Italian marble and the
walls had reproductions of frescos from Pompeii. Statues

from various Roman ruins had been reproduced and were placed in strategic positions near the tables. Vines clung to sections of brick along the walls and the restaurant opened out at the center into a two-leveled affair with skylights and balconies. Waiters, busboys, and formally attired maître d's bustled about, doing a brisk business.

"Good evening," said a dark-suited man. "How many will you be?"

"We're dining with Mr. Jacobs."

"Ah, yes." His expression shifted from one of critical appraisal into a professional smile. "He's waiting for you in the bar. Your table will be ready in a few minutes. Please follow me."

Annie brought up the rear, her head turning left to right as she tried to glimpse what was going on in the rooms that opened out from the central room. They passed a buffet table full of dazzling pastries, set like so many colored gems. Beyond the desserts was a canopied smorgasbord. The maître d' continued up a flight of wooden stairs to where the bar stood, recessed on a balcony.

"Vanessa!" Rick rose to greet her, taking her by the hand and placing a kiss to one side of her mouth.

"Rick, this is my friend, Annie Abrams."

He took her hand in his and shook it gently, smiling directly into her eyes. "I'm glad you were able to join us," he said graciously. "Are you in town for long?"

"Just a couple of days," she told him, accepting the chair he pulled back for her. "I haven't really spent much time in New York since my husband was in residence at Columbia Presbyterian. That was five years ago."

"Let's drink to the first of many visits," Rick said as he signaled for the waiter.

Vanessa took the seat on his other side. "I'll have a Campari and soda," she told the silver-haired Italian who paused for their order.

He nodded imperceptibly and turned to Annie, who giggled. "You wouldn't think this would be such a big decision, right?" The waiter nodded, and waited, his pen poised expectantly.

She swallowed, unable to think of what she wanted to drink. Whenever she went out, Mark was always with her, and they had a bottle of wine. But it just didn't seem appropriate to order wine for herself. "I'll have a beer, I guess."

"Any particular kind, signorina?"

"Do you have a Bud? A Budweiser," she corrected herself.

"We only serve Italian beer, signorina."

"Oh."

He rattled off the names of the brands. Annie wasn't enjoying the attention. She wished she could simply throw back an answer at him in an offhanded manner, but she didn't dare try to repeat the long, foreign-sounding words.

"I think the lady would enjoy a gin and tonic," Rick jumped in, "and I'll have another Bombay Martini."

He smiled warmly at Annie, and it was a gesture she could respond to. She giggled and shrugged. "Country mouse flunks city test."

"They can be intimidating in New York."

"Especially here," Vanessa confirmed.

"But doesn't that kind of spoil the fun of dining out"—

she asked her question directly to Rick "when your waiter thinks he's better than you?" She turned to Vanessa.

"Once you taste the food, you'll forgive a lot," she answered. "And after a while you get used to their attitude. I hardly even notice anymore."

Rick nodded, but had something to add. "It isn't that they think they are better than we are, but this city breeds a special brand of waiter and waitress. Most of them have other professions—jobs they can't make a living at like painting, or ballet, or—"

"Photography?" Vanessa interrupted.

"You're one of the privileged few who support themselves with their art. You don't know how envied you are."

Annie nodded vehemently.

Rick continued. "That waiter is probably a sculptor or something, and only has this job because he has two kids and a wife to support. He wants to make sure you don't mistake him for a mere waiter."

Annie considered. "Now I feel bad for criticizing him. It's just that he made me feel pretty stupid."

"Pride has funny ways of expressing itself," Vanessa explained.

"Besides, you're not wrong to have noticed. Just because their behavior can be rationalized doesn't mean their arrogance doesn't sting. Your sensitivity is refreshing," he promised her. "Reminds us of how jaded we are, right, Vanessa?"

"I've only been back for two weeks," she protested. "It'll take me at least a month to get my skin thick again." Vanessa grinned, in time for the approaching waiter to think it was meant for him. "I think our table is ready."

Vanessa led the way to the table while Rick escorted Annie. He sure was being nice to her. Vanessa wondered if he felt personally responsible for the waiter's behavior or for making the whole evening fun. She let the waiter pull out the chair for her and watched Rick do the same for Annie. Could it be that Rick was attentive to Annie because he found her attractive?

"Gosh," Annie whispered breathlessly, opening the menu and staring inside. "It's written in Italian." She looked up at Vanessa. "Can you actually read it?"

Vanessa minimized her ability with an offhanded gesture. "I never spent enough time in Italy to really learn the language. But I can ask directions to the Coliseum and read a menu. What do you feel like having? The stuffed *calamari* is terrific."

Rick closed his menu. "I've always let her do the ordering. She's never failed me in the past."

Annie wondered just how often they dined together. From the look in Rick's eyes he was clearly smitten, but Vanessa wore the usual look of indifference, as if she'd never even noticed how attractive he was, how blue his eyes were or the suggestion of a dimple in his chin when he smiled. It didn't seem to matter to her that he knew the right clothes to wear, the right drinks to order. Vanessa responded to his attentiveness about as enthusiastically as a sea turtle hunts for sharks. Annie admired her friend's independence as much as she ever had, but wasn't she perhaps missing something? How could it hurt her career to enjoy Rick's attention?

The waiter left with their dinner order, and another returned with a second round of drinks.

"To your decision, then?" Rick raised his glass to Vanessa's.

Annie clinked glasses but looked puzzled. Vanessa explained. "I promised Rick I'd let him know tonight about the Laos-Cambodia assignment."

"What'll it be, Vanessa?"

"I've decided to try to make a life for myself in one place."

"And I'll bet it isn't Cambodia," he kidded.

Vanessa nodded. "That's right. I'm going to try to make a go of it in New York."

Annie grinned openly. "Why, I'd say that's reason to celebrate." She squeezed her friend's hand and continued smiling. "Good thing Phil's apartment is big enough for the two of us."

"Two of us?" Now Vanessa looked puzzled.

"Because I plan to visit you as much as you'll let me."

Rick pursed his lips. "Yes, I'd say there is cause to celebrate." He smiled at Annie, then at Vanessa. "At the risk of speaking on my own behalf, instead of for *Time,* I'm glad to have you for a crosstown neighbor," he said. "Any idea where you'll look for studio space? I have a friend who might—"

"Actually, I'm already settled."

His surprise was obvious. "I'm impressed. Even Gina Gilmour, with all her connections, took a month to find her studio."

"The great thing about Philip Abrams's apartment is that there is room for me to live and work. His maid's quarters were sitting empty."

"She made the laundry room into her darkroom," Annie said. "The pantry is set up for layouts, the—"

"Sounds very impressive. So you'll work out of your apartment exclusively, then?"

"For the time being. Until I find something else, or I'm evicted, whichever comes first."

"Oh, Phil will never make you leave. His apartment sits empty all year."

"Phil's your husband?"

"My brother-in-law. My husband's older brother." Vanessa thought she noticed a darkening to Rick's features, but he continued to smile. "Is your husband in town, too?"

"Oh, no," Annie told him. "He's at home, with our son."

"How old is your boy?"

"Nearly six. He starts school next fall."

"Bet he's cute, if he takes after his mom."

"He looks like his father," Annie answered.

"And he's adorable," Vanessa added.

Rick lifted the bottle of Pouilly-Fuisse and raised the level midway in both women's glasses before refilling his own. "This *ossobuco* is fantastic," he remarked. "How are your *tortellini*, Annie?"

"Excellent," she announced, forking another stuffed pasta. "You don't know how wonderful it is not to cook tonight."

"But I thought you liked to cook," Vanessa protested. "You do it so well."

"Oh, I guess I don't mind it, really, but night after night it gets tiring after a while."

Rick nodded, as if he understood. "Funny, but I've grown tired of dining out after all these years. Nothing would appeal to me more than a nice home-cooked meal."

"Sometime I'll have to cook a dinner for you, then," she promised. She glanced at Vanessa. "Maybe next time I come down we could invite Rick over for supper. I bet he'd love my chicken cacciatore."

"I thought you just said you were tired of cooking?" Vanessa reminded her.

"Well, cooking for guests isn't the same, really."

Vanessa swallowed a bite of squid. "How is your work going, Rick? Are you still having problems with that article you're editing?"

"Yes, I suspect the author sometimes exaggerates, but I don't know enough about the place to question him properly."

"Rick's editing an afterpiece on a canyon that was flooded several years ago," Vanessa explained. "You know, before-and-after shots, some commentary about the ecological effects—"

"We brought out a book ten years ago on Glen Canyon, and now we're doing a follow-up."

"Glen Canyon, by the Colorado River?"

"That's right." He put down his fork. "Have you heard of it?"

"If it's the same place I'm thinking of, my dad took the family there once on holiday, when I was a kid."

"When it was still a canyon? Before it was flooded?"

"That's right. We camped in the dry ravines for two weeks. I'll never forget that place, it was so magical. Like another world, another time."

"I'm sure it is —I wish my writer felt as tied to the true memory as you do."

The waiter cleared their plates.

"What do you say we move up to Café Roma for dessert and espresso?"

"Sounds like a good idea to me. Annie?"

"Whatever you suggest." She wanted to see the insides of as many places in New York as she could. When she'd lived here before she'd been too timid to explore areas like Little Italy or Greenwich Village. She was being recharged by the multitude of impressions. "Is it far from here?"

"Just a few blocks. We can walk." He summoned the waiter back and received the bill, paying for it with a credit card. Annie would have liked to know how much their dinners had cost, but she knew it wasn't proper to ask such questions.

Vanessa seemed less concerned with what was proper. "Let's split that, Rick. There's no need for you to treat us."

"It's my pleasure, really. Besides, I can deduct it as a business expense."

Vanessa acquiesced. "In that case, all right, but I'm picking up dessert."

Annie threw her shawl over her shoulders as they entered the streets. The sidewalk was wide enough to walk three abreast. Rick took the position next to the street, and Vanessa took the inside, keeping Annie in the middle. She felt like Dorothy in *The Wizard of Oz*, off for an adventure, heading for the Emerald City. Her fantasy broke when she tried to imagine which of her two companions was the Tin Man, and which the Scarecrow. Certainly Rick had a heart of gold, and Vanessa had never lacked for courage.

"What are you working on, Vanessa?"

"A number of things—a sitting for a book jacket with Lisa Bach on Monday, a portrait of Paloma Picasso next Wednesday but those won't take much time. What I'm most excited about is an idea I've just presented to an editor at Harper and Row."

Rick nodded. "What's the subject matter, or is it too soon to ask?" He steered them into a crowded little coffee shop, and to a tiny round table near the front window,

"Sure, I can tell you. The project's titled *The Bowery: Portrait of Change.*"

"A book about the bums? Isn't that a little lower depths for an Ansel?"

"I have to work on what interests me, Rick. Besides, the Bowery has only been skid row since the Depression. Lillian Russell used to sing there. People dressed in their finest and came there to kick up their heels. It was a veritable midway of carnivals and sideshows before the blue-collar workers took it over to build Manhattan's elevated subways."

"How can you photograph what isn't there anymore?"

"It is still rich in lore. The old theaters are still standing. The Palace Hotel is still there. Much of the cultural history of New York can be read in the places left on the Bowery."

"You sound really excited about it."

"I am. In fact, I should probably get home soon. I'm meeting with my collaborator—a writer named Ched Royales—first thing in the morning, so I have to be up early."

"For the first time in years I don't have to get up until I feel like it." Annie stretched her arms above her head. "I might just sleep till noon."

Rick ran a piece of lemon peel around the rim of his demitasse and dropped it into the thick black brew. "I hoped we could continue on from here. I know a great room for listening to jazz. Joel Wilson is performing at Greene Street."

"Who's that?"

"Joel Wilson?" He looked surprised. "He's the greatest male vocalist alive."

"I don't know anything about jazz, but I'd love to hear him." She turned to her friend. "Would it be all right if we stopped in for just a little while?"

Vanessa checked her watch. "I really don't think I should. My pictures will come out blurred if I don't have enough sleep. Maybe we can hear him another time."

"He's only in town this weekend," Rick advised. "What if I take Annie along with me? I'll make sure she gets home safely."

Vanessa didn't much like the idea of them going off alone, but it was too late to change her mind about going and she did have to be alert the following morning. Besides, she didn't like to tell Annie she shouldn't go. "Will you bring her home by cab?"

"I'll rent a limousine if that will make you feel more secure."

"A cab will suffice, but ride uptown with her."

"I won't let her out of my sight until she's opened the door to the apartment. She's safe in my hands."

CHAPTER THIRTEEN

"Hold on, Lisa, let me adjust the light." Vanessa turned the hooded spot directly on her subject. "How's that?"

"It's blinding," said Lisa Bach, hugging herself against a plain white background screen, her long dark hair billowing around her.

"Let me adjust it. Good." Vanessa stood back and viewed her subject through the Hasselblad camera. "If I can get some high-contrast light and shadow on your face, I think it will make a strong portrait, and in keeping with what you want. It will give the planes and bones of your face a sculptural quality."

"You're the professional here," responded Lisa. "I've admired your work, and your father's, for years. I'd be a fool to second-guess you."

"An ideal subject. Now, just sit still."

Vanessa was all around her, the shutter of her Hasselblad clicking at top speed from every angle at varying distances.

"Good, Lisa. Now look at me. Hold it."

The young author turned to gaze over her shoulder at the photographer. Instantly Vanessa got the effect she was after. The cords and ligaments of Lisa's neck stood out at a sloping angle to her head, giving a kind of resolve to the delicate face. Indeed, it might have been the head of the Olympian Juno.

"Enough?" The subject slid off her stool when the photographer nodded. "Thank you so much, Vanessa. A book jacket photo is such a tricky business, you simply can't trust it to just anyone."

"I'm complimented." Vanessa brought the roll of film to the end of its spool, then popped it out. "Unless I'm sadly mistaken, I think we've got just what you want here."

"My editor was insistent." Lisa reached for her light cloth jacket on the back of the chair. "You know, it's the packaging that often sells the book. And he felt very strongly that the author of *The Eternal Goddess* shouldn't look like a wimp."

"Is it a love story?"

"Nothing so overworked." Lisa Bach gave a nervous laugh. "It's just what the title says, a study on the different aspects of the female goddess through time and culture."

"Interesting."

"Yes. And no two are exactly alike. Kali isn't Cybele, and neither is like the Virgin Mary."

"Have you drawn any conclusions, then? About women?"

"Only that we are very complicated. Our powers of healing and destruction are staggering."

"I never guessed we had such power." Vanessa smiled.

"We do and don't know it." Lisa slipped into her jacket, picked up her purse from the same chair, and started for the door. "We've allowed it to become submerged. The really fascinating question is why we have lost sight of it."

"Did you find the answer?" Vanessa stopped with her for a moment in the hallway.

"I'm hot on the trail."

Vanessa smiled and looked down at Lisa. She hadn't realized how short her subject was, partly because she moved with such confidence. She was even a bit brassy, but Vanessa liked her for it.

"I'll have the contact sheets in a couple of days. Why don't you stop up on Wednesday, and we'll go over them to see if there's something you want enlarged."

"See you Wednesday."

Vanessa closed the door behind her and suddenly everything seemed deathly still. It was still relatively early on a Monday night.

Automatically her hand slid to the end of the table and picked up the well-fingered letter she'd received from her father that afternoon. Her reading of it was equally reflexive, since she had already memorized the words. Yes, she was sure he had done a masterful job of the presidential family, even if the country had found itself the victim of another terrible tropical storm. The country may have been reduced to muddy rubble, but Clemens Ansel would get all the dignity possible into the Hidalgo face of Lopez Portillo. Having finished the job, he was photographing the ancient capital of the Aztecs, Tenochtitlan, being dug up right in the heart of modern Mexico City. For a moment she felt a pang of envy, but when she recalled her delightful hour with Lisa Bach, and her own archaeological odyssey to the Bowery that morning, she felt better. It was just that his letter was so emotionally *distant*.

She took a long, hot shower, put on a pair of lime-green pajamas with chocolate-brown trim, and got into bed. A strip of exposed film marked her place in the book she was reading by Mary Renault. But not even the secret life of Alexander the Great, as told by his eunuch, was enough to calm her restlessness. Putting the book down, she realized why she was so anxious.

Where was Annie? Why wasn't she home?

The small alarm on her night table read ten minutes after ten.

It wasn't the hour. By New York standards the night was just starting. But over the long weekend Annie had spent in Manhattan, Vanessa had seen her only fleetingly. They'd hardly even had time to speak. If she had known what the upshot would be of that dinner at Il Cortile, she never would have invited Annie along. Every day, from the time she had left the two of them outside Café Roma, Annie had been with Rick.

Damn, it made her furious! Why should she be put in this position? On the other hand, she reasoned, Annie was an adult. Vanessa wasn't her keeper. Yet she was her best friend, and friends—real friends—did assume some responsibility, even if only by way of a word or two. But why was she so angry with Annie? Could she be jealous of the time she preferred to spend with Rick?

The day following their Greene Street date Rick had taken Annie to the Edward Hopper opening at the Whitney Museum. They'd ridden in a horse-drawn hansom cab through Central Park, My God! Could Rick have found anything more corny? But Annie had loved it. She was like a young bird on her first solo flight, chirping away about how wonderful it was to be flying in the ratified air of the New York cultural scene.

He had taken her to dinner at Raoul's, in SoHo. It looks like an ordinary bar, Annie had remarked, beaming, but *the food* and the interesting types of people who come there to dine!

Vanessa shook her head pityingly. Annie was such a country mouse!

For three days and four nights Vanessa had waited for an opportunity to show Annie her own work, to discuss some of the decisions she had made in her own life, to hear more about what was going on in the heart of her childhood friend, but Annie seemed far more interested in exploring the town, on the arm of *Time's* most eligible editor.

The sound of the elevator interrupted her thoughts. She listened closely, but it stopped on the floor below.

Ridiculous. She was like an anxious mother waiting for her daughter's return from her first date.

Yet how could Annie be doing this? For Rick's part, it was perfectly understandable. He was simply a big city boy, compulsive about women. But that her friend should have found him attractive? Didn't Annie know she was playing with dynamite? Driving over a bumpy road with a packet of nitroglycerine in her lap? How could she take such risks with such a wonderful husband and child back home?

Shush, she told herself. Who are you to talk? You didn't invite Mark's kiss, but you didn't turn away from it, either. In fact you wanted him so badly it eclipsed the physical ache of the fall. Why should you make assumptions about Annie's behavior when your own indicts you of the same dangerous moves?

The elevator stopped, this time, on her floor. Quickly

she turned off her bedside light before she heard a key turn and the door open.

Vanessa held her breath. It wasn't as though she were eavesdropping, exactly. If she'd been able to turn invisible and disappear, she would've done so. Sitting in a darkened room pretending to be asleep was the next best thing to not being there at all.

She heard footsteps, then glasses clinking. There was some muffled conversation in which she made out Rick's voice, but not the words. Words weren't necessary to get the picture, however. It was all conveyed in the tone, which was giddy and conspiratorial. They laughed a lot together.

Yet why shouldn't Annie laugh? She realized, by contrast, how deeply somber her friend had been in Vermont. She had come back to New York afraid that Annie was becoming a dour individual, if no less sweet and caring. The sound of their laughter reminded Vanessa of how easily her childhood friend could be moved to mirth. Yes, Annie seemed like a different woman from the one she'd been with in New England, closer to the friend she'd grown up with. Suddenly she was grateful and relieved that the laughter had returned.

When the laughter was replaced by a pregnant silence, Vanessa began to worry again. More accurately, she was seized by a wave of panic. Her pulse quickened, until the faint sounds of whispering ensued. The front door creaked open, but there was silence again. Were they kissing good-night? What in the world was Annie doing?

She heard footsteps approaching the maid's quarters. They became tentative outside of her bedroom; then, slowly, the door opened.

Vanessa's first impulse was to close her eyes, lie perfectly still, and affect the heavy, regular breathing of deep sleep. Instead she sat up, flicked on the light.

" 'Nessa, sorry to wake you."

"That's all right, Annie."

She looked positively vibrant in her yellow eyelet cotton dress. It highlighted her blond hair and tanned skin, the dewy blue of her eyes, and the only piece of jewelry she wore, a gold wedding band.

She sat at the edge of the bed and Vanessa was reminded of Lisa Bach's description of her book: she could even glimpse those staggering powers of healing and destruction in Annie. No wonder women had submerged them. They were too overwhelming to face day after day.

"Have you been asleep long?"

Vanessa shook her head. "No. To tell you the truth, I wasn't asleep at all. I was just lying here in the dark."

Her friend considered the response for a moment, then nodded. "Couldn't you sleep?"

"I was too anxious."

"I see." Annie gazed down at her hands and caught sight of the ring. She looked up quickly, the excitement that had shown in her eyes transformed into worry.

"Have you been enjoying yourself?" Vanessa sounded self-conscious, even to her own ears.

"Very much. I haven't had so much fun—felt so glad to be alive—in— in—I don't remember how long."

"I'd hoped we'd at least have a moment to talk before you went home tomorrow. You said you were anxious to show me your clippings."

"I did want your advice, but I left them with Rick."

149

"I see." Vanessa tried not to sound wounded.

"I *do* want to talk," Annie hastened to add. "That's why I came in."

Vanessa studied her friend. The ground of their relation-ship was shifting beneath them and she felt the tremors acutely. "Now that you're here, I don't quite know what to say." She bit her lip and turned her head to the side.

Vanessa felt guilty, jealous, and protective all at the same time. "What's going on, Annie?"

"Don't be too hard on me, 'Nessa. "

"Do you know what you're doing?" Vanessa tried to keep her voice soft.

"But I haven't—"

"Oh, I'm not saying you've slept with him or anything like that. It doesn't matter. What does matter is that you're courting disaster at the expense of your husband and child."

"Vanessa!" Annie stood up and began to pace back and forth in front of the bed. Her eyes shot sparks, like stones rubbed against flint. "How dare you judge me that way?"

"Annie, I was only—" she tried to retreat.

"What do you know about how it feels to live the kind of life I've been living? Do you know what it is to feel more like a *function* than a human being?"

"Annie—"

"No, let me finish!"

Vanessa laid her hands deliberately on top of the blanket and waited.

"You always say the grass is greener, and maybe it is true. But from where I sit, you know nothing about the

150

endless, numbing repetitions of domesticity. You are free to fly around the world. You have access to the finest art, conversation, and company. And you sit there and look at me with something approaching righteousness—"

"Please, Annie, no more." She reached out with one hand. "I apologize. Really, I'm sorry." Tears rolled down Vanessa's cheeks. She hadn't meant to criticize her friend. She only wanted the ground to stop shifting.

Annie stopped her pacing and came over to the bedside. "You've got to understand— I'm more alive than I've been since you knew me in Virginia. This weekend I've felt things that I'd forgotten existed."

"I do understand." Vanessa nodded, wiping her cheek with the back of her hand. As much as she longed for the solid ground of their friendship, she had to admit that they'd both changed. Still, she could be supportive.

"Do you know how it feels to find yourself like that again? It's like a . . . a resurrection."

The Eternal Goddess come alive, thought Vanessa, but she knew better than to say it.

"Guess what?" Annie jumped up from her perch on the bed, too excited to remain seated. She was again transformed into a child with a secret.

"What?" Vanessa smiled encouragingly.

"Tonight Rick asked me to rewrite the essay on Glen Canyon! Can you imagine that, Vanessa! On Saturday I showed him some of the things I've written, and he said they were first rate. He didn't even care that I'd only published in the local paper. And if it works out, he says there might be other projects I can do."

"But won't you have to be in the city to do that?"

"Not full time. I can take work up with me to Vermont. But it does mean I'll have an excuse to come in to New York more often. Maybe with some regularity, even." Annie reached out and hugged her friend. "Oh, Vanessa, it's like getting a reprieve."

Vanessa let her gaze wander over Annie's shoulder. She noted, almost absently, the way the lights and the table had been set up, with shelves for her printed work and cubbyholes for her contacts. Each of those attempts to organize and secure her life appeared so desperate, so insubstantial, when faced with the whirlwind of human need: her own, Annie's, and Mark's.

The room seemed to dissolve into chaos as she patted Annie's back reassuringly, but the blur was just a momentary renewal of her tears. If only someone would grant her a reprieve from the feelings inside herself!

"Vanessa?"

From the single word she recognized the voice. "Hello, Mark." Her own voice sounded scratchy, as if the tightness in her throat were constricting her vocal cords. "How are you doing?"

"All right, I guess." He paused. "Say, I'm calling for Annie. Is she still there?"

His question surprised her. "No, she's on her way home. Didn't she reach you? I know she tried several times. "

"Well, we were out a lot."

"Did you go fishing?"

"Fishing, yes, and camping and hiking, and Saturday we rented a canoe that we hauled to the Green River. Our lunch got soaked and so did we, but you know, Danny really got the hang of handling an oar."

In her delight she forgot her reserve. "I would love to have been there."

"That would have made it even better." For a second he was silent, as if imagining the three of them tucked into the tent. "Danny wants to know when his 'Nessa is coming back. He misses you."

"I miss him, too." She couldn't think about Danny too much or her heart ached.

"And, to be truthful," Mark added, "there is someone else who wants to know when you're coming back."

His words touched her deeply. They also frightened her, the way Annie had the previous night. Where was the order? Where were the rules? What would happen if they followed their hearts instead of their heads?

"I love Danny," she told him, "and if I'm honest, I have to say I am drawn to you, Mark. But that's the problem. Annie's still my best friend."

"I know," he said, the gravity falling heavily on the two words. "And she's my wife."

There was silence on both ends of the line.

"I guess I'd better start home now." His patients had been seen for the day, and he'd made no plans for his lunch hour. "I have a lot of dishes to do if she's going to be home this afternoon." He sounded resigned, but not happy. "I don't want to spoil her vacation by reminding her what slobs she lives with."

Vanessa forced herself to laugh. "I'm sure you'll both be appreciated," she said, and hoped it would be true.

CHAPTER FOURTEEN

Annie bought her ticket for the train beneath the great marble arch at the Forty-Second Street side of Grand Central Station. The train was already boarding when she reached the gate, and she found herself a window seat in a forward car. It was virtually empty, with the exception of a couple of college kids on their way to Bard or SUNY Albany, and a handful of residents on their way to Ossining, Croton-on-Hudson, or Mechanicville.

She closed her eyes for just a second and again found herself in Rick's maroon-carpeted office, sitting on the couch with a photo layout of Glen Canyon spread on the table in front of them. The rusts and ochres of the rocks, the deep-shadowed reflections of trees on the water, merged with the colors in the office: the mahogany desk, off-white walls, the tanned leather couch and huge armchairs. Rick and she were floating together in this sea of color, between towering cliffs, as if down a great river. She had dozed off when the sudden lurch of the train woke her, as the river in her dream carried them to a dangerous waterfall.

The train emerged from the tunnel, where the tenements of Harlem and The Bronx formed a backdrop that made her think of the microscopic life of Glen Canyon: the lichens, insects, and tiny animals she had found so

155

exciting when, as a child, she had explored the dry canyon bed and walls.

The streets here were also teeming with life. The cluttered strivings of humanity might be no more than the organic growth of moss on a stone.

Yes, but to be able to make some sense of the pattern, even for a moment, to rise far enough out of the mold to make a statement with one's life, seemed to her a wonderful thing.

Up in Vermont she was just one of the innumerable forms of life on the side of the rock, but in Manhattan she had viewed the works of Rothko at the Guggenheim, and had spoken with the literary community at a cocktail party. Here she had felt her life expand into something more.

The buildings melted into the trees and lawns of suburbia. Eventually those, too, gave way to the wonderful expanse of the Hudson River. It was as glorious a ride as she had ever taken—this train to Albany. She'd taken a seat on the left side, to follow the twists and turns of the river, with a clear view of the Palisades on the far side. She tried to lose herself in the coves and marshes, the old boneyard with the ghostly hulls of retired naval ships; but even the castles built during the early part of the century by eccentric millionaires could not stop her from replaying the events of the weekend.

At first it had been a casual flirtation that Annie had found merely diverting. After dinner and the Café Roma, Rick had walked her through the streets of SoHo, where he'd given her a tour of the cast-iron architecture and shown her some of the artists' bars. They had made their way to Greene Street, where the music and atmosphere had enthralled her. She had absorbed it all, hungry for new impressions. Apparently Rick had been engaged by her utter enthusiasm.

On the way home, in the back of a taxi, he had stolen a kiss. It was a peculiar position to be in, and Annie had found herself giving in to the moment. At first she had rationalized by saying that it would have been juvenile—even a bit prude—for her to have made a big deal out of it. Besides, her spontaneous affection for him had made it a pleasant task. Afterward, she had of course reminded him that she had a husband and a child in Vermont.

"I see," he had mused. "Does that mean you don't want to see me anymore?"

"I should be the one asking that question," she responded. They'd agreed that the time they'd spent together was too good to give up.

"Does that mean I can't kiss you again?" He pursued her.

She bit her lip but didn't answer.

The following day he had taken her to the Rothko retrospective at the Guggenheim. Around the huge snail-shell of a structure, at the very top of the circular ramp, she had gazed down and taken in at a glance the life's work of the late master. His large canvases of pure color were brighter during his middle years, turning to somber monochromatic blacks and grays toward the end, just before a final burst into full effulgence.

"It's almost embarrassing to see this deeply into someone's soul," she'd told Rick.

"What do you mean?"

"It's like seeing someone naked. Or perhaps I'm seeing myself, my own life in it." She laughed. "I'm just not used to such a powerful artistic statement."

"That's why you should spend more time down here," he had insisted. "You're made for this world."

At that point Rick had touched her more deeply than she had meant to let him. At first he had been a play-mate, someone with whom to share the surface of her New York "experiment," for in truth she had come to New York hoping to be renewed by the change of scene. Suddenly, he had become a guide to an inner experience.

In his office he had shown her the Glen Canyon piece and had asked for her comments on certain portions of the text. When he had offered to hire her to rewrite the essay, she had felt such a rush of gratitude she was nearly moved to tears. It was as though she had finally been pulled out of the anonymous grays of Rothko's mel-ancholy and placed in the midst of his luminous reds and golds.

"If you like the work, and are as quick as I think you are" Rick had touched her hand—"then perhaps you can do more work on a free-lance basis."

The very thought of it!

The kisses, also, had moved from the sheer innocence of novelty to something more profound. Even Rick had hesitated before saying good-bye.

Had she felt guilty?

A little, perhaps, but she had in fact been carried by a current far too powerful to resist. Besides, it was not on-ly exhilarating, it had been life-giving. Yes, it seemed as if her life depended upon it. She felt, as she had tried to explain to Vanessa, whole for the first time in years. Did she feel remorse? It was like asking a starving person if he felt guilty for eating a piece of bread at a banquet.

How she would handle it was yet another considera-
tion. She had already learned by experience that being
an adult meant compromise on many levels. The gallant
knight, the ardent swain—these were myths of her
childhood. Had Mark ever embodied one of them? As a
young doctor he'd had the kind of intense compassion
that had made him seem larger than life. He had cared
so much. With his beautiful hands he had been able to
soothe the more hidden pains in her life. For the first
two years, yes, he had, in fact, been her knight errant.

She had learned a great deal since that time. He was
only human, and his humanity made demands on her
that she had worn herself out trying to meet.

"Why, it's Mrs. Abrams. I thought it was you from the
rear, but I could only see the top of your head over the
seat."

Annie was wrenched from her meditation to find the
coiffed, middle-aged specter of Mrs. Dumont, wife of the
hospital's chief surgeon, sitting behind her.

"Oh, hello, Mrs. Dumont."

"Madge, darling. No need to stand on ceremony. May
I join you?"

"Of course," said Annie, though she hated to have her
solitude interrupted.

"What a glorious train ride." Mrs. Dumont nestled her
matronly body into the seat. Her immense bosom heaved
when she spoke. "New York is fine, twice a year. A little
shopping, then I am grateful to get back home. And you,
Annie dear?"

"Yes, a little shopping."

She let her end of the conversation drop, and picked
up the threads of the internal monologue she'd been hav-

ing before Mrs. Dumont arrived. How would she handle her situation? She knew that it was impossible to have it all, but if she could have a little taste of it now and then, there might be enough nourishment to make the rest of her life work.

Rick, as exciting as he was, as ardent and supportive, was no more the knight in shining armor than Mark. She had not yet been afflicted with his idiosyncrasies; perhaps if she could accept the limitations of their relationship, she never would be disappointed. Yes, that was the answer. She'd take what was most generously offered by Rick, and ask no more. She'd have more to give to Mark from her renewed supply.

"And did you hear about Mercy's boy?" Mrs. Dumont was saying. "They sent him to the juvenile counselor, who recommended he come for regular treatment at the hospital's psychiatric clinic. But he just refused." She shook her head. "They've lost all control over him. But then, bringing up a boy without a father in the house must be very trying."

"I'm sure."

"Just the other day Mercy was telling me she had done what she could. But she has to work, and being the legal secretary for a Supreme Court judge is a demanding job."

"Yes, I imagine it is."

Annie thought she would go crazy if she had to listen to much more of this talk, and was pleased to see they were coming into Albany. Soon she would be rid of Mrs. Dumont. It was Rick she'd have to deal with. But she knew how she was going to do it. From now on she would be the model wife and mother. No more complaints. If she could just have a piece of life for herself—moments partaking of the exciting things Rick had exposed her to—then all would be well. She *could* get through it. Mark would have his meals on time. Danny would find her more interested in his world. She'd be saved.

"Well, after all that" Mrs. Dumont didn't even bother to see if Annie was listening—"the boy went out and burnt the barn" at McGowan's Bridge. You know the one by the manmade lake? Burnt it down to the ground. Now, I ask you, what could have been going through his head to do such a thing? What could he have been thinking? The world has changed for the worse, I'm sure of it."

Annie silently disagreed. The changes would save her.

CHAPTER FIFTEEN

Mark pulled the car into the lot in time to see the train move into the station. Just in time, he thought. He'd pushed the speed limit excessively because he didn't want to keep his wife waiting. He'd been halfway out the office when Mrs. Watson had rushed in with a feverish baby in her arms. He knew it wouldn't sit well to be late for Annie's return, but he also knew some things were more important than punctuality. Annie would just have to understand. Doctoring meant helping people, whenever there was the need. However, he was glad to have fulfilled both his obligation to his patient and his wife.

He reached the platform in time to see a conductor giving Annie a hand down the stairs. He watched her glance around tentatively, until she spotted him, and raised her hand to signal him.

"Annie, you look great!"

She smiled broadly. "I feel great," she answered, putting her hand on his arm while he kissed her cheek.

"Oh, hello, Mrs. Dumont. I didn't know you'd been away."

"Just for an overnight. Good to see you, Mark."

"Can we offer you a ride into Sherbroke?"

"No, thank you. Walt's in Albany. He'll be here shortly, I suspect."

"Would you like us to wait with you?"

"There's no need. Run along, now, you two."

Mark waved good-bye and shouldered Annie's bag. He watched her sideways as they made their way back to the Toyota, and he realized it wasn't her looks that were different, but that she looked relaxed. Happy. Simultaneously he grasped that he had been dreading her return. In her absence he hadn't had to worry about her dissatisfaction; listen to her complaints.

"You had a good time, then?" he asked as he opened the car door for her.

"It was wonderful from the minute I arrived until the minute I left," She didn't tell him how much she hated to return. "I must have walked a hundred miles over the last three days."

"You sure don't look tired." In fact she looked as though she'd spent a three-day rest cure instead of bustling through the city that depleted his energy. "I thought you and Vanessa would stay up all night discussing old times."

Annie reached over the front seat and dropped her purse in the back beside her suitcase. "Actually, we didn't talk much this visit." Mark raised his eyebrows quizzically. "She was pretty busy, with work and all." She fastened her seatbelt. "So I explored the city without her."

Again his eyebrows flexed upward. "That sounds like an adventure. Were you all right?"

She laughed. "I got turned around in my directions at times, but nothing worse than that. I saw a lot."

Mark listened to her description of the Whitney Museum, of the jazz club she'd been to, the musician she'd heard, the hours she'd spent absorbed in the books at the Gotham Book Mart, and the literary party she'd attended in the private rooms upstairs. She bubbled on enthusiastically, and Mark repeatedly took his eyes off the road to watch her, she seemed so unlike herself.

"You did all this without Vanessa? On your own?"

"I went shopping a couple of times by myself, but Vanessa introduced me to some of her friends, and they introduced me to others. I met a lot of interesting people."

"Who are Vanessa's friends?"

"Oh, she seems to know everybody, but no one person particularly well. She doesn't seem to let people get too close."

"So who are these friends?" He was interested for his own information as much as curious about the quality of his wife's visit.

Annie rattled off a list of some of the people she had met, giving what details she could. As she talked about them, she realized she knew what each of them did for a living, but little else. It had been a source of some embarrassment to her, she recalled, whenever someone inquired what *she* did for a living. "I was the only person who didn't have a career," she told her husband. She didn't bother to add that it had been Rick who'd saved her from excessive embarrassment by introducing her as a free-lance writer from Vermont. He'd said it with such confidence that she'd begun to think of herself in the same way!

"This Rick guy, is he Vanessa's current boyfriend?" From all Annie said, it sounded like he was the most frequent visitor.

"They might have been lovers, but I don't think they are now," she told him, sharing her suspicions. "Vanessa maintains the same distance with him she keeps with all the others," She pondered. "Rick seems like the kind of guy who wants more involvement."

Mark considered what she'd told him. Vanessa's life was becoming clearer to him, her behavior more predictable. He wondered if all the men fell for her as completely as he had, and if perhaps such an immediate reaction frightened her. Maybe she just didn't like being pursued. He couldn't blame her if it happened as often as Annie suggested it did. It would be the cool, indifferent lover who would finally rouse her interest. "So, Vanessa keeps them all at arm's distance?"

"It seems so." She thought for a minute. "In fact, I can't think of another real friend she has."

"Other than you?"

"Yes." She thought back to their weekend. "And sometimes I feel as if we've grown apart. She doesn't confide the way she used to."

"Have you asked her why not?"

Annie didn't answer immediately. Slowly she realized that over the long weekend, she'd been too engrossed in her own adventure to ask about the seeming change in Vanessa's style. She *assumed* Vanessa liked living in New York City, because she'd told Rick she planned to make it her base, but how did she feel, say, about her father? Was she pleased with the assignments she was getting? "Oh, Vanessa's all right, I guess. She always manages. Besides, no one in her position has reason to be unhappy."

Mark thought about all the people he knew who

seemed to have everything and still found cause for complaint. He'd never heard Vanessa whine, but somehow he didn't think she was as blissful as Annie made her out to be. A woman of such passions must find it hard to bury her feelings. But then, what did he know about women's passions? He swung the car into Sherbroke's downtown. Maybe all her passions were channeled into her work.

"Should we stop in town for groceries? What do you want for supper tonight?"

Mark looked surprised. "We've been invited out, remember?"

Annie tilted her head quizzically. "Out?"

"The hospital dinner. I told you."

"I must have forgotten," she answered casually, calling on her resolve not to show her reluctance. "Whose house is it at?" She forced the questions without missing a beat. "What time do we have to be there?"

"Not until six thirty," he told her, relieved that she hadn't launched into a litany of complaints. He was forever cajoling her into coming, and then would feel responsible when she ended up having a lousy time. Tonight's dinner was especially important to him. He'd been appointed as head of the new wing, an honor most physicians didn't receive so early in their careers. It was a tribute to him and he wanted her present. Her absence would have diminished the event, both socially and personally. "It's at the Plunketts' house. By the way, I've made arrangements for a baby-sitter."

"Louise?"

"No, I tried her, but she'd already promised the Hartwells she'd take care of their boy. Laurie Young's agreed to sit for us."

"Laurie?" Annie's brow furrowed.

"You don't like Laurie anymore? Danny loves her."

Annie shrugged. "Laurie's good with him, I know, and she's always been reliable, but I think she had someone over last time we were out."

"A boy?"

Annie nodded.

"If you think you're right, just tell her you don't want her to have company while we're out. She'll listen."

Just the kind of confrontation Annie hated most. She'd find her own way to deal with the problem. Next time she'd make sure she called Louise in time. "Who's with Danny now?"

"He's been with Mrs. Colby all day."

"We'd better pick him up right away. She's bound to be weary."

"I thought we could take advantage of the time, and have a quiet hour to ourselves."

She knew what he was thinking, but she couldn't yield to him just then. "Let's take a quiet hour later, okay?" She smiled wistfully. "I haven't seen my son for days."

"Well, he's dying to see you, too."

Annie played with Danny for the rest of the afternoon, walking with him along the side of the road while he collected rocks. When they reached the old mill, they turned back, and by the time they were home, both his pockets were filled, and she had heard all the details of his weekend with his father.

At first Annie had been a little hurt that he hadn't

168

seemed to miss her much, that he'd had such a good time without her. But after a minute her priorities righted themselves. She was glad he wasn't harboring a resentment; it would make her future trips to New York that much easier to arrange.

Back at the house she stayed in his room with him, playing with the two new miniature racing cars she had brought back for him.

"Come on," she invited, after an hour. "I'll cook you some dinner."

He followed her into the kitchen, his toys in one hand. "Are you and Daddy going out?"

"Uh huh."

"Will I be asleep when you get home?"

"Laurie will put you to bed."

He smiled. He liked Laurie. She let him stay up to watch television. "Will you bring me home cake?"

"If they have any," she promised, taking the skillet down from the rack over the stove. "What would you rather have for dinner, a hamburger, tuna and noodles, or macaroni?"

"Hamburger!"

She made a little salad, and he picked out the cucumbers and olives while the patty cooked.

"We should be thinking of going soon." Mark poked his head into the kitchen. She could see he had put on a clean shirt. By rote he twisted a knot into his tie and straightened it in the window reflection. "I'll watch the burger while you dress."

"Thanks." She untied her apron. "There is milk in the fridge and applesauce if he wants some." As she left the room, she heard Danny explaining how to toast the buns *slightly.*

Laurie rang the doorbell as Annie slid up the zipper on her red sleeveless dress. Since Mark had put on a tie, she added earrings and a single string of pearls. One never knew for sure what the dress code would be. Sometimes she'd take care, only to find no one else had bothered; it was even worse when she wore the same outfit she'd worn all day, and everyone else appeared spruced. Now she just followed Mark's cue.

"What's tonight's occasion?" she asked, as they turned onto Vesper Street.

He found a spot behind a line of parked cars. "Fundraiser for the new wing of the hospital."

"Will all the wives be here?"

"I expect so." He studied her closely as she walked ahead of him toward the house. So far no complaints, but she didn't want to be there, he knew. He wondered what it would take to interest her in community activities.

"Mark, good to see you!" A plain-faced but smiling Mrs. Plunkett greeted him. "And Annie, how nice of you to come."

"Hello, Mark." Dr. Plunkett held out his hand to welcome his young colleague. He smiled warmly at Annie. "You're just in time to settle a dispute for us," he said, leading Mark into the middle of a small cluster of dark-suited men holding drinks in the living room.

"Aren't men rude?" Mary Plunkett invited Annie into her confidence. "Ches didn't even ask what you'd like to drink."

"What do you have?"

Annie carried her gin and tonic to the edge of the circle Mark dominated. He was explaining to three wealthy

170

patrons the need for a new wing in the hospital.

"There isn't a burns center within a two-hundred-mile radius of Sherbroke. When Larry Heller's boy was burned last fall, it took nearly two hours before he received treatment. They had to fly him clear to Boston. If we'd been set up here, he'd have had a chance of surviving. Harvey Madison wouldn't be scarred if we'd been able to treat him immediately."

"But you say the new wing would house an orthopedic center as well?" the balding man with a pink complexion asked. "Wouldn't it be wiser to take one step at a time?"

"Our staff is capable of handling both improvements at once, sir. And neither venture is a risk. As it is, we have so many broken bones during the ski season, we have to send half *or more* out of the county. It is a known fact that every year the hospital administration struggles to balance the budget. The orthopedic center would pay for itself—and earn back your investment, if I may be presumptuous, Mr. Kelly— in the next five years."

There were further questions from the other potential contributors, but Annie didn't stay to hear them. She wandered out of the living room, through the den, and into the kitchen, where she heard the laughter of women's voices. In a house full of familiar faces she was without a friend. For a minute she wished Vanessa were with her, to prove what kind of tedium she had to put up with, but the new Vanessa might be contrary enough actually to enjoy the gathering.

"Hello, dear." Madge Dumont opened the circle of women to welcome her. "Annie and I spent the day in New York together," she told the others, "only neither of us knew it, right, dear?"

171

She let out a hearty laugh and left Annie to explain. "We met on the train, coming home."

"The last time I went into New York, I couldn't wait to get out. It's so dirty!" Sue Hanover dusted her tiny white hands. She was a mousy woman, about Annie's age, with three little girls. Her husband specialized in the ears, noses, and throats of Windham County.

"You couldn't get me into that city with a team of horses," Lucy Parker admitted.

"You've never been?" Annie was shocked.

"No, and I never will, if I have anything to say."

Annie was about to inquire why, when Margaret Given came into the room. "Glad to find you all together," she said, her pleasant voice rising from deep within a sizable bosom, and aired through a stationary smile.

For as long as Annie had known the gynecologist's wife, she had never seen her without that smile. Wasn't she ever unhappy?

"Girls!" The stately matron settled herself on the stool by the counter. "It's going to take all of us to complete our share of the fund-raising. Sue, you said you'd canvass the downtown section. You think you'll be able to convince all the store owners of their obligation?"

"I'll bend whatever arms I have to," Sue answered the leader.

"I think I can enlist the service organizations," Mrs. Given announced. "Now, what about the rural community? Annie, your husband has lots of patients out there. Do you think you can handle it?"

"I don't think I could, really," she said shyly.

"I'll take that group," Sally Neighbors volunteered. She worked part-time in the post office, and knew most of the rural deliveries.

"Good. Then we need someone to supervise the bake sales each week." Margaret Given spoke as from a mental list. "And someone to solicit the churches."

"I'd probably have some luck with the church community," Madge Dumont answered.

"Could you supervise the girl scouts' bake sale Saturday mornings?" The question was directed at Annie.

"I wish I had the time to volunteer, but I'm afraid I'm very busy these days."

"You have time for shopping trips to New York," Madge Dumont challenged, and the look in her eye reminded Annie that she'd never liked the woman.

"We all have families to care for," Mrs. Given reminded her. "Surely you can find time for one morning a week—"

She was not going to be trapped into a committee project that didn't interest her. "As I said, I would like to help, but I don't have the time to spare. I've just accepted a writing assignment while I was in New York."

"Really?" The gynecologist's wife asked the question, but every eyebrow shot up. "This is the first we've heard that you're planning to move."

"Nothing so drastic as all that," she quickly corrected. "The nice thing about writing is that it travels well. I won't have to go in but once or twice a month, but my spare time will be taken up with the work."

"Well, I'll just have to see to the bake sales myself, then," Mrs. Given finished. "Unless one of you others has time to carry Mrs. Abrams's load."

"I think I have Saturdays free," Sally Neighbors contributed, smiling so sweetly at Annie that she couldn't

173

tell if there was something behind it.

"Now that our business is settled, shall we lay the table for dinner? I suspect our men will be hungry before long."

Annie hated to be induced into this task, as much as she resented the assumption that as a doctor's wife she'd be free to raise funds for the hospital. None of these women, she realized, with the exception of Sally, who helped out at the post office, had jobs. Their worlds revolved around their husbands', and they were expected to be not only content, but cheerful with their situation. Maybe *they* were content, but Annie wanted more. She accepted the tureen of soup from her hostess and carried it into the dining room. Setting it on the far end of the buffet table, she disappeared into the living room instead of returning to the kitchen.

Dr. Hanover approached her. "You're Dr. Abrams's wife, aren't you? I know who all the other wives belong to."

She had been introduced to him before, on more than one occasion, but she hadn't seen him in years. Though he and Mark were on the same staff, they were not close friends outside of work. "Good to see you, Dr. Hanover."

"This is Jack Hindrik. He and his wife, Ginny, just moved to Sherbroke, and they are very enthusiastic about the new wing."

"Your husband is quite a salesman, Mrs. Abrams," he said jubilantly. "You must be proud of him."

"Of course she is," Dr. Hanover answered. "We're all proud of Mark. Best loved doctor in the entire community. If I worked the hours he did, my Susie would divorce me," he said, confident that this was the last thing his

174

wife would ever do. "You must be a patient woman, Ann."

He was talking for the other man's benefit, and Annie didn't feel an answer was necessary. "How do you like Sherbroke, Mr. Hindrik? Have you been here long?"

"They bought the old Thompson house," the doctor answered for him. "Completely restored it."

"That's a lovely house," Annie remarked diplomatically. "And you like it here." She wasn't particularly interested, but it kept her from having to help in the kitchen. She wondered if the other women were discussing her news.

"Love it. Wouldn't leave for the world. Can't wait to plug my maples next February. I've got sixty acres full of syrup just waiting to be tapped."

Apparently that was enough for him, Annie considered. But then, he was retired. Maybe he'd had a full life already and was ready to settle down.

"Do you work for the hospital, too?"

Annie smiled. "I'm afraid nursing has never appealed to me.

"Annie has a young son," Dr. Hanover answered, as if to explain it all.

"I see." The other man nodded, enjoying the vision of the pretty young wife at home with her son. It gave his world a nice order.

"And I am a free-lance writer," she added, feeling some need to defend herself.

"You are?" both men chorused.

"For the local paper?" the newcomer asked.

"Right now I'm working on a photo-essay for *Time* magazine."

"Mark never told me that." The doctor seemed distraught at not having known.

"It's a new development. I just got this job." There was no need for him to know it was her first.

"Come join us, Mark." The newcomer stepped back to welcome the young doctor into their conversation. "You must be very proud."

"Proud?"

"Of your wife's accomplishments."

Mark hid whatever surprise he must have been experiencing. "Yes, I am always proud of Annie."

"I didn't know we had a celebrity in our town," Dr. Hanover exclaimed.

"I'd hardly say that," Annie wanted to stop him. She wished she'd never spoken.

"But *Time* magazine, Mrs. Abrams. It takes real clout to work for them."

"This is my first assignment for them," she said, hoping Mark wouldn't speak until she could explain. "I haven't had time to tell Mark about this particular job. I just got back from New York today." She was rushing ahead. "Vanessa's editor at *Time* asked me to rewrite an article on Glen Canyon, Mark. Isn't that good news?"

He wasn't sure how to respond, but followed Annie's lead with a smile. "It's great news," he said, and laid his arm around her shoulder. "Just great."

"There, I think the ladies want us for dinner." Dr. Hanover held out his arm to Annie. "Shall we walk in?"

"You dropped quite a bomb on me tonight," Mark admitted on their way home from the supper. "I wish you had prepared me for it."

"I was going to tell you tonight." She stared straight ahead into the darkness, the headlights like beams into the unknown. "Are you mad?"

"Stunned." He turned on the heater. The night had turned chill. "What will this job mean to our lives?"

"I don't think it will change much." She covered a yawn with her hand. "I don't have to be in New York for another two weeks. If the editor likes my work, he said he'd hire me for more. I don't think I'd ever have to go in for more than a few days, two or three times a month."

"I have to go to New York in August myself."

"Oh—?"

"I want to visit my parents' grave."

"Your yearly sojourn?"

"That's right."

Mark didn't say anything more. For a mile or two they rode along in silence. "Is this Vanessa's friend, Rick, the one you're working for?"

"Yes." She hoped he didn't press for more information. She didn't want to confuse the issue of her work with her attraction for Rick. "The job means a great deal to me, Mark. I've been dying for something to occupy my mind, something to fulfill—"

"I was thinking it might be the right time to have another child, now that Daniel's starting school."

"I don't want another baby," she answered decisively. "At least not now," she softened her reply. "I want to work, and this job is the perfect opportunity."

He bit his lip. "As long as it doesn't rob Danny of his mother, or me of my wife, I guess it's all right. I hope it will make you happy."

"It will," she promised. Already she could feel it.

CHAPTER SIXTEEN

The cabbie dropped Mark at the steel gate of King David Cemetery, in Ridgewood. He preferred to leave his car in Manhattan, not to have to negotiate traffic before and after his yearly visit to his parents. He paid his fare, walked beneath the arch with the name of the cemetery overhead, and took the gravel path to the main building on the side of the road, glancing briefly at the map of plots. It was like a map of city streets and buildings. The City of the Dead, where his parents now resided. He really didn't have to look at the map. He knew the way.

Whenever he came to the cemetery he had the same thought. It was a city whose population increased every year. In fact, Cities of the Dead all over the world existed alongside those of the living, whose numbers they equaled. Moreover, in spite of the efforts of professionals like himself who spent their lives probing the mystery of the human machine, the population of that city would continue to grow.

Physician, heal thyself, he thought.

He took a path to the right and followed it for about half a mile before stopping at a plot with two white marble stones surrounded by yews. It appeared to have been tended, which is what he'd come to make sure of. Also, he had come to stand before his parents in death as he had in life, to talk with them during this period of stress.

He had come to consult them before his marriage, brimming with joy, to tell them he was about to spend his life with a wonderful girl named Annie. At the birth of his son, their grandchild, he had whispered the child's name to the stone. And when he was deciding to leave what might have become a burgeoning New York City practice to settle in rural Vermont, he had asked their advice. The only answer he'd heard was the sound of his own heart beating. "Listen to your heart"; he accepted that as the answer.

But what was his heart saying now?

"Mom, Dad, I don't know what to do," he whispered, and knelt before his father's grave. "Annie and I have drifted apart."

His father, he knew, would have told him to bite the bullet, to do whatever was necessary to save the marriage, to keep the family together. Theirs had been a sturdy family. His parents, having spilled onto the shores of Ellis Island, had made their way to the Lower East Side of New York to find that the terms of existence meant struggle. They had been through the Great Depression, his father in a tailor shop, his mother taking in washing. Still, they had managed to send both their boys to college. His brother had vowed never to be poor again and lived the life he had promised himself. Mark had always felt the fragility of his parents' health in the harshness of their lives; he'd seen his father's face worn with fatigue, borne witness to the rheumatic heart that had eventually killed his mother. His vow had been to help his parents and those like them. The Abramses had been proud of both their sons.

They would have urged him to lay down the law to his

wife. It was their way, and from the grave he heard the instruction.

"But my wife wants to leave me," he protested, then stopped himself. No, it wasn't only Annie. He couldn't blame it all on her. She was struggling to discover the truth of her feelings, and that was all one could do. He recalled his feelings for Vanessa, how he'd tried to disregard them at first, to think of her merely as a dear friend. But since that day by the stream, when she had fallen, and he had kissed her before he'd realized what he was doing, the pull had been too strong to ignore. It wasn't just a physical attraction, though that was there, too. Rather, he had the sense of being completely at home with her, knew he could say aloud whatever existed in his most private thoughts. He had turned toward Vanessa as a flower turns toward the sun.

Adultery? A prelude to adultery?

It couldn't be summed up so simply. No, it would be wrong to punish himself for feeling what he did; as wrong as for him to blame Annie for her feelings. And what about Vanessa, who was caught in the middle? Certainly what he felt had to be shared by her as well, was too powerful a force to be his alone. It was almost as if, at times, they didn't need words at all. He had understood the alarm in her eyes when he tried to speak with her before she left Vermont. All he could do, in his present confusion, was to keep himself from making demands on either Vanessa or Annie. But it was getting harder. He thought about Vanessa incessantly, wanted to see her, if only for a moment. If he could just see her, it might relieve his emptiness, enough for him to take the drive back to Vermont with some peace of mind. He'd just call, and drop up to Philip's apartment on some pre-tense. A cup of coffee with her would be enough.

"What shall I do? Dad? Mom? Tell me. Save the family at any cost? No. It doesn't work like that anymore. You two had a common struggle. Today everyone wants to make his own way. In the world I live in, unless you are true to yourself, you have nothing to give to anyone else. Can you understand that?"

He listened, but there was only silence.

"It's different now," he tried again to explain.

It was his mother's advice that he heard. As a boy of fifteen he had been forced to fight with two tough kids from the Irish section. One boy had called him a sissy and tried to take away his first-baseman's mitt. Mark had thrown him to the ground, wanted to hit him but pulled back, rose, and walked away. He could still recall the helpless expression on his antagonist's face.

"There's no easy answer," his mother had told him afterward, in the safety of their kitchen. "You did what you had to. I can only repeat the words of the prophet Micah: *'Be just, love mercy, and walk humbly with thy God.'* I know you, Mark. You will always do that."

His eyes filled and he chanted the words of the Kaddish, the Hebrew prayer for the dead. It was a marvelous prayer; in it one expressed grief for the loss, then was encouraged to rejoice at the life remaining. When he was finished, he bent down and picked up two pieces of white gravel. Finally, he placed a stone on top of each of the graves, as was the custom, then turned and walked away.

CHAPTER
SEVENTEEN

August, one hot breath beyond the Dog Days. Late summer in Manhattan, where pigeons roosting in the eaves purr like fat, airborne kittens.

At a little after ten in the morning, the sun was a luminous disc in an ice-blue sky. It was a crystal morning, with a breeze from the northwest blowing all the industrial air out to sea so that the edges of things seemed etched into the horizon. Vanessa lay back down on her chaise longue in a brief, two-piece bathing suit, remarking to herself that the day was so clear she could distinguish the faults and striations of the distant cliffs abutting New Jersey.

The passing weeks had been good to her. Vanessa had made her decision to remain in Manhattan, in spite of the fact that the image of Mark continued in her mind. She'd ceased trying to control this, to block him out. Instead she made the image a co-conspirator, talking with it in her quiet moments, sharing feelings and ideas she might have shared with the real person. In doing this, she reasoned, Mark became an imaginary friend, something quite apart from the factual man who had inspired the fantasy. It was harmless, made her feel a bit like a child with a teddy bear. There was no harm done; in fact, it gave her moments of intimacy she might not otherwise have had.

It also helped her to accept Annie's now regular visits to Manhattan. Two or three times a month her friend blew through town like a whirlwind, full of exacerbated energy. A dam whose floodgates were open, Annie poured herself into what was quickly becoming an alternative life.

Vanessa wondered how Mark was taking it, but never inquired, not even of her imaginary friend. She simply wished him well, soothed him if she thought he was upset, allowed him to ease her if she felt in need of comfort. For the rest she tried not to get in the middle of Annie and Mark's relationship.

Besides, there had been plenty to keep her busy. So much so that she hadn't had time to cultivate any new relationships of her own. Is it really that I don't have time, she wondered? It would be a kind of irony if the imaginary Mark were all she needed. She knew that before she could form another bond, she would have to let the imaginary one go. But she wasn't ready to do that. Not yet. Soon, but not yet.

Vanessa sighed as the sun penetrated her sunscreened body, kneaded her muscles like a practiced masseuse. Again she found herself talking to the imaginary friend. She felt as if he were lying on the chaise longue next to her, dressed for a fishing expedition in his brown chinos and blue-and-white-plaid flannel shirt. Aren't you hot? She asked. He nodded. Well, then, could he tell her why she felt such comfort in his overdressed presence? No, he shook his head. He couldn't explain it, except to say that he took equal comfort in hers, which was underdressed and beautiful. Vanessa blushed, embarrassed at the likelihood she was complimenting herself. Except that in this game she played, Mark had taken on a life of his own. It's magic, she said. He smiled. She closed her eyes and lay back.

It was her first full day off in months. She had completed the Bowery photo-essay, the text for which was being written by the writer Ched Royales, an old friend who lived down on Great Jones Street. She had put off portrait sittings for another week, and refused any magazine assignments until after Labor Day, when the vacationers returned from Martha's Vineyard, East Hampton, and St. Tropez. And Annie wasn't due back for one of her weekends for another five days.

My God, she thought, what a transformation her best friend had undergone. Annie had had her blond hair straightened, and had taken to wearing clothes that accentuated her femininity, instead of her girlishness, like off-the-shoulder blouses. Nor did Annie waste a moment's time in small talk or somber reflection. She whipped through the apartment and the streets of Manhattan like a force of nature. Sure, it pleased Vanessa to see her friend happy, but it was also taxing, and she worried about the long-range effects. They had shied away from sharing any real confidences; and yet the bond of their friendship was secure enough to hold through troubled times, and while it hadn't yet reached a comfortable new level, she was pretty sure it would.

Her breathing grew shallower, and Vanessa drifted off into the warmth that engulfed her.

The phone interrupted her peace.

"Vanessa, this is Mark. Am I disturbing you?"

"No, not at all," she said, but a shiver ran up and down her spine like a winter chill. "I'm just sunning myself on the terrace."

"I'm over on Park Avenue, at the office of an old friend. Would you mind if I came by for a minute?"

"No, I—"

"There are some papers I need to pick up. If you're busy I can be in and out before you know it."

"Don't be silly, Mark." She regained her composure. "We could have lunch."

"About twelve?" He tried to sound calm.

"That will be fine."

"Great. See you later."

She returned to the chaise longue, but her imaginary Mark was no longer there. Nor could she summon him to her side. He had been reabsorbed in the real one, and this made her feel a vulnerability she hadn't experienced since her return from Vermont in June.

Vanessa felt excitement and apprehension in equal measure as she lay back in the sun: she wanted to see Mark, but how could she defend herself against a man she'd been telling her most intimate secrets to for months!

She shifted position, unable to find one that would restore her former comfort. Even the sun had become harsher, more abusive. Forget it, Vanessa told herself. She rose, showered, then dressed, and still had time left to run down to the corner delicatessen to pick up some lunch.

By the time the buzzer rang, she had set the table with a tabouli salad, cucumbers and onions vinaigrette, a cold potato soup, and iced tea.

When she opened the door, Mark stood there, tall and tanned, his brown hair shot through with golden highlights. He was dressed casually, in a dark-blue alligator knit shirt and light tan slacks.

"Good to see you, Vanessa," he said, looking directly into her eyes, as if to communicate a deeper greeting.

She broke the intensity with a noncommittal smile. "Come on in, Mark."

She was prepared carefully to sidestep the physical contact of an embrace, but he walked past her without even stretching out his hand. Vanessa felt a disappointment she immediately masked, but she had more difficulty hiding the sense of familiarity she felt in his presence, and wondered if it was the fruit of her illusory intimacy.

"I hope I didn't interrupt your afternoon."

"Stop being apologetic." She walked over to the table. "Lunch is ready. I can't think of a pleasanter way to spend it.

"Thank you." He sat down at the head of the table, facing the terrace. "I thought about calling you last night, to let you know I was coming into the city."

"I was out, I'm afraid. A friend of my father's was just in from Mexico."

"How is he?"

"Clemens? Fine, I guess. I receive a letter from time to time. Apparently he's gone from Mexico to Belize, to do some underwater photography."

"Do you wish you were with him?"

"No." Vanessa shook her head. "I'm happy to be where I am." She lowered her eyes. At that precise moment she was speaking the absolute truth.

"This is marvelous, Vanessa—" He took another heaping forkful of the tabouli. "I don't know how you do it.

Hold down a career, move around the most exciting circles in New York, and throw together elegant meals for your country cousins."

"I make a great pitcher of iced tea," she admitted, picking up a cucumber. "The rest is from the deli."

Mark grinned, caught in his attempt to compliment her. "Well, from the way Annie describes your life in the fast lane, I get dizzy just thinking about it."

"She tries to do everything in a few days." Vanessa watched him spoon his soup. "I can ration my time."

"I see." He put his spoon down and just stared at her.

His look unnerved her. Vanessa broke the silence. "Did you come here to talk about Annie?" That was a tricky subject, but it was less personal to discuss her friend than to talk about the feelings between Mark and her.

He nodded. "In part." He, too, understood the danger of addressing his feelings. And yet he'd have to, if he continued to sit with her much longer. "I don't know what to make of this whole thing."

"What do you mean?"

He forced his thoughts to Annie. "What's happening to my wife? She's changed."

"In what way?" Now she stared at him intently.

"Just look at her." He held his hands out, as if to indicate the answer was as obvious as his open palms.

"She looks wonderful to me. Better than I've ever seen her."

"Yes, I know." He shook his head. "She looks ravishing."

"Doesn't that please you?"

"It would, if I thought she was happy."

"Isn't she?"

"On the surface of it. She's always cheerful. Dinner is always served with a smile, and on time. She never complains anymore. When a chore needs to be done, she hops to it. If Danny makes a demand on her, she's there to meet it.

"I don't understand, Mark." Vanessa took a sip of the soup. "Sounds to me like everything is better than it was."

"I'm a doctor. I diagnose things every day from symptoms." He set down his glass. "Something is going on under that surface, and I can't figure out what it is."

He stared down at the table, and Vanessa felt a sudden, sympathetic twinge. Yes, it must all be very confusing for him.

"Mark, isn't it better to have Annie's spirits up than where they were when I came to visit you?"

"Yes, but—" He gestured with his hands in exasperation. His next words came out almost in a whisper. "I hardly know the woman I'm living with!"

"Who is she?"

"I don't know. I hardly see her. She disappears into the study every night to work, and when I touch her, it's like touching a total stranger." He stared straight ahead, past the terrace and beyond.

Vanessa waited until she was sure he had said everything he was thinking. "As I see it, Annie is discovering herself in ways that are new and exciting for her."

"I'm not denying it," he protested. "I wouldn't think to deprive her of her work, or her trips, if that is what is making her happy. But it's not the Annie I married."

"Do you expect people to remain the same all their

lives?"

"Makes me sound old fashioned, doesn't it?" He conceded this with a smile. "But we did build our lives and have a child on certain assumptions."

"I understand that," she agreed. "But you can't always diagram your life, and expect it to follow as you've planned." If she had foreseen her hunger for him she might have been able to avoid it. "I've been gypsying around since I was a child, and thought I always would. But suddenly the idea of staying in one place, of drawing the circle of intimacy closer, appeals to me." She lowered her eyes as she spoke. This was the closest she'd come to speaking her true desires. "Annie, on the other hand—" she looked up and met his eyes, "—has never been able to test herself in the world as you and I have."

"That's great for Annie, but every time she comes down here to find herself, Danny is without a mother."

"Would you prefer your son to have a mother who is constantly on the edge of a nervous breakdown?"

Neither of them so much as looked at the food in front of them.

Vanessa had played the devil's advocate, yet all the while she had spoken on Annie's behalf she had felt the acuteness of Mark's pain. And she could imagine what the situation must be doing to Danny.

"Listen." Mark traced an invisible line on the surface of the wooden table. "I have an idea." He glanced up, but couldn't engage her expectant eyes. He had to sound casual if he were going to ask his question, and there was no way to feign nonchalance when looking deep into her eyes. "You spoke of spending time in Vermont," he started, "maybe even photographing the children and the landscape. How about it? I know Danny would love to see you."

"Mark." She felt her face color.

"Please, Vanessa." He let her see the importance of his request.

"Can't you see what we'd be doing?" Her words came out more sharply than she had meant them to. "Can't you see?" she repeated softly. After all, she wasn't angry at him, but frustrated by the danger of the situation. She had to struggle to resist the temptation, when she wanted, more than anything, to accept his invitation.

"I guess it wouldn't work," he answered, nodding, his defenses reconstructed to disguise his real feelings. "I know your life down here is full. Annie has told me about your suitors—"

"Don't be a fool!" Now she was angry. He refused to see what was really happening. "That's not the reason, and you know it. As much as I wish it were otherwise, I haven't been able to keep you out of my thoughts since I got here."

"No, I wasn't sure." Her declaration dissolved his defenses.

"Can't you see it doesn't matter how many invitations I get from smooth corporate executives?" She was up and pacing the room. "They mean nothing to me. Nothing." She sat back down, as if exhausted from admitting her feelings. "I spend half my time confiding in an imaginary friend who looks just like you."

"If that's how you're feeling, why not come up and spend some time with me? Us," he corrected himself, reaching across the table and taking both her hands in his.

"Because we'd be courting disaster." Her eyes turned dark with regret. "As much as I care for you, Annie is still my best friend."

"Christ!" He let go of her hands and leaned back in his chair. "I can't stand the irony of it." He threw his napkin onto the table. "I've got a wife who doesn't want to be with me, and a woman who does, but can't because of my wife. I don't believe it."

Vanessa shook her head sympathetically, but spoke firmly. "There's nothing we can do, Mark, as long as she's your wife."

"Her body's up there, but not her soul. I'm starved, Vanessa. You say Annie has a right to grow in whatever direction she must, but don't I have a right to some emotional nourishment, too?"

"Of course you do." There was suffering in both of their eyes, but it was as though they were separated by an invisible barrier that neither of them could surmount.

"But as long as Annie is still living with you, and the two of you haven't talked about the problem, what can you expect me to do? I can't be your mistress, Mark. That would make everyone miserable."

"You're right." He turned aside. "Of course, you're right."

"When you and Annie have worked it out, then we'll see. Until then, Mark, how can I get any more involved than I already am?"

He nodded, then lifted his fork to play with the tabouli. "I'm so confused, Vanessa. I'm losing my wife. My marriage is empty. It's all like a bad dream, except for you." He took her hand carefully into his. "I love you, Vanessa."

192

She didn't answer him. Nor, it appeared, did he expect an answer. But the declaration seemed to lift his spirits some and he began to eat again. They finished the rest of the meal in relative silence. It was as though they had both relieved themselves of the heavy unspoken burden and were free again just to savor the moments between them.

Vanessa cleared the table while Mark disappeared into his brother's study. He might as well pick up the deed to his parents' burial plot, as long as he was there. Finding the document, he placed it in his briefcase, and announced he was ready to leave.

"Are you going back to Vermont tonight?" Vanessa asked, afraid of the fantasy that lurked at the door of her question.

"I wouldn't have to." He smiled. "Is that an invitation?"

"Go on." She pushed him playfully to the door of the apartment. "Don't make me reject you anymore."

He stopped at the threshold, his hands on her arms. "Thanks, Vanessa. Talking to you helped."

"Don't do anything rash." An expression of alarm fell over her face.

"This has nothing to do with you, Vanessa. Even if I didn't feel about you as I do, I'd still have to deal with the situation. I know that now. But your honesty—knowing how you feel—has helped me tremendously."

"I hope everything works out, Mark."

"One way or another."

"I don't want to lose either of you. How can I keep you both in my life when you're pulling me in opposite directions?"

"Shhh." Mark brought her into his arms so gently it felt more like comfort than excitement. "There is a right thing to do, Vanessa, and a right way to treat the situation. We'll find it."

He continued to stroke her back until she grew calm. He held her at arm's length for a moment, then drew her toward him again and hugged her warmly. Reluctant to let go, they did, nonetheless, and parted with a feeling of renewed confidence.

Mark's assurance lasted all the way down the elevator and out onto the street. But Vanessa's began to fade the moment she closed the door and was alone above the apartments and rooftops of Manhattan.

CHAPTER EIGHTEEN

"But it's his first week in school."

"I told you Monday I'd have to be in the city Thursday."

"For another long weekend, I suppose." The expression on Mark's face was not pleasant. He couldn't believe his wife valued her work more than her child.

"You act as if I'm going on a vacation!"

"I don't care if you're going to discover the cure for lung cancer. Your child needs you!"

"Don't shout at me," she yelled back. "Danny understands. It's only you who's making a fuss."

Mark slammed his hand down on the kitchen counter. "You're unwilling to see that your job is interfering with your duties at home."

Annie stared at him blankly. "How can you say that?" Ever since she started going to New York she'd made certain that the house had been run to perfection. "Where do you find fault with my performance?"

"That's it exactly." He paced the length of the room. "It's all performance. You may be gone only a handful of days each month, but even when you're here, you're absent emotionally. I almost prefer your complaints."

"You don't want me to be happy, do you? You're jealous!"

"Jealous?" He looked back over his shoulder at her.

"Of my other life." She met his stare. "You resent my trips to New York because you can't control me there." Her voice had risen again, and she'd resumed her pacing. "You want to deprive me of the only joy I have. You can't stand to see me free. The role you've tied me to is suffocating."

"You believe that?" Mark's voice was unsympathetic in its volume. She had put him on the defensive when he thought she should be feeling remorse for the strain she was putting on their family. "Your son is taking the biggest step of his life this week, and after three days you plan to desert him, to work on some stupid article?"

"It isn't stupid, and I'm not deserting him. We are both his parents, remember? What stops you from seeing him off to school for two lousy days?"

"Are you forgetting that I have a job?"

"You seem to have forgotten my job."

They stood at a distance, glaring at each other, their anger seething beneath the temporary silence.

"I think you're a failure at your first job."

"How dare you—" Annie clenched her hand and closed the few steps between them with a swift stride. "You don't care if I'm happy. You just want me to play the game your way." She pounded his chest with her fist. "I won't! I won't do it!" She tried to hit him, but he caught her wrists and held them tightly. "Let go! You're hurting me," she insisted, through tears now brimming in her eyes.

"Mama!" Danny hurried into the room but stopped short when he saw them. "Papa!" There was terror in his voice.

Mark released his grip at once, and Annie rubbed her

reddened wrists, stifling back tears. "Go back to your room, Daniel," she commanded.

"No." The boy was unwilling to be sent away. "Why are you fighting?"

"We weren't exactly fighting." Mark reached out to touch the boy's shoulder, but he pulled away.

"Yes, you were."

Annie had regained control enough to answer him. "Your daddy and I were having a disagreement. You know how you sometimes fight with Joshua."

"But you always say no hitting."

"That's right. We weren't going to hurt each other. Everything's okay now. Don't you worry."

He scrutinized his parents. Everything didn't look okay.

Annie created a cheery attitude. "Are you almost ready for school?"

"I can't find my belt."

"I'll help you look for it." She was glad to have an excuse to drop the argument. "Let's try the den. Come on, now." She held out a hand to the reluctant follower. "We have to hurry. You don't want to be late."

He didn't budge. "I don't want to go to school anymore."

"Of course you do," she prompted. "You told me how much you liked your teacher."

"Are you going to fight when I'm gone?" He worried.

"No, son. We've stopped fighting."

"Mom, are you going to pick me up after school?"

"Your daddy wants to pick you up today, so he can see your class."

"You're going to see 'Nessa again?"

Annie didn't look over at her husband. "Remember, I told you I have to work this week. I want you to be a big boy while I'm gone. No tears, promise—"

"You're coming back?" He addressed his fears directly.

"I'll be back in time to fix you lunch on Saturday."

"And you won't fight anymore?"

"We won't. Now let's find that belt, or we'll both be late."

How could Mark deny her a chance to fulfill herself? She thought angrily as she searched under the den sofa for Danny's belt. He had no right to keep her from the one thing she loved. She was doing everything she could to keep up her end of the familial responsibility, though increasingly she wished she could give all her time to her work. To him it might just be a stupid article, but she was making a place for herself, and she'd be damned if she'd give it up, for Mark or anyone.

She found Danny's belt in the bathroom hamper, still woven onto a pair of denims. "Don't forget to tie your shoelaces," she called back to him, throwing together the things she'd need for her trip to New York.

The change of season made packing difficult. Just when she'd figured out which of her summer clothes translated into city fashion, the season was past. She'd have to bring along a couple of dresses and let Vanessa advise her. She couldn't wait until she got her first paycheck. With her own money she would be free to buy herself some new clothes. She was so angry with Mark, she didn't ever want to ask his permission again.

"We haven't finished this discussion." Mark stuck his head into their bedroom, his face still dark with anger.

"We have for now," she said, swinging her suitcase up

off the bed and grabbing her coat. "If you want a ride to your office, you'd better come now," she said on her way into the spare bedroom to fetch her briefcase. "I'm taking the bus into Albany and it leaves from Main Street in thirty minutes."

"Annie." He was firm in his insistence.

"There's nothing more to talk about, Mark. We promised Danny we wouldn't fight."

CHAPTER NINETEEN

"You've done a wonderful job with it, Annie, really. I couldn't be more pleased." Rick stood before the storyboard on which the captioned photos that accompanied the article were pinned. Dressed in shirt-sleeves and gray slacks, his red tie pulled down below an unbuttoned collar, he was the complete professional.

"What is it, Rick?" she asked. "I can hear the hesitation in your voice."

She sat on the couch, watched him pace around the storyboard, stop, then start pacing again. The tension of the moment was so great it almost made her forget the tension from which she had fled. Mark's angry voice still echoed in her ears. She could still hear her son, asking if she'd be coming back to him.

Annie had tried to flee those voices with a vengeance. In her flight she'd not even dropped her overnight bag off at Vanessa's, but had come straight from Grand Central to Rick's office. Here, the tension was of a different order, tinged with the excitement of her expectations. Would he like what she had done? Would he consider giving her more work? If so, it would make a legitimate woman out of her far more than marriage had ever done. Her anticipation was almost enough to block out those voices she'd left behind, but not quite. They bled through the moment like muffled whispers. She raised her voice in an attempt to blot them out.

"Tell me, Rick. What's the problem?"

"Nothing you've done." He stopped, patted her on the shoulder. "It's just that, well, it'll never make it past the editorial committee."

"Why"

He walked back around his desk, sat on the swivel chair, and propped his feet up on the blotter. With an automatic gesture he picked up the unlit pipe from the ashtray in front of him and started to suck on it.

"I can't see what's wrong with it," Annie insisted. "The photos are gorgeous, and the text is a perfectly accurate description of what happened."

"As far as it goes, Annie. But you don't know those sharks in the conference room. They're going to get this piece in front of them and tear it apart. I can smell the blood."

"I don't get it."

"This is a rough game. More than half of the pieces we commission never see print. And every editor on the staff brings his article into that committee room prepared for battle. Every other editor comes in with a critical eye, ready to kill it. That's the way the game is played."

"But all the time and money we've put into this?" Annie shook her head.

"Exactly. I've put in a considerable amount of both, and it won't look good for me when it's shot down." He sighed, and sucked harder on his pipe.

"Tell me what's wrong. Maybe we can correct it."

"Wait, I'm trying to put my finger on it."

"If I read this in a magazine, I'd be intrigued. It's a fine piece, Rick."

"Sure, for the Sierra Club, or one of those other ecologically oriented publications, like *Natural History* or the *Smithsonian*."

"What's wrong with that?"

"We're a magazine that's oriented, not to hard news, exactly, but to the dramatic qualities of an event. There's simply not enough drama in this piece. The other editors are going to look at it and yawn."

"I'm sorry, Rick."

"Then they're going to ask me why I spent so much time and money on it."

"Why did you?"

"Because it appealed to me. Damn it, there is drama in this piece. There was tremendous controversy surrounding the flooding of this canyon."

"I recall." She warmed to his growing enthusiasm. "There were the archaeologists who said that the flood would wash away valuable clues to the earlier forms of life on this continent."

"And their opposition was the folks who expected to make a lot of money on a new recreational center," Rick chimed in. "Not to mention the people who simply needed a water supply to live."

"I remember something about a protest from the native Indians, about an ancient burial ground that would be violated by the flood."

"That's an angle." Rick sat bolt upright, jotted down a couple of notes on a pad of yellow legal-sized paper. "Was there a curse on the burial ground? Did the souls of those ancient Indians come back to make life difficult? Great idea, Annie!"

"We'll just have to get more of that into the article,

Rick." Annie sipped the last tepid remains of a cup of coffee.

"Damn it, Annie, we're going to have to fly to Utah and do some pretty fierce interviewing, fast."

"Rick, I—"

"Don't let me down now, Annie. I need your help."

He gave her his earnest blue-eyed stare. "You know both the article and what it needs. You've also spent time out there as a girl, and have a real feeling for the place. You're my ace in the hole."

The thought of going out to Glen Canyon once again appealed to her greatly. Not only that, she would be doing original work on the piece, have a chance at hardcore reporting. It was an opportunity she couldn't turn down. By the same token, how could she go back home to Mark and Danny after their little scene that morning, and announce that she was off for an unspecified length of time to the Southwest?

"We'll leave next Tuesday," he said, marking his calendar. "It'll only take us a few days. At most a week," said Rick, mistaking her indecision for surprise.

"I'd love to, Rick, but—"

"No buts, Annie. It's a way for me to pull my ass out of the fire, and for you to get a foothold in the business. I may even be able to arrange a byline for you."

"A byline." She sounded incredulous.

"If everything goes according to plan. Wouldn't you like to have your name tacked onto a major article?"

"Of course I would."

"Then, it's settled."

What would they say when she told them? It didn't matter. She couldn't turn down such an opportunity.

"It's settled," he repeated. "Right?"

"Okay, Rick."

"That's my sweetheart."

In a minute he switched on the intercom and gave his secretary instructions to book passage for two to Cedar City·, plus a car to be picked up at the airport. "Make it four-wheel drive," he instructed, in case they needed to camp.

"Isn't this going to be expensive?" Annie couldn't ask Mark to pay for her trip.

"Expense is all relative. You are more than worth the cost of airfare, and when the committee reads the piece, they'll think they've gotten off cheap."

He lit his pipe, and suddenly the air was full of Balkan tobacco. "I feel better already." He exhaled a plume of smoke. "What do you say we celebrate tonight with dinner at Lutèce?"

She ·was about to tell him she had always wanted to go to Lutèce when his phone rang. He spoke a few words into the receiver, then handed it to Annie.

"It's for you."

"Who could—" She took it from him and heard Vanessa's voice at the other end. It was shrill, practically hysterical. It made her blood run cold.

"Annie! Thank God I've found you."

"What is it?"

"I just spoke to Mark—"

"No reason to get upset, Vanessa. We just had a run of the mill marital dispute—"

"It's not that, Annie. There's been an accident."

Annie didn't say anything, but pictures of tragedy rushed past the floodgates of her mind, and with them the inexorable sensation of culpability. Whatever had occurred, she had been at the root of it.

"There was a fire, and Danny got caught in it."

"Oh, God—" Annie went pale, the phone slid from her hand.

Rick was up and out from behind the desk in a flash. "What is it?"

"My little boy—"

He helped Annie to the couch, then picked up the dangling receiver.

"No, give it to me." Annie held out her hand. "Vanessa, is he—"

"He's all right. Mark pulled him out in time."

"Is Mark hurt?"

"He's all right, too, but he wants you to come back."

"Vanessa, what am I going to do?"

"Wait right there, I'll be down as fast as I can. I'm going up with you."

Rick had poured her another cup of coffee, spiked with a shot of cognac, and made her stretch out on the couch. He tried to comfort her, but she was frantic with guilt and worry.

Vanessa was there in twenty minutes. With Annie on her arm they caught a cab in time for the three o'clock train out of Grand Central.

Annie was ashen. She walked like a woman in a fog, placing each foot tentatively to make sure the ground beneath was solid before shifting her weight. Vanessa felt as though she were with a sleepwalker and didn't say anything that would jar her awake. Slowly, however, Annie woke by herself, and both women could see the size and shape of the precipice before which she stood.

"What did he say?" Annie asked finally, as the train pulled into Croton-on-Hudson.

"Just what I told you. There was a fire and Danny got caught in it."

"In the house?"

"No, I don't think so. I was so shocked by the fact of it, I wasn't listening for details—just that he and Mark were all right. I called back but no one is answering."

"If anything happened to Danny—" Annie shook her head back and forth to dispel the image behind her eyes—"I don't know what I would have done."

"Easy, Annie," her friend soothed, noticing the color beginning to return to Annie's cheeks.

"We had a fight this morning before I came into New York."

"I know," she answered, nodding.

"It wasn't pretty. Mark accused me of being emotionally absent, and I told him he was trying to suffocate me."

"Stop blaming yourself, Annie."

They were silent again, until just before Albany, when Annie mumbled something under her breath.

"What did you say?" Vanessa asked her.

Annie shook her head, but upon her friend's insistence she repeated what she had said in a monotone that, once again, sounded like the ravings of a somnambulist.

"I said, 'I can't blame myself and I can't be myself, what else is left?' "

No sooner had Annie and Vanessa set foot on the platform of the Albany station than Mrs. Dumont swooped down on them like an avenging angel, her magnanimous bosom contained in a light-blue linen suit.

"There you are, poor dear. I've been waiting for you." She took Annie's free arm and peered over at Vanessa. "I'm Madge Dumont. My husband's the chief surgeon. I didn't think the bus appropriate, and poor Dr. Abrams is too distraught to leave his son."

"You're very kind to pick us up." Vanessa forced a smile. "I'm Vanessa Ansel."

"Kindness has nothing to do with it, dear girl. In this part of the country, if we don't help each other out, we're goners. There's the car. Poor baby, she looks like she's in shock."

"I'll be all right." Annie's voice was soft, but firm.

"Here we are." Mrs. Dumont put a key in the door of a deep red pick-up. "There's room for all three of us in front."

"Do you know what happened?" asked Annie, sandwiched between them.

"Lord, yes, I do." She frowned. "Very strange."

"Maybe we should wait," Vanessa cautioned.

"No," insisted Annie. "I'd like to know."

"Well, we're not sure exactly how he ended up in the Colbys' barn. I guess he just came home after school, and there was no one around to keep an eye on him. Dr. Abrams was in his study, working, no doubt. You know, these medical men never stop. It isn't easy being a doctor's wife," she spoke to Vanessa. "But it does have its rewards."

"I'm sure," Vanessa told her.

"So he got into the barn, and he had some matches, you know, plain old kitchen matches. No one was around, so, naturally, the child started playing with

208

them. One of the matches he struck must have caught. Just a spark will do it, honey. You know, the Colby's' barn is full of hay, and it's been a dry summer. Doesn't take much to set it off."

"Oh, no," groaned Annie.

"It went up like a brush fire. Luckily Dr. Abrams has a view of the barn through his window. He saw the smoke and rushed out. Danny was trapped inside, but your husband went right in through the flames and carried him out . . ."

Vanessa put her arm around Annie, who was weeping on her shoulder. "I think we've heard enough—"

"Fortunately, Mark found a horse blanket, stamped it out before the fire got out of hand, Mrs. Dumont continued, undaunted." One wall of the barn was scorched but otherwise, everything is ok."

"And Mark, is he all right?" Vanessa asked.

"Fortunately, he wasn't hurt, either. Maybe now you can see how important the new facilities are, Ann." Mrs. Dumont sounded like a schoolteacher lecturing a refractory pupil. "I know you said you don't have time for fund raising, that you're busy with more important things, but maybe you can see now how important it is to take care of things back home."

Vanessa rushed to her friend's defense. "I don't think this is the time for a lecture, Mrs. Dumont."

"It's all right, Vanessa." Annie sat up, dried her eyes. She addressed Mrs. Dumont formally. "I appreciate your coming to pick us up, Mrs. Dumont. However, I don't think this incident gives you the right to pass judgment on me."

"I didn't mean to do that, dear. Lord, no." The doctor's

wife shook her head. "But I was just thinking about Mercy's boy, the neglected child grown up into a regular arsonist and I—"

She didn't complete the sentence. The Abrams's driveway came up suddenly on her right.

Mark and Dr. Dumont were talking in the living room when Annie came in, followed by Vanessa and Mrs. Dumont.

"How is he?" asked Annie, and anxiously looked around the room as though the answer to her question lay secreted in a distant corner.

"Calm yourself, Ann," said Dr. Dumont in a voice calculated to act as a soporific. "One hand was burned slightly, but nothing serious. He's very lucky."

"We're all very lucky," put in Mark, barely concealing the blame and anger in his voice.

"Can I see him?"

"Sit down for a moment." Dr. Dumont patted the couch. "You don't want to rush in and upset the boy." Annie chose to sit in an easy chair.

Vanessa noticed that her friend's hands had started to tremble. "Are you all right?"

"I just need a moment."

"Would you like something for your nerves?" Dr. Dumont started to open his black bag.

"No, please." She shook her head.

"Come, darling, I think we've done all we can for the moment." Mrs. Dumont stood in the doorway.

"Perhaps you're right." The doctor slipped into his twill jacket, picked up his bag, and walked over to join his wife. "If you need me, Mark, don't hesitate to call.

Any time, day or night."

"Thanks, Walt. I appreciate all you've done."

"Think nothing of it."

After the Dumonts left, the three of them sat in silence until Annie spoke.

"I want to see my child."

She didn't wait for an answer, but rose and tiptoed to the bedroom door, as if she were walking on a fragile membrane.

"Mommy! Mommy!" Danny sat bolt upright in bed at the sight of Annie's face.

"Oh, Danny," she cried, as she rushed to her son's bedside, bent down, and pressed his small body gingerly to hers. She felt the texture of his blue cotton pajamas, his silky, uncombed hair. He still smelled like a baby to her. She cradled his head on her shoulder until he pushed her away.

"I'm all right, Mommy. But look at this." He held up his right hand. There was some adhesive wrapped across the wrist, and she could see a slight blister beneath the bandage. Gently, she took his wounded hand in hers. "You should have seen it, Mommy. The fire got real big."

"Were you frightened?"

He nodded.

She turned her face away and let go of his hand to wipe away the tears that had begun to stream down her cheeks. "Don't cry, Mommy," his tone was urgent, solicitous. "Really, I didn't get hurt."

"Thank God, Danny." She hugged him again.

"Can I come in?" It was Vanessa. Mark was with her, but he remained at the threshold of the room.

"'Nessa!" Danny's eyes filled with excitement. "You

should have been here. It was such a big fire I thought it was going to burn down *everything.*"

"You have to be more careful." She leaned over and gave the boy a hug. "Matches are serious business."

"I know." He put his head down, guilty for a moment. "I won't do it again."

"Perhaps Danny should get some sleep now. How about it, son?" Mark's phrasing indicated that this was an order, not a question.

"Oh, Dad. Can't I visit with Mommy and 'Nessa a little?"

"Later. I want you to rest now."

"See you in a while, Danny." Vanessa rose and joined Mark at the door.

Annie followed reluctantly.

"Mama, promise you'll see me later?"

"I promise." She turned off the light. "Try to sleep a bit, baby. It will help your hand to heal."

"Okay." He turned on his side, put his unhurt hand under the pillow, and drew his knees up to his chest.

Annie walked back to his bedside for one last kiss. It brought a smile to Danny's face as he closed his eyes to sleep.

"We have to talk." Mark broke the silence, turning from the view out the living room window.

"I'll make coffee." Vanessa was up and on her way to the kitchen.

Annie sat on the couch, smoothing her skirt with the flat of her hands. All she could think of was her child's face above the counterpane. How did it feel from inside of him? She didn't think he hated her, but clearly he'd felt abandoned, betrayed, let them know that his world was going up in smoke.

"This arrangement is not working." Mark regarded Annie. "I'm not blaming you—don't misunderstand." He was trying to remain objective. "I'm just making an observation."

Annie nodded. "You know I've tried, in every way I know how."

"I understand. He kept his voice low, cool. "I've seen it coming, I guess, but tried to pretend the problem didn't exist." He gave an ironic chuckle. "If I treated my patients that way I'd soon be out of business."

"What can we do?" Annie threw up her hands. She felt tears brimming once again.

"What do you want, Annie?" His voice was an urgent whisper. He placed his elbows on his knees and leaned toward her.

"I want something of my own."

"But don't you see that in order to make a marriage work you've got to want it more than anything else in the world? Do you want to make your life with us?"

"I can't go back to the way things were." Her voice choked, as though a valve in her throat were trying to hold back her words.

"You mean you can't give up this idea of a career?"

"What if I asked you to give up your practice, Mark? If I said that in order to make the marriage work we'd have to move to a place where I'd have something to do?"

"Like New York?"

"Yes. Or Boston. Or San Francisco."

"Out of the question." His face turned red. He stood and started pacing back and forth like a caged grizzly.

"But didn't you just say that to make a marriage work you had to—"

"You know what I mean!" He stopped in his tracks, cut her off in midsentence.

"I know exactly what you mean." Her voice grew louder. "You mean that it's perfectly all right for me to sacrifice a part of myself, the part that wants to be something more than the wife of a country doctor."

"You married a country doctor!"

"Wrong. I married a man."

"It's not as though you didn't know what you were getting."

"Does that mean I have to remain forever exactly who I was when you married me?"

"Just tell me what you want." Mark slumped back into his easy chair.

"I want to find something of my own, Mark." Her voice was almost timid. "I'm not the same woman I was when we married. I don't fit that mold anymore. Every time I try to squeeze into it, I get hurt."

"You haven't answered my question. What do you want?"

"Time. I want time to think, to be alone." Annie's words came out in an impassioned cry. "I don't know why that's so difficult to say." She wrung her hands, determined to speak her mind, however painful it was. "I went right from my parents' care into yours, Mark. I never had a chance to find out what it's like to be alone in the world."

"The time to grow up is before you have a child, Annie, not afterward." He paused and softened his tone. "If it were just you and me, I'd give you my blessing and tell

you to go out and find yourself. But we have Daniel."
Although he fought to contain himself, he became strident. "What shall I tell him when he asks me where his mother is?"

"If I could be the mother you and Danny want me to be, I would. I tried, but I can't do it." She wiped away a stream of tears. "Do you think I want to cause my child pain? I don't want him burning down barns." She shook her head, as if to dispel an unspeakable vision.

"But you can just turn your back on him?"

"You asked me what I wanted, Mark? I'll tell you." Annie's jaw set in thoughtful resolve. "I want two weeks. I have an opportunity to do an article that interests me greatly, and after that I'll be able to tell you more. But I need the time to think. Two weeks isn't forever."

"No, but it's a long time to be absent from the home. How about ten days?"

"This is ridiculous." Annie shook her head. "Here we are bargaining over time as if—"

"As if it were precious," he cut her off. "It is precious. And every day you leave me alone to care for Danny *and* my practice is one more day of stress for me."

"You can make arrangements. . . ."

"Even if I leave Danny with a sitter all day, I have to get him up for school, feed him, put him to bed at night, and deal with his emotional responses. My God, woman! Be realistic. Put yourself in my place."

Mark stopped speaking a second before Vanessa entered the room with a tray.

Annie conceded, to end the argument. "All right, Mark. Ten days."

Vanessa set down the tray on the table and was about

to slip away when Mark called her name. "Vanessa, don't go. We've finished, and, besides, you're one of the family."

"I just wish there was something I could do to ease things for you both."

"We seem to have reached an agreement, of sorts." He looked at Annie and she held his gaze.

"Vanessa and I can still catch the eight o'clock train back to Manhattan," Annie said, glancing at her watch. She paused. "I'm taking ten days for myself, Vanessa. Mark has agreed to give me that much time."

"What is your reaction, Vanessa?" Mark crossed his legs and stared at the woman standing by the table.

"That's not fair. I can't take sides. I can hardly pretend to be objective."

There was a silence, which was filled with the sound of Danny's voice calling from the bedroom for his mama.

"He's overexcited," said Mark. "Perhaps I'll sedate him so he can sleep."

"No." Annie stood and walked to the bedroom. "A few minutes with one of his storybooks is the best sedation." Quickly she slipped into the child's room, closing the door behind her.

He held onto her, reluctant to let go; asked if she'd be leaving again. Soon, Annie told him, brushing his hair back from his forehead. But she'd be back. There was something very important she had to do. Danny asked if she had to see patients, like Daddy. It was similar, she assured him. But she wanted him to know that although he couldn't see her, she would be thinking of him, and sending him messages through the air; that if he listened real hard, he might be able to hear her. And will you be able to hear me if I speak to you, he wanted to know. Yes, she said, because she'd be listening real hard, too.

"Mommy," he said slipping further under the covers, "read me a story."

She chose a favorite of her own, Maurice Sendak's *Where the Wild Things Are,* about a little boy named Max dressed in a wolf suit who journeys in his sleep to a land in which he becomes king of the Wild Things.

Danny had drifted off to his own kingdom of Wild Things before she was halfway done, but she continued reading till the end, knowing that the sound of her voice followed him on his journey, and that it would have to sustain him for the next ten days.

"How can I leave this child?" She closed the book and stared at her sleeping son. A pang shot through her stomach, like the blade of a knife. She saw herself with Rick, pursuing the assignment in Utah, and knew she had no choice. "I'll be worthless if I stay," she whispered. "This way I'll be worth more to you in the long run."

Annie flipped through the pages of the book on her lap, then stopped at the illustration of Max in his bedroom, before his journey, hand on hip, defiant in his wolf suit. "That's me, too," she told her sleeping son.

CHAPTER TWENTY

"Not now, Daniel—" Mark threw his papers into his briefcase, his instruments into his black leather bag, and took a frantic last look around his study before closing the door behind him. Not only was he going to have to rush his morning rounds at the hospital, but he'd have to finish his report for the board during his lunch break. Grabbing a piece of cold toast from his son's breakfast dish, Mark felt as though he would forever be reaching the station just as the train disappeared down the tracks. He'd lost all sense of order, as if he'd been taking care of his son alone forever. It was hard to believe that only five of the ten days had passed. There wasn't enough time to do it all anymore, as if the days had shrunk from twenty-four hours to twelve. How could one small boy consume so much time? He felt a pang of guilt and wished he'd been more sympathetic with Annie. There had to be a solution, somewhere. He'd just have to sleep less. Maybe Danny would understand if they cut out next weekend's fishing trip.

"Daniel? You ready to go?" Where the hell was he? One minute he was underfoot with a question Mark didn't have time to answer, the next he was nowhere to be found. Opening the back door, he scanned the yard, looked south to the grove of sycamores. No Danny. Back inside, he called again, searched from room to room and was about to try the Colby's' house when he found his son standing in the corner of his bedroom.

"For Christ's sake, Danny, I've been calling you!" He reached for the boy's jacket and pulled one little arm into the sleeve. "Why is it so much trouble for you to dress yourself?" He forced the two zipper parts together and yanked the teeth into the key. At the sight of his son's vacant eyes, however, Mark stopped short. He looked down at the listless figure, the thin, stooped shoulders, the bowed head. "Danny? Is something wrong?"

"No." His voice was flat, void of feeling. He picked absently at the skin in the palm of his hand, but didn't look up.

Mark knelt down to his level, sought his eyes, but his son seemed to look right through him. "Don't you feel well?" His tone was less impatient now, though he hadn't forgotten how late he was running. "Tell me what's bothering you."

Danny's eyes were glazed but his forehead felt cool. Still he wouldn't answer. Mark glanced at his watch. Already he should be at the hospital. His day would never recover from this late a start.

"Daniel?" His voice resumed some of his former insistence. "If nothing is wrong, could we please go? I have patients who need me." Danny looked up, a light flashed through his eyes like anger, but, as quickly as it appeared, it dimmed. "Don't you want to go to school?"

"No"

Mark waited, but the boy⸱ refused to say more. Danny stared at his hand until Mark lifted the boy's chin. "What *would* you like to do?" he asked with exaggerated patience.

"Can I stay with you today?"

Mark hesitated, but only for an instant, not long enough for Danny to notice. "You don't want to go to school?"

"Not today."

Again Mark hesitated, this time more visibly. "You know, I have a lot of work to do. People are depending on me to help make them better." Even as he spoke, he knew that his son was counting on him for precisely the same attention.

"I know." He looked back down at the floor, fiddled with his jacket zipper.

"It isn't a good idea to skip school," he cautioned, but Mark instinctively knew that wasn't the issue. Painfully he realized that he needed his boy as much as his son needed him. They were in this together. "How would you like to come along on rounds with me?"

Danny's face brightened, and, except for a tremor in his lower lip, there was no sign of his misery.

"Of course you'll have to let me work with my patients." Jane could keep an eye on him while he wrote his report for the board meeting; maybe even take him to Kroger's for a hamburger. "And I'll have office visits this afternoon. Can you entertain yourself?"

The boy nodded. "I just want to stay with you."

Danny's neediness cut him deeply. How could Mark have been so blind to his son's suffering? He reached across and placed his hand on his son's shoulder. "We'll be all right," he said softly, holding him tightly against his chest.

For the first time since his mother had left, he felt safe enough to shed tears.

Mark suddenly understood how much strength it must have taken for him to act brave. He must have felt as though his world were teetering on the brink of extinction. Mark wished he could squeeze dry his son's reservoir of tears. He felt helpless to heal his own son. Now that he understood, he would be patient, take the time to listen.

And as if Danny heard his father's silent promise, his crying subsided, and for a long moment neither moved. They held the embrace until Danny's breathing grew more regular, until he started to pull free.

"You're not mad at me?"

Mark shook his head, his heart breaking. "I'd like to spend the day with you more than anything else in the world."

By the time they reached the hospital, the last traces of morning fog had been lifted by the dry September heat. Soon the leaves would be changing, Mark thought. There was another month yet to fill the woodshed, another four or five weeks to enjoy the green. Each fall the brilliant foliage distracted him from the temperature's rapid decline. In fact, it was the combination of warm days and chill nights that turned the leaves their incandescent shades of red, orange, and yellow. Curious, Mark thought, crossing the parking lot to the hospital entrance, that although he'd watched the seasons change some hundred times, he asked the same question year after year, had never ceased to wonder at the drama.

Danny let go of his hand, ran ahead, and pulled open the heavy front door. Mark usually slipped in the side, but his son showed a preference for the ceremony of passing the first-floor nurses' station and accepting greetings on his father's behalf. Mark remembered how he'd felt as a child, walking down the street in his father's company. His father was the most important man in the world! Was that his son's fantasy? Was Mark larger than life to his little boy? Funny, but after all these years he still felt that the one on the other end of the hand-holding was the really special one.

"Hi, Margaret." He didn't pause in his stride but kept up the even pace down the marble hall. "Hello, Dr. Hanover."

Mark nodded at his colleagues, smiled at the nurses. He was glad Danny had come along. It made the day feel like a Saturday.

"Come on, Dan." Mark took the boy's hand at the end of the next corridor. "We're going to say hello to Mrs. Whitney."

Danny turned shy at the door to her room and reached up for the security of his father's hand. He lagged behind a half step, and when his father stopped at the bedside, he peered around to find a tiny white-haired woman with a smile as timid as his own.

"Mrs. Whitney, this is my son, Daniel."

The woman greeted him shyly, her voice hoarse, a little weak. "Thank you for coming to see me, Daniel." She folded her hands across her breast. "My daughter won't be in today and I was just thinking how much I'd miss seeing my little grandson."

"What's his name?" Danny asked, taking a step forward. "Is he as old as me?"

Mrs. Whitney smiled, seemed to look less tired. "I think you're probably a little older." She smiled at Mark. "His name is Matthew and he's blond like you, too."

Mark set his bag onto the bedside table and opened it. "Sounds like you're feeling better today," he said, touching his hand gently to her arm for a minute before taking her pulse. The previous day she'd been unable to disguise her discomfort, had been impatient with her illness and with him for not begin able to do anything more. Today her pulse was even, her color good, her pressure down. She looked as though she'd reclaimed her interest in life.

Mark removed the stethoscope from his ears. "Well done, Mrs. Whitney. At this rate you'll be home in a week." He wrote something on the chart. "We should have the test results on your hemoglobin this afternoon. I'll be in this evening, before you go to sleep."

"Will you bring Daniel to visit me again?"

Mark looked down at his son. "Would you like to come back tonight?"

"Yep." He stared at Mrs. Whitney. "You'll still be here?"

She wondered how this must all look to him. "Yes, I'll still be here."

Mark took Danny's hand and led him from the room. He had a dozen more patients to see and there was never enough time to visit for long. Danny made the few minutes feel less two-dimensional. "It's fun working with you along, Danny. Did you like Mrs. Whitney?" he asked, picking up another chart from the nurses' station.

"Yeah." He thought a minute. "Is she sick?"

Mark looked up from reading the vitals on his next patient. "She has a bad heart."

"Bad?"

Mark understood the confusion. "She's a good woman,

but her heart doesn't always work right."

"It breaks?"

"Sort of. It breaks down. Like your flashlight, when it needs new batteries."

"Oh." That made sense to him. "Do you think she'll give me one of her candies tonight?"

Mark grinned. He had noticed the unopened box of chocolates; he had wondered the same thing in passing. "You can ask her. She might share." He opened a door and led him into a small private room. "Danny, this is Mrs. Stickney."

Danny didn't complain about being hungry until right before the last patient. "One more stop and we'll break for lunch," Mark promised. "Can you wait?"

"Yep." He turned the corner and walked beside his father into the last ward and was brought up short to discover that the dozen beds were full of children. He wondered why they weren't sick at home. Maybe they didn't have mothers to take care of them when they were sick. He didn't think he'd like to bring his bed into the hospital. "Dad"—he pulled at his father's hand "will I have to come here next time I'm sick?"

Mark stopped and closed the chart he'd been reading. "Not unless you get very sick," he answered him, "and I think you are looking pretty healthy these days. Does it scare you, this room?"

"Uh-huh." Danny chewed on his forefinger while he stared over at a little girl. Beside her, another little girl sat up against a pillow, making two stuffed animals play with each other. "Hey, I have a raccoon, too," he said, loud enough for her to hear.

Mark followed his gaze. "Why don't you go on over and ask what its name is?" He nodded his head encouragingly. "It's all right, I'll be here, with Marie."

Danny looked at Marie, a big girl with brown braided hair, before crossing the ward to examine the other child's stuffed raccoon.

They ate lunch in Mark's office. Danny told him about the girl's tonsils. "She said it hurt to have them pulled."

Mark imagined that Danny saw them as two teeth at the back of the throat, and was pleased that he didn't sound overly concerned with the news. "Did she tell you about the ice cream?"

Danny's eyes twinkled. "Yep. She said they didn't make her brush her teeth, either."

"She'd probably taste the ice cream more if she did." Danny started to consider, then saw his dad's eyes light up with humor, and knew he was kidding. "How would you like to walk to Kroger's for an ice cream?"

Danny stood up, shedding crumbs on the carpet. "Can I have a double?"

Again Mark smiled. "Sure." He reached into his pocket and handed him a couple of dollars. "Ask Jane if she'll go with you, and make sure you ask if she'd like a cone, too."

"All right. What kind do *you* want?"

Mark deliberated. "Rocky Road." Danny turned to go and Mark pulled out the report he had to finish. By the time Danny returned with the cone he had the thrust of what he wanted to say composed. Before his first patient arrived, he sat with his son, enjoying the simple pleasure of marshmallow, walnuts, and of course the melting chocolate.

They didn't actually spend time together that afternoon. The patients filed in one after another. Occasionally, he'd glimpse his son sitting quietly in the waiting room, flipping through the well-worn magazines. Twice he heard patients politely disengage themselves from what sounded like a serious conversation; no one failed to remark on his son's vibrance.

By the time Jane closed the door on the last mother and daughter of the day, Danny was ready to go home.

"Don't forget we're coming back to see Mrs. Whitney tonight," said Mark.

"After dinner?" Danny yawned.

"We'll eat early."

"Good. I'm hungry."

"Yes, and you'll want to get home for a good night's sleep"

"Yep, I don't want to be tired for school tomorrow."

CHAPTER
TWENTY-ONE

When the phone rang, Vanessa was sitting out on the patio trying to identify constellations in the night sky. She had managed to find Orion, Taurus, and Canis Major with the help of a small diagram in the form of a wheel that, when adjusted to the proper time and date, became an accurate map of a particular heaven.

Our lives, she thought, couldn't be determined by the stars, or they would be more orderly.

Mark's frantic phone call early that morning had left her unable to do anything requiring sustained concentration. He had called because Danny was ill and needed more attention than he alone could give him; but it wasn't the news that upset her as much as the fact that she was once again in the middle. Mark had been unable to reach Annie in Cedar City. "If you talk to her before I do," he had said, "tell her she needs to come home."

All day she'd dwelt on their situation. It would have been futile to attempt to work. Fortunately it was a slow period, one in which Vanessa had time to lie back, take a breath, and look around her. The majority of those who availed themselves of her talents were just beginning to trickle back from their summer holidays. She had time to walk around and gaze like a tourist at things she never saw in the midst of her frenzied activity.

Sirius, the brightest star in the constellation Canis

Major, winked down at her. She wondered if her father was walking under the winking eye of that star at this very moment, and what he was doing, when the phone rang. She dropped her map of the heavens, rose from the chaise longue, and answered the phone before it had rung a fourth time.

"Vanessa?"

"Annie, thank God. I've been hoping you'd call."

"You sound out of breath."

"I was on the balcony. Listen, Annie—"

"Vanessa, I'm so excited," she interrupted. "Today we interviewed the head of Indian affairs. Tomorrow we're going to take a white-water trip, see a part of the canyon seldom seen. The people here are so ready to talk, give information, help us out."

"Annie, Mark called this morning. He's been trying to reach you."

"Oh?" The enthusiasm drained from her. "What did he want?"

"He wants you to come home."

"When I'm through here, I will. In another week, as we agreed."

"No, Annie. He wants you to come back immediately. Danny's sick and someone has to stay with him." She went on to explain that he was running a fever. "He has a sore throat, achy bones, all the symptoms of the flu. Mark sounded overwhelmed."

"I simply can't come back yet," said Annie after a brief silence. "If I leave now, everything I've struggled for will be lost. Listen, I know it's a lot to ask, but are you terribly busy now?"

"No," responded Vanessa, missing her friend's point.

"As a matter of fact, I'm sitting here stargazing, or was, before you phoned."

"No, I mean, do you have commitments for the next week? People, work, that kind of thing?"

"What are you thinking, Annie?"

"I couldn't ask this of anyone else, but I know you'll understand. You're my sister in a way that's more real than most blood relatives. Will you go up and take care of Danny?" When she heard no answer forthcoming she added, "Please."

"I don't think that's such a good idea," Vanessa finally replied.

"Vanessa, if I go back now and become a nursemaid, it's all over for me." Her voice choked. "I mean it. It's over.

"Annie, it's so. . . loaded. Don't you see?"

"Look, you like it up there. Danny adores you, and so does Mark."

That's part of the problem, Vanessa wanted to say. The other part of it is that I adore him. But she held her tongue and Annie rushed on, sensing her advantage.

"It's a wonderful time of year to be there. You'll be able to take your camera and shoot all kinds of things. And it's just for a week. I'm begging you."

"All right." She sighed. "If it's agreeable to Mark."

"I know it will be. He needs help, a little support. You'll give it to him willingly. Even if I went back, I'd begrudge every inch I gave. You have no idea how important this trip is to me."

"Okay, Annie." Vanessa gave in. "If that's what you want."

"It is. One day perhaps I'll be able to return the favor."

"Perhaps," said Vanessa.

CHAPTER
TWENTY-TWO

"I don't think I know how to cook macaroni and cheese, Danny."

The boy climbed out of the white wicker chair and crossed to the counter. "I'll show you, it's easy." He pointed to the shelf of cookbooks and poked at a tattered red-and-white one. "That will tell you how."

Vanessa reluctantly accepted the binder and flipped open the cover. Scanning the index for noodles, she came upon a variety of dishes and settled on the simplest-sounding one: macaroni-and-cheese bake. It called for one-half cup milk, one pound cheese. "Do we have cheese?"

"Yep." He opened the refrigerator door. "Do you want the white kind or the yellow?"

"I don't know." The recipe book didn't specify. "Which does your mother use?"

"White, I think."

Vanessa shrugged. "Then, we'll use white. Grab the milk while you have the door open." She returned to the directions. "And butter, too."

Danny tucked the package of cheese beneath his arm and used both hands to pick up the milk. "I can't get hold of it good enough."

Vanessa looked up, distracted. "Here, I'll take it." Great mother she was turning out to be. "Listen, you're just over the 'flu. Sit down and rest."

He sat back down in the wicker chair, his eyes fixed upon her." You're supposed to *grate* the cheese, not slice it."

Vanessa brushed back her hair from her face. "How do you know so much about cooking?" she asked, nonplussed. "And where is the grater?" she continued, opening a couple of drawers without finding utensils.

Danny had the grater between his hands before Vanessa noticed he'd climbed out of his chair.

"Are you sure you wouldn't rather turn on TV?"

"No, it's more fun watching you cook. Do you want me to light the oven?"

She stared at the little sous-chef. "No. Now, sit back in your chair, and next time I need something, *tell* me where it is." Leaning back over the worn recipe, she read the amounts of salt and pepper the casserole needed, and the temperature at which it was supposed to be cooked. With Danny's help she located the dish that would hold the milky concoction, and dumped it all in, relieved when the oven door fell shut behind it.

"That's done, now what?" It was the first meal she'd ever cooked, and though it wasn't cordon bleu, she was proud of her accomplishment. "Shall we set the table?"

"Aren't you going to make a salad?"

"Oh, right, a salad." She flipped the pages, looking for a recipe, but didn't find one. Anybody could make a salad. She'd eaten enough of them. "What else do you like besides lettuce?"

Danny listed a number of his favorite vegetables, and she added a few others she found in the bin.

"Dad likes onion, but I don't, so Mom leaves it out,"

Danny volunteered.

"How 'bout if we make the salad in separate bowls," she suggested, dropping the items onto the cutting board. "That way we make everyone happy." She cut the cucumber into chunks, the tomato into wedges, tore the lettuce into bite-size pieces, and sprinkled sunflower seeds over the top.

"Ick." He made a face. "What did you do that for?"

Vanessa looked up, hurt. "They taste good in a salad."

"Mom never put them in." He didn't know what to make of the addition, but he didn't think he'd like it.

"If you don't like them, you can pick them out," she amended. "But try them. You might like them, all right?" He nodded. "What about salad dressing?"

He pointed to a jar on the window ledge. "Mom uses that."

"But what does she put in it?"

He shrugged. "I don't know."

"Is there a recipe?"

"I don't know, Mom always—" He stopped, seeing his father open the back door. "Hi, Daddy."

"Are you feeling well enough to be out of bed?"

"Vanessa needed help cooking dinner."

"Do you know how to make salad dressing?" she asked Mark.

"You don't?"

"I never said I could cook."

He raised his eyebrows and peered through the glass door into the oven. "That looks promising."

She beamed. "My debut. Dinner will be ready in a few minutes."

"Without dressing." He was smiling fully now, and if

they had been alone, he wouldn't have been able to resist his urge to embrace her. But Danny was watching, and it would have confused him to see his father kissing a woman other than his mother. Not to mention Vanessa. She hadn't agreed to become his lover when she stepped in for Annie. He mustn't make assumptions. "Let's try some of this"—he splashed vinegar into the bottom of an empty jar—"and some of this." He added oil. "Shake, and let's see how it tastes."

Vanessa stuck her finger into the jar, and made a horrible face. "Ick," she imitated Danny.

Mark tasted it for himself. "You're right." He shrugged. "I never said I could cook, either."

"We can just eat macaroni," Danny contributed.

Vanessa popped open the oven door and lifted the lid to the casserole dish. "Oh, no, we can't," she said, disappointed to find the mixture burnt on the edges but mushy in the middle. "Something went wrong."

Mark came to her side. "I think you're supposed to cook the noodles separately," he said, removing one of the half-baked shells, "and grease the pan, but I don't know what went wrong with the liquid."

Vanessa put it on the counter, defeated. "What are we going to do?" Filling in for Annie was more difficult than she assumed it would be, but for other reasons.

"Dad could always cook scrambled eggs," Danny jumped in, rather enjoying the chaos.

He laughed heartily. "I can see us now—" He smiled broadly at Vanessa, then at his son. "Eating scrambled eggs every meal for the next week."

"At least it's something."

In fact, Mark's scrambled eggs were rather spectacular. He added a touch of cayenne pepper to spice up the dish, along with the tomatoes and sunflower seeds from the aborted salad. Vanessa burnt every slice of bread she dropped into the toaster, and Mark poured her a beer to cheer her up. Danny watched with absolute delight, enjoying the activity in the disorganized kitchen, as a theater critic might appreciate a well-timed farce. Mark seemed pleased with his successful dinner, but suggested they eat downtown the following night. In the meantime Vanessa vowed to master cooking, even if it killed her, and Mark said they'd probably all die from her attempts.

Long after the eggs were gone from the plates, and the coffee cooled in the cups, they sat at the big round table, making jokes to amuse each other, telling stories that couldn't be true. When Danny dropped off to sleep, they jointly carried him to his room, and when he was tucked under the covers Mark and Vanessa stayed by his bedside, their mood somber but happy.

Together they returned to the table to finish the coffee. "He seems to be taking it all very well," Vanessa whispered, smoothing back the strand of hair that fell into her eyes. "Almost as well as his father."

"What do you mean by that?" He looked at Vanessa in her jeans and red pullover sweater; her face radiated a kind of insistent well-being, and the lines of her body flowed beneath her clothes. She was beautiful, and he wanted to go over and hold her before she could answer him, but he remained seated across the table.

"Just what I said. You seem to have adjusted quite easily yourself. No sorrow, no obvious remorse."

"You're right." He leaned back in the chair and considered for a moment. "You know, I've slipped into a routine with you so easily I haven't even thought to tell you how good it feels. No, don't turn away. I mean it."

"I know you do." She met his gaze. "It feels good to me, too."

"I never have to ask you for help. It seems my back is always covered. I'm used to looking everywhere for booby traps. No, I mean it. With Annie, the smallest negotiation can be a power struggle. What a relief not to have to enter into silent battle."

"It must have been difficult for Annie, also." Vanessa spoke without lowering her eyes as she sipped her coffee.

"You want my real, unedited feelings?"

"I'm not sure."

"Well, I'm going to let you see them, Vanessa, because if I don't let off a little steam, one day I might explode. What I feel is this: I am sad, relieved, and angry, occasionally all at the same time. "

"Sounds a little like a high-wire act," said Vanessa.

"I'm sad that the woman I married has chosen to act like a rebellious adolescent. . . ."

"Mark, you're talking about my friend."

"Well, it's true. And besides, I'm your friend, too." He sat back and sighed. "I guess it isn't fair to you to dump out all of this. I'm sorry."

"No, don't be." She wanted to go over and touch his shoulder, cradle his head, but she sat there, attempting to convey her feeling with her voice and eyes. "The way you see it isn't entirely charitable. Annie has to do what she's doing, Mark, just as your responses are also natural human responses."

"I know," he answered with a nod. "Of course, you're

right. Annie doesn't have a choice. Whenever I realize that, I am overcome by an immense sadness."

"And the relief?"

"That's the best part. She's forced me to let go. I've been dependent on her, too. I might never have given up on the idea of making it work if she hadn't forced my hand."

"Have you given up on it? Already?"

"At certain moments. And those are accompanied by a wave of relief. It's difficult to let go, Vanessa. In some way perhaps Annie is the more courageous of the two of us. She wants more for herself than the struggle we had with each other. I do, too."

His last words were soft, confessional. When he gazed at the woman across from him, all he could think of was how much he wanted her. She felt to him like a safe harbor after a relentless storm. In the time she had been there with him, they had worked as a team, and he felt the rebirth of a feeling that had gotten buried: trust. And with trust came his buried longing. Yes, he thought, I do want more for myself. I want what you have to give me.

"The difficulties for me are obvious." She poured herself more coffee. "I'm sure you understand what they are. I'm also sure you know how good it is for me, Mark. What we share has been very valuable." An invisible bond stretched taut between them, felt almost strong enough to pull them like sympathetic magnetic poles across the table until they met in the center.

"I don't even care that you're a lousy housekeeper," Mark said, glancing around the room.

Vanessa followed his gaze to the dishes piled high in

the sink. There were coats thrown over the couch in the living room, wood chips by the stove, Danny's toy soldiers in disarray on the battlefield of the hallway carpet.

"A good thing you don't," said Vanessa.

They both laughed. Looking at the world around them, the casual litter, the warm, lived-in nest gave them back the design of their collective personality.

"It's wonderful." He chuckled.

And they both laughed again, a series of sustained, life-giving bursts that built up to a crescendo, allowing them to glimpse the truth: they were enjoying each other, savoring the moment. What they had to give each other transcended roles.

CHAPTER
TWENTY-THREE

Everything was set. Her equipment was packed and waiting by the front door so that when Mark pulled in with the car she could dash off. And you mustn't linger, she reminded herself, pulling her sweater over her head. Already the sun had cast a rosy glow over the mountains, and she would lose the quality of light if she delayed. There would be time to talk later, *after* she'd finished her work.

Ahhh, the temptations!

Not that she wanted to work less; on the contrary, she was repeatedly inspired by the awesome beauty of the landscape, wanted to capture it all before she had to leave Vermont. No, her interest in work hadn't waned; rather, other desires had surfaced to compete for her time. She'd never have believed that a few minutes with Mark over a cup of coffee would threaten her commitment to her work. And who'd have believed she'd found equal pleasure in playing with Danny as she had in finding new subjects?

"Where's Dad?" Danny wandered into the hallway while she was checking her hair in the mirror. She smiled. "He's on his way home. He said he wanted to take a hike with you before dinner, all right?"

Danny's eyes lit up. "We could go to the top of Mount Cedar."

"Well, that might be a little far." He had gone back to school that morning but she didn't want to risk a relapse of his 'flu. Maybe they could spend Saturday morning hiking, she thought. "Why don't you put on your hiking shoes, so you'll be ready to leave when he gets here?" She glanced at her wristwatch. Where was he? She was as impatient to see him, she realized, as she was to leave.

"Papa's on the phone," Danny called from the kitchen. She hadn't even heard it ring, but hurried to take the call. "Mark? Where are you? "

"Unfortunately, I'm still at the hospital. One of my patients decided to have her baby this afternoon. I'm sorry, Vanessa, but I can't get away."

"Oh—" She sat down in the breakfast nook, a complexity of feelings threatening to overwhelm her. She *understood* that he wasn't intentionally staying away to keep her from her work, but that didn't cancel the frustration she felt. Sure, she could wait until another day to photograph the falls, but she couldn't operate without some inspiration, and that, unfortunately, didn't come on demand. And what about Danny? He was looking forward to some time alone with his father, as much, she guessed, as she needed a few hours alone with herself.

"I don't think the birth will take long," he was saying. "This is her third baby and they tend to slip out—" He was interrupted by a question from someone on the hospital staff. Vanessa could hear he was busy. He returned to the phone. "Sorry—things are a little frantic here."

"Well—" She wanted to make it easy for him, wished she could say it was all right, that she'd find time for her work later, but she couldn't find words that sounded convincing. "Well," she repeated. "I'll see you when you get home."

He could hear the disappointment in her voice as clearly as the attempt to disguise it. "I wish there were something I could do." He was frustrated, too.

"I'll tell Danny. He'll understand."

"Listen." He suddenly had an idea. "If you want to drop him at the baby-sitter's, the number is by the phone in the hallway. I could pick him up when I'm finished. You could still have time to take pictures."

Vanessa considered. She really did need some time with her camera, out of the house, surrounded by nature. As much as she loved playing the surrogate mother, it wasn't all there was to her. Her photography would always be her lifeline, had been her stability since she was a little girl. It was her fix on reality. Adjusting the light and focusing the lens to capture the angle she wanted to preserve was as fundamental to her as meditation was to a monk. In the long run she'd be more understanding, far more patient if she took a few hours for herself, sunk into her art. "That's a good idea," she said.

She was feeling better, less disappointed. "I hope it's an easy birth," she added. "And Mark, would you mind picking up Chinese food or something so we don't have to cook when we get home?"

"Sure." He considered. "How about a couple of barbecued chickens and some coleslaw."

"Sounds good." They had some dessert left from the previous night. "See you later."

Now she'd really have to hurry. Ten minutes could dramatically affect the quality of light.

"Danny?" She found him in his room, working on his

model airplane. "Your dad's tied up at the hospital. He won't be home for a while yet, so I'm going to take you to the sitter's—"

"You're going to leave me?" He looked up with wide, questioning eyes.

"Just for a few hours. Your dad will pick you up on his way home."

"Where are you going?" His lips pressed together tightly.

"Up to the mountain to photograph the falls," she explained. "And if I don't hurry I'll lose the light. Can you gather some of your toys so we can go?"

"Can't I go with you?"

"Not today." She offered a compensation. "But this weekend we can go for a hike, up Mount Cedar, if you like."

"Why not today?"

"Because I have to work, Danny." How could she explain that this was her job, that she had to treat it seriously or it would suffer, would become little more than a hobby? "I need to concentrate."

"But I'd be quiet."

The look in his eyes penetrated her determination. "Oh, Danny," she said, exasperated. "I wish I could, but—"

He continued to stare at her, daring her to continue, and again she was torn between what she wanted to do and what she thought she should be doing. Part of her wanted to take him along, but she didn't know how wise it would be; part of her needed time to be alone with her work, but she didn't know if she could concentrate if he was elsewhere feeling abandoned. As a child she remembered pleading with her father to take her along, and she remembered restraining the plea she felt like making as an adult. Maybe she'd just stay home, she thought, but that didn't feel good, either. "If you think you can let me work, you can come along."

The distrust disappeared from his eyes, replaced by a cautious smile. "Can I bring my airplane?"

"Anything you want, but *please,* hurry."

He was on his feet and into his jacket before she had her equipment bag slung over her shoulder.

"How are we going to get to the falls?" he asked, walking beside her down the road.

"I thought we'd hitch a ride." She reached down and took his hand. "We won't accept a ride unless we like the driver," she added. She had hitchhiked with Clemens all over Europe, had learned to make a quick appraisal. She waved down a passing car.

"That's Mr. Holcomb," Danny informed her. "I like him."

'That's good enough for me." She bent down and peered into the car. "Would you mind giving us a lift down the road?'

The light was still good by the time they reached the falls. Quickly Vanessa unloaded her bag and set up the tripod for the series of time-exposed shots she'd anticipated. From an extraordinary height a thin veil of water streamed down a mossy, fern-imbedded wall, feeding a small but deep pool of cold, crystal-clear water near her feet. A few weeks from now the flow would be too forceful to be this close, depending of course on the rains; in a few months the greenery would be gone, too. That would make another good subject, she pondered, pressing the shutter to suspend the view in front of her. Under her breath she counted to five, added another five seconds' exposure for effect, then released the button, reenacting the natural speed of the falls.

Danny, true to his word, remained silent, but Vanessa was acutely aware of his presence. He perched on a nearby rock, his model airplane in hand all but ignored, his attention riveted to his godmother and her camera. Vanessa could hear his questions forming, could see by his expression that he was straining to understand. All at once she was transported back through time, to her earliest memory of sitting with her father, watching him work. He, too, had insisted she sit quietly if she wanted to observe.

She recalled her father's refusal to let her touch his camera equipment. It wasn't until after her mother had died that he invited her into the private, mysterious world of his work. He was far from the perfect father, Vanessa knew, but she gave him credit for picking up the pieces of their shattered world, for making a kind of home for her. Some mothers give their children milk and cookies after school, some fathers help their kids with homework. Vanessa had always felt deprived because she didn't have what other kids had. Now she felt that comparison was unjust. Clemens *had* given her something valuable, not to be underrated because it wasn't typical. He had shared what was most important to him, had shown her how to order a world that sometimes moved too fast, often threatened to overwhelm her. No matter what else happened in her life, she'd always have her art.

The expression Danny wore might well have been hers at his age. She wondered if she felt close to him because he reminded her of herself as a child. But that was too simple an answer. They were different in many ways: she'd had no more interest in model airplanes than he had in dolls, and yet, those were but superficial differences, Vanessa knew. The similarities were all too real. Danny's world, like her own, was coming apart at the seams.

"Danny?" She reversed the film in the camera, popped open the back, and lifted out a completed roll. "Would you like to try taking a picture?"

"Could I?" He put down his airplane and hurried toward her.

"Sure." She thought to let him use the digital camera she had in her bag, then changed her mind and dropped a new roll of film into the chamber, advanced it to the first frame, and reinstated the heavy Hasselblad back on the tripod. There would be enough for him to think about without trying to hold it steady. She adjusted the mount. "Climb up here, so you can reach."

"What do I do?" He clambered up on a rock so he was tall enough to see through the viewfinder.

"First "—she dropped back so there was nothing between him and the camera—"find something you'd like to make into a picture."

He took his eye away from the camera, and began searching the setting for something of interest.

"If you look for your subject through the lens, you'll have a better idea of what can be captured."

"Oh." He squinted into the viewfinder again.

"Use one hand to turn the camera." She turned the

instrument swivel on the tripod. "When you see something you like, tell me, and we'll stop moving the camera."

"Okay . . ." He continued looking as Vanessa moved
the camera from left to right. "Now, stop."

"Can you see your picture clearly, or is it blurred?"

"Kind of blurry."

"Then turn this part—" She fitted his hand over the
focus ring and turned it slowly. "Tell me when it starts
getting clear."

"No . . . no . . . it's getting better. . .all right . . . Stop!"

The light meter was already set. She would save the
more complicated instruction for another day, after he'd
mastered the basics. "Now all you have to do is push this
button."

"Like this?" The lens clicked shut.

"Like that."

He looked up, proud. "When can we see the picture?"

She shrugged. "Maybe tomorrow." Mark had said she
could set up her enlarger in the utility room, if she liked.
Earlier that day she had sufficiently darkened the bathroom to develop the six rolls of film she'd shot since her
arrival. "When you get home from school tomorrow, we
could print up some of our pictures." She was anxious to
see her work, too.

"Not tonight?"

"Tonight your father will want to spend time with us,"
she reminded him. Vanessa grinned, remembering the
impatience she had experienced as a child, always wanting to see her pictures at once. She was glad he was enthusiastic. Working in the darkroom was demanding,
and it took a strong interest to balance the tedium. It

would be fun for her, too, to have him working with her. "But tomorrow, first thing after school, I would love to teach you how to make a print."

"Can I take another picture now?"

"Sure." She adjusted the aperture to compensate for the decreasing daylight. "Take a couple more, then let's head home for dinner." She hoped they'd get a ride back. . . that Mark would be home when they got there. She had a sudden, irrepressible urge to be with him, to share the details of her day. So what else was new, she chided herself, then turned her attention back to the steady stream of Danny's questions.

CHAPTER TWENTY-FOUR

"Why don't you help Danny into his pajamas while I do these dishes?" Mark lifted the three plates off the table and carried them to the counter.

"All right. Do you feel like having a bath tonight?" she asked the towheaded boy.

"Not tonight," he said, scampering out of his seat.

Mark laughed. "That's a question that's better not asked. Annie usually—" He stopped himself. "Usually we just toss him into the tub when he's too dirty to struggle."

Vanessa encircled the boy in both arms and peered down at his neck. "I can still see some white meat. Guess you can wait another night." In truth it was hard work bathing Danny and she was looking forward to that part of the day when her time was her own.

"I'll be up in time to read you a story," Mark promised, as she led Danny out of the kitchen.

"Do you love me, 'Nessa?"

"Of course I do."

"Tomorrow, when I get home from school, are you going to be here?"

She kissed him lightly on the cheek. "Step into these," she said holding out the bottom half of his fireman red pajamas. "I'll be here for a while longer. Is that all right?"

"Uh huh," he said, slipping in between the sheets. "Will you stay here when Mama comes home?"

"How come all the questions tonight?" She'd been with him for a week and this was the first time he'd questioned her.

"I was just thinking . . ."

"Thinking, huh?" She could imagine him wondering what was happening. As far as he'd been told, his mother was still away on a business trip and Vanessa was staying with him until she came back. But the question of Annie's return was as unclear to her as to the boy. Annie had called to say she was back in New York but not ready to return to Vermont. She had asked Vanessa to remain another week, and Mark had agreed to the arrangement. "I'll stay as long as I'm needed," she assured him, tucking the cover beneath his chin. "And wanted," she added with a laugh. "Leave the worry to the adults, okay?"

"Okay." He seemed content to obey. "Will you read me a story before Dad gets here?"

"How about, I start a story and let him finish it?"

Mark joined them halfway through *The Night Kitchen*. It was the same story Danny wanted to read every night, though he had lots of books, and Vanessa guessed it was because he could recite the words.

When they had closed the door on *The Night Kitchen,* and Danny had been convinced there'd be no more stories, they shut out the light, leaving the door slightly ajar, and returned to the living room.

"Boy, am I tired." Vanessa collapsed on the couch, kicking her feet up onto the ottoman.

"Shall I make a fire?" Mark asked, opening the dual doors to the wood-burning stove. "The temperature's dropped again."

"As long as I don't have to carry in logs tonight." She didn't think she could get up just then for anything.

"We brought in enough wood yesterday to last all week," Mark answered, stuffing a bundle of dry kindling on top of crumpled newspaper. "You don't have to do a thing except relax."

She let out a breath and sank further into the cushions. She could understand Annie's weariness after six years of caring for the energetic boy, but she still couldn't fathom the resentment. Sure, Vanessa was tired. She'd put in a long, full day, but the sense of accomplishment at its completion was every bit as satisfying as the work she did in the city. Today she'd watched Danny master the game of Chinese checkers, and grow accomplished enough to beat an old pro like herself, in less than two hours. To witness his little mind expanding fulfilled her as thoroughly as catching the right light for a photograph of Prince Andrew. Whatever Annie was doing, Vanessa hoped it was giving her as much pleasure as Mark and Danny gave her.

"What are you thinking?" Mark settled into the armchair beside the sofa. "You look a hundred miles away."

She smiled. "Actually, I was thinking about Annie," she told him, "and how different things will be when she returns."

Mark frowned. "I thought you might be thinking about her. Do you ever think about us?"

"Us? I've been sharing your home for the past week. I treat Danny like a son. We act like we've been married for years. Whenever I have a spare minute, yes, I think about us. Do you?"

"To the detriment of my patients, I'm afraid. I'm scheduled for surgery tomorrow, and I'm almost scared to go."

Vanessa laughed. "My thoughts haven't been quite so desperate lately." She had been distracted in New York, when she wanted to be with him all the time, but now that she spent every day with him, she wasn't so crazy with longing. Occasionally there were pangs of desire, but for the most part she felt relaxed. "I feel wonderful, if you must know."

He nodded. He did, too. It seemed so natural to be living with her. Annie's absence had turned out to be more of a relief than a trial, now that Vanessa was here. Danny seemed easy enough with the change. On the whole, Mark felt settled and happy in his new situation. "We haven't had a moment's struggle adjusting, have we?"

"No. It's been easy," Vanessa remarked.

"Except for one thing."

She looked at him. "One thing?" Maybe he wasn't as happy as she was. Maybe there were things that didn't sit well with him. If he was uncomfortable, she should know now. "What's wrong?"

"Every night we put Danny to bed, have ourselves a quiet evening, then disappear into separate bedrooms. For myself, I would sleep far better with you in my arms."

She wanted to stop him from pursuing this train of thought, but knew she couldn't. She, too, lay in bed each night wishing to be with him, falling asleep to the sound of his even breathing. It would have been easy enough to have followed him into his bedroom, but the thought of Annie had kept her out of his bed. After all, even if this hiatus led to a separation, they were still married.

Mark watched her, waiting for some kind of reply. "Don't you want me, too? Somehow I can't believe these feelings are one sided."

She sat up to face him and smoothed her dark hair back with one hand. "If I was drawn to you before, Mark, you can imagine how I feel now."

In the last week her affection had burgeoned into full-grown love. There was no other word for it. Every time she saw him, the surging inside of her grew more intense. Even first thing in the morning, with his eyes half-closed with sleep, his hair tousled, he was beautiful to her. He wasn't perfect, but he was everything she wanted. "I'd love to fall asleep in your arms, you know that, if only. . ." She faltered.

"How long are we going to use Annie as an excuse?" There wasn't any anger in his voice, only frustration. "We've got our own happiness to consider. You don't see her concerned with anyone's happiness but her own, do you?"

"It's a tricky situation."

"It's a bloody mess, if you ask me." He fumed for a minute, remembering Annie's misconstrued priorities. "Except for the fact that you're here now, I have little to thank her for," he said definitively. "And it isn't fair that you and I have to deprive ourselves of something we both want and need!"

"That's not Annie's decision, but mine."

"Then give me a good reason, other than Annie, why you won't share my bed." He stared at her with desperation flooding his eyes. "I want you, Vanessa. I need you."

She wanted him so badly she could feel him inside of her. "But what will happen to us when Annie comes back?"

"Do you really think she will?"

"Of course." Vanessa shook her head. "Given enough time, she'll realize what she's given up and want it all back. If only I hadn't . . ."

"You have no reason to blame yourself." Mark poured them both a glass of brandy. "She and I have been ignoring a problem that has to be faced." He handed a glass to Vanessa. "You've given both of us—all three of us—a reason for wanting something better in our lives. That is cause for celebration. We have a right to reach for what we want."

"I don't know. . . ." She set down her drink on the coffee table and rose. "I feel too guilty, too responsible." She wanted to flee. "I think I should go to my room now."

"Vanessa—" Mark blocked her exit and took her by the shoulders. His grip was gentle but insistent. "Running away won't solve anything."

"But I don't think I could stand to lie with you tonight, then give you up next week when Annie returns." She tried to get past him, but he wouldn't let her. "I can't lose what I haven't had," she reasoned.

"Even if she does come back, it takes two to reconcile. You won't have to give up anything. I promise."

Vanessa looked at him sadly, pressed her lips firmly together, and turned away. "Mark, I'll see you in the morning."

In the bathroom she slipped out of her clothes and into the shower. Greater than her fear of becoming addicted to Mark was the thought of interfering with the re-construction of his marriage. Sure, Annie had gone away, but only to get enough distance to make a clear-headed decision. Mark might not miss her yet, but eight years of marriage was a long time. He'd said that Vanessa had been the catalyst for their separation. How could she live with the guilt of keeping Danny from his natural parents?

She shut off the spray of hot water and reached for a towel. Wrapping herself, she stepped out of the stall and unpinned her hair, letting it fall to its full length.

In a minute she was cozy in her flannel nightgown, feeling somewhat better covered with chaste primroses and violets. She brushed her hair to a gossamer sheen and hung up the damp towel before returning to her bedroom.

"Oh. . ."

"I came to say good night." Mark was beside her in the hall. "I wouldn't sleep, thinking I'd upset you."

"I'll be all right." There was no need to bring up her guilty feelings again. He was standing very close to her and she fought the urge to yield to his embrace. She wanted him; only her mind said no. "Besides, it isn't you who has upset me . . . it's the situation we're caught in."

"You know, in all the important ways, we're already lovers."

She knew that was true, and nodded.

"It doesn't make sense to me. People meet in bars, ex-change names, and go home to share the same bed, sometimes for only one night. Here we are, living under the same roof, yet denying the physical side to the love we both feel."

She listened, her eyes cast down at the carpet.

"It's too late already to avoid the hurt. If we were forced apart now . . ." He faltered. "Well, we'd have to deal with that problem."

"Yes." Her voice was shaky.

"Our choice isn't whether we sleep together or not, but whether we bury the feelings that bind us. I love you, Vanessa. Doesn't that count for something?"

She nodded, afraid that if she tried to answer him, she'd break into tears. If only she could grab hold of the moment, and cherish it while it lasted, without worrying about the future. He had said he loved her, and she believed he meant it. Perhaps there was something worse than losing what she'd had but briefly: *never to have had him at all*.

"What is it, love?" He closed his hands over hers, waiting.

If only for tonight, she wanted to be his completely. They might only have this, but at least it would be theirs to cherish forever. "I love you, too, Mark."

"I promise you won't be sorry."

"What about Danny?" She had to be practical. "He wakes up so early."

"We'll set the alarm." She was right. It wasn't a good idea to confuse the boy, until they'd sorted it out for themselves. "Now, no more excuses. Come."

She hesitated at the door to his bedroom. "Let's go to my room, instead," she suggested.

"Yes, that would be better," he responded, and placing both hands on her shoulders, he guided her across the hall.

Switching on the light beside her bed, and watching

the yellow glow spread over them, she wasn't sure if she should turn back the bedspread or undress first. What had seemed resolved a minute ago was now fraught with new anxiety. She wasn't sure if she knew *how* to make love to Mark. No, she hadn't reached her age a virgin— she had experimented in college and had been with a practiced lover in Rome—but she had never embraced a man with the deep emotion the act was supposed to address. She cared for Mark—she wanted to please him, but she didn't know how to begin.

Mark seemed less aware of the problem. Standing only inches from her, he brought her into his arms. Knowing that before too much longer she'd be his completely, he was no longer in a hurry.

Lifting Vanessa's chin with his finger, he watched her close her violet-blue eyes, and before he did the same, he felt the exquisite sensation of her lips full against his. For one unhurried moment their lips touched without moving, until she began to tremble. Before the trembling claimed him, too, he pressed his mouth firmly to hers and held her more tightly in his arms. "Shhh, love should be a celebration." Vanessa felt her resistance dissolve in response to his reassurance. She had forgotten how good it felt to be held, how essential it was to be touched. In his arms she felt the strength of his desire: but what startled her most was the hunger inside her. Since Mark had first kissed her, she'd been aware of a craving only he could satisfy; yet that need was minor compared to what he presently stimulated. She was torn between rushing to meet his desire, throwing herself at him with sheer abandon, and wanting to savor the heightened tension of their first embrace.

He continued to rock her, as if to some unheard melody. She swayed in his arms, as if they'd been dancing for years. If only their lives could continue simply like this, the world around them caught in the net of their feelings for each other. "I love you, Mark," she whispered. "I always will."

There was a bittersweet quality to her words, and he felt his heart ache to relieve it. "My love." He kissed her ear beneath a veil of dark hair. "We will be addressing our love for a long, long time."

"For a long, long time," she repeated softly, as if trying to convince herself. "Our love." All her secret lamentation was replaced by the joy his words had made her feel.

Starting with the top one, Mark started to unbutton the front of her nightgown, his fingers accomplishing their feat as effortlessly as if tying a surgical knot.

"I've imagined making love to you a hundred times," he admitted, trailing his finger down the strip of exposed skin where the material had fallen open. "I know exactly what you look like," he added. He had visualized every inch of her body, from her small, upturned breasts and silky black hair to the slope of her buttocks; he knew what she'd smell like, what her skin would taste like, what shape were her thighs.

She grinned. "So you've been imagining, too?" She'd envisioned running her fingers through his hair, her hands over his broad shoulders. She'd pictured his back, muscular and tan, his legs long and lean. She lowered her eyes from his face and busied herself with the row of buttons on his shirt.

Hairs peeked out above the first button. Farther down

his chest they grew darker, without gold highlights. Mark held in his breath when she pulled the tails out of his trousers and edged the shirt off his shoulders.

He slid her nightgown over her shoulders, too, and dropped his eyes. He wasn't disappointed that, in fact, her breasts were much fuller, the nipples larger than he had assumed. Her waist was even smaller, and the skin stretched across it was as soft as mink. He felt her quiver beneath his touch.

"Don't forget to set the alarm," she murmured between kisses.

"Right." Impatiently he pulled himself away and fiddled with the clock on the bureau. "Six?"

"Better make it five, just in case."

She'd been wrong to worry. As with everything else, they were natural together. His arm found its niche beneath her back, and she wound her arm under his neck. They were a perfect fit.

There was no longer any question of going slow. She wanted him as badly as he wanted her, and one touch would tell him how ready she was. She imagined how he'd feel inside of her: the slow sweet pressure of his entry, the deeper pleasure of his total exploration, the heightened sensation of repeated entrance. But nothing in her fantasies prepared her for the intensity of his actual touch. However urgently he sought her, his touch was always gentle. He moved ahead purposefully but was never impatient; while vigorous in his lovemaking, he was never aggressive. He reached for what he wanted, then handled it with supreme delicacy.

In close embrace Vanessa came to understand more about the man she loved than through all their previous communications. She felt him shudder within her and she was lifted by a series of sensations that converged into one blinding light. It eclipsed every thought, every image.

And when they slept, they slept as one.

CHAPTER
TWENTY-FIVE

"Good to see you, Ms. Ansel," The uniformed doorman tipped his gray cap. "Have you been away on vacation?"

"Spending some time in the country, Charles."

"Couldn't pick a better time for it. It must be beautiful now, with the leaves changing." He followed her inside. "Mrs. Abrams already has the mail."

"Is she at home?"

"I believe she's upstairs right now."

The October sun shone its burnished light through the paneled windows of the Art Deco lobby. All over the world light was different at various times of the year. In the Far East and the Riviera, colors had a luminosity they had nowhere else. A tomato in Antibes and Bangkok was redder than a tomato in London or Los Angeles. Summer light in New York had a whiteness that bleached the colors, as if the skyline had been dipped in Clorox; but as the season moved toward fall, it gained a golden quality that was more mysterious than all the jade in the Orient. The cast of light seemed to catch the immutable beneath the surface of constant change, if only for a moment. Or was it simply the afterglow of her time in Vermont, the amazing grace of the love she had felt from Mark and Danny and carried with her still?

A physicist might explain the differing qualities of light in terms of the angle of refraction and the curvature of the earth. But there was no physicist in the world who could reduce the sensations she was feeling to photons or quantums. Emotions were the real mystery.

As a photographer, she always sought the elusive emotional quality beneath the image. Even Danny could aim a camera at a scene and dilate the shutter. But not everyone could sense the meaning beneath an image: compose it and capture it.

The pictures she had taken this week reflected an intuition heightened by all that she had felt inside. Her love for Mark had opened up an emotional lens more profound than she had ever guessed existed. Using the camera as its extension, she had probed deep into the heart of those rural children's faces, and the mystery of the mushroom-laden forests. She couldn't give all her attention to the wonders of nature, she knew; she had returned to New York because she couldn't neglect her professional obligations any longer. Even if she didn't stay overnight, she had to pick up material to work on in Vermont and make contact with a number of clients. *Vogue* had been after her to take on an assignment, and if she could accept the work without being kept long from Mark and Danny, she would be happy.

Her mood changed as the elevator rose steadily. The glow she had been feeling receded, and a shadow of apprehension held the foreground of her inner landscape as the elevator doors slid open.

Annie was coming in from the terrace with a tray of empty dishes and a sheaf of manuscript. When Vanessa opened the front door, she stopped. They faced each other dumbly, as if for a split second both were held in suspension.

Annie was the first to move. She put down her tray on the table and ran to embrace the other. "Vanessa!" She hugged her firmly, then stepped back.

"Annie! You look wonderful!" Vanessa regarded her friend. Annie's skin had achieved a deep golden hue, and her hair shone a dozen complimentary shades of blond. She radiated a healthy vitality.

"I feel wonderful, thanks to you." She took Vanessa's arm and led her to the sofa. "It was a glorious trip, Vanessa. Not only Utah and Glen Canyon, but the detective work, finding the material."

Annie was bubbling. Her spirits were so high that her words were like tiny helium balloons, pulling her whole body up. She couldn't sit, or stand in one place, but paced back and forth as she continued the description of her time in the Southwest.

"It was amazing to watch Rick. Now I know how a real professional works. He sniffed out the relevant issues, and the essential people to interview, the way a hound sniffs quail. Really, we got everything we needed in half the time."

"So, it's finished?"

"The research is, but the job's not complete until I introduce the new material into the piece. That's why I needed more time. Oh, 'Nessa, it's all so exciting. This is more than I had hoped for. I am so happy. I feel like I'm worth something again. I don't think I'll ever be the same." Her look of elation faded into a frown. "Is everything all right at home?"

"Yes, Annie," she assured her, though hearing the word "home" made her stomach instantly knot. "Everything's just fine." Vanessa spoke in a deliberately calm voice. Behind her cool facade, however, she felt panic. During Annie's flight of enthusiasm she had almost forgotten the ecstasy of her own experience; up until a short time ago she'd been filled with an equally soaring joy.

Annie's voice was suddenly timid. "And Danny?"

"He's fine. They're both just fine."

"Does he ask for me?" Annie fell back on the sofa.

"Who? Mark or Danny?" The minute she asked, she was sorry. She knew that Annie had meant her child. What contrary impulse had baited that hook?

"Somehow, I don't think Mark misses me very much." She lowered her head. "He must be as relieved as I am."

"You're relieved?" That was why Vanessa had asked the loaded question, she realized—to get information. She was trying to protect herself, yet in the process she had manipulated her friend's emotions. It depressed her to find herself dealing with Annie this way.

"I have to confess that I *am* greatly relieved," Annie went on. "These past weeks have been the fullest and happiest of my life. My only regret is Danny. I wanted to call him many times, but each time I fought the urge. It's so hard to know the right thing to do for a child."

Vanessa reassured her as sincerely as she could. "He asks about you but we've kept him busy, and he gets lots of attention."

"I'm sure he does." She gave a half smile that was more an expression of vulnerability than pleasure. "Probably had a better quality of attention, too." She waved her hand to dismiss any protest. "No, don't be polite with me. It's better to be honest. I love Danny a great deal but in these weeks of upheaval I've done some

266

soul-searching."

"And what have you found out?"

"I may be confused about a lot of things, but I know I love my son." She paused to gather courage. "And I hate motherhood."

"Annie!"

"Please don't act shocked. I'm sure there are countless women, good women, who feel the same. It's just not a fashionable admission."

"But what will you do?"

"I don't know yet." Annie rubbed her neck, as if a stiffness in the muscles had just set in. "But no matter what my decision is, I have to be honest with myself."

"In the meantime, what about your son?"

"Without begging that question, it's a good thing for both Danny and me that you're around. You are probably more patient with him than I ever was or could be. You'd make a smashing mother, 'Nessa, do you know that?"

"Funny," Vanessa remarked, speaking openly. "If you had told me that a month ago I would have laughed. But now I think you might be right. At the very least this experience has opened a whole new world of feelings to me; for that I'm grateful, Annie."

Vanessa reached out to touch her hand, but Annie turned away. For a moment neither woman spoke, but the silence said it all.

"You don't mind going back to Vermont?" Annie finally asked.

"No. In fact, if I want to catch the last train out tonight, I should get started with my business."

"You can't stay over? We could go out to dinner."

"I wish I could, but I promised I'd be back. I just came

267

in to investigate a few assignments and to let my editors know I'm still available. Is it all right if I make a few calls now?"

"No, go ahead, make yourself at home."

Vanessa picked up her bag and started for the studio. At the door she stopped and turned. "Maybe we can have a drink this afternoon, before I go."

Annie seemed to brighten. "That would be nice, Vanessa. I'd like to have a chance to talk."

CHAPTER
TWENTY-SIX

Annie tried to work, but her attention kept lapsing. After a couple of desultory efforts she pushed the papers aside and made herself a gin and tonic. Squeezing a wedge of lime into the glass, she went back out onto the terrace, sat in a chair, sipped, and waited.

They had returned last week and she hadn't seen Rick since he'd dropped her off in a taxi in the middle of the afternoon. He hadn't called her that night, or the one after. His parting words to her had been "I'll be in touch."

Wasn't that rather formal, after the relationship they'd built? One said "I'll be in touch" to an acquaintance, or a business associate, not to a familiar. She had even let him know that she'd moved out of her house, had left her husband and child, to be in Manhattan. When she'd been here for weekends only, they'd seen each other every night. Wasn't it ironic that now that she'd begun living here, she'd hardly seen him at all?

Perhaps not. She had heard of men who wanted only what they couldn't have, what was slightly forbidden or inaccessible. These were men frightened of real intimacy. Could Rick, with his quick intelligence, his almost feminine intuitiveness, be such a man?

Vanessa had hinted as much, but Annie hadn't been able to see it. She'd ascribed it to just the slightest touch of jealousy. Why not? Vanessa was as capable of that as anyone.

Intimacy hadn't seemed to frighten him when they had been in Utah. On the contrary, Rick had fed on the fires of her confidence, her personal disclosures, her enthusiasms and disappointments. He had opened her eyes to the world, made her a companion on his unique journey. What greater intimacy could there be?

The sun was sinking behind the Palisades. A slight chill curled around her shoulders. It was getting dark earlier. Already the leaves were falling. Soon they would all be gone. Where would she be then?

She finished her drink inside, showered, and changed into a pair of jeans topped by a turtleneck sweater. Back in the living room, she paced the floor, feeling how large the room could be. She missed Vanessa's voice, the presence of another person. Their talk had whetted her appetite for company.

At first she hadn't minded the time alone. It had been a relief from the constant demands of the home she'd left. It seemed the greatest luxury imaginable to be able to sit quietly, read a book, watch TV, or do nothing. Not until last night had she felt a listlessness creeping over her. To deal with it, she had sent out for Chinese food and played several of Philip's albums at top volume. Neither Beethoven nor Miles Davis had helped, but the original cast album of *Oklahoma!* had finally had her dancing, and singing aloud, as though her living room were a proscenium stage. She had retired exhausted. Well, there was always *Carousel or South Pacific* for tonight, but Annie didn't think she could hack being the musical queen of stage and screen yet another night on Riverside

Drive.

Taking the bit in her teeth, she went to the phone and dialed Rick's number. The phone rang five times before he picked it up.

"Hello?"

"Rick, it's Annie."

"Annie, old girl, how are you? You caught me on my way out."

"I just wanted to find out how you are."

"Fine! Great! Hold on a minute." He turned aside and whispered something to another party, but she couldn't hear a response because he cupped his hand over the receiver. "Annie, can I talk to you tomorrow? I'm right in the middle of something and I was just—"

"On your way out. Yes, I heard you."

"Good girl. I'll be in touch."

She gently disengaged the line, with something like heartburn rising in her chest. It was a real physical pain, and she reeled back a couple of steps, as though struck by a physical blow. She was too young for a heart attack! She stood up and waited for the pain to pass. In its place a hot flush of anger fanned its hooded serpentine head.

"That louse," she said, softly at first. "That shallow, rotten son of a bitch!" The words made her feel better, and for several minutes she stood there calling out every possible invective she could summon. Afterward, breathless, she sat down to muster her resources.

It was amazing how quickly her moods shifted. One minute she was flying high, then she was in pain; the next, enraged, and, finally, just plain tired. But, if she were true to her present form, her fatigue would vanish, and once again she'd be thinking of her byline, soaring high with the literary eagles.

After a halfhearted version of "When I Marry Mr. Snow," she turned off the music. Her voice was not cooperating. Surely Rick was not her only resource in this great city. Hadn't she met a number of people?

Sitting down with the phone, she tried to remember some of those people who had extended her the invitation to call. One in particular sprang to mind. She'd met Alicia Thomas, the actress, at the Gotham Book Mart, and then again after the theater when Rick had taken her to dinner at "21."

Annie dialed the number she had scribbled hastily in her phone book. This time it rang only twice before it was picked up.

"Hello, hello, hello," came the rat-a-tat answer. "This is Alicia. I am not in at the moment, but if you have a message, please leave it at the sound of the tone."

Annie felt stupid. After the first hello she had started speaking, as though a person had answered the phone. It was only after she had gotten out her pitiful introduction, and the other voice had gone right on talking, that Annie realized her call was being processed by an answering machine.

She didn't bother to leave a message.

Her next call was to the novelist Ched Royales, a soft-spoken young man Vanessa had introduced her to one night in the East Village. This time the phone was answered by a human being.

"Hello?"

"Ched?"

"Yes?"

272

"This is Annie Abrams."

"Who?"

"Annie Abrams."

"The name sounds familiar, but I can't place the face. Have we met?"

"Vanessa Ansel's friend," she reminded him. "I met you at La Mama, after the Peter Brook play."

"Yes, of course, Annie. From Vermont."

"That's right. Only I'm no longer in Vermont. I've moved to Manhattan."

"Decided to live on the edge?"

"Yes." She relaxed some. "I was getting ready to have dinner, and I thought I'd do some exploring. Would you like to meet me downtown? If you're not doing anything, that is. I remember you told me to give you a call."

"Of course, and I meant it. It's just that, well, I have another engagement tonight. Some other time, perhaps?"

"Sure," said Annie. "Some other time."

She reached two more answering machines, one with a full forty-five seconds of the Eroica Symphony through a kazoo, before she decided to forget it. Was New York a city populated by answering machines?

The hunger to be with people, however, was too great to deny. She picked up her jacket, put it over her arm, and went downstairs. The black doorman, Everett, gave her a cheerful greeting.

The last time she'd lived in New York, she'd been separated from all the activity by a baby carriage. Though much of the activity had fascinated her, she'd been half glad for the protection of motherhood. She simply hadn't been ready. Now, she thought she was.

Walking up Broadway restored some of her balance. That was the marvelous thing about being in New York. Anytime, day or night, she could walk out onto the street and find a whole tapestry of life before her. Here Black, Chinese, Hindu, Latino, and every other race imaginable rubbed shoulders, each with their own dreams, language, cuisine. This in itself was almost enough to make life a continuous adventure.

She checked the movie marquee at Eighty-Third Street, but there was nothing she wanted to see. People were already lining up for the next show. The line started in front of the box office and wound around the block.

A few blocks farther uptown she stopped in front of a steel-and-glass facade, with potted plants hanging in the window, and music drifting out from the jukebox. A board with a menu announced a fare of burgers, salads, quiche, and omelettes. The place was called Trapper's, and the three or four casually dressed young men in their early thirties wished Annie pleasant good evening as she entered. The friendly greeting made her feel better immediately.

The place was busy. A maître d' in a blue button down shirt and crimson tie told her there were no tables at the moment, but she could give him her name and have a drink at the bar while she waited. Or, if she preferred, she could eat at the bar.

Annie gave him her name.

A middle-aged couple left two barstools vacant. Annie slid up on one of them. There were imitation Tiffany lamps over the bar, and a smoked mirror that Annie stared into as she ordered a gin and tonic from the mustachioed bartender. She was positioned near the service end, so waitresses in black aprons scurried around her, calling out their orders: A well-groomed man in a lightweight, pearl-gray three-piece suit, sandy hair, and wire-rimmed glasses took the stool beside her.

"Pardon me, miss," the man beside her spoke.

"Yes?"

"You wouldn't be interested in buying some life insurance, would you?"

Annie looked at him, trying to guess what he meant. After a moment she determined that he had meant just what he said, and answered no.

"That's too bad." He shook his head and moped over his drink. It was a frothy green drink, and looked more like medicine than liquor.

"Why is that too bad?" She sipped through her straw.

"Because I'm an insurance salesman at the end of his tether, I've been short of my quota for the last six months. I can feel the axe falling right now."

"I'm terribly sorry."

"So am I. I'll probably be going back into women's shoes before the end of the month."

"Have you thought of real estate?" She tried to cheer him up.

"No. Have you thought about dinner?"

"I'm sorry. I'm waiting for someone," she told him.

"Next time you see me, you know what I'm going to have tattooed on my forehead?" She shook her head, trying not to meet his eye. "Born to Lose."

She was about to tell him that such a move would really curtail his career options, but decided against further involvement. He was hardly her idea of a dinner companion. She had enough troubles of her own.

"Abasynia," said Born-to-Lose, slipping off his barstool. He was replaced by one of a group of men, already slightly drunk and whooping it up.

"Eight beers," said her neighbor, who had a two-day beard and wore a red T-shirt.

The press of people in the back of her was becoming uncomfortable. She saw the place was filling up with men. All around her they were cruising the women who came in alone, or in pairs. It was a singles bar, she realized, and suddenly felt out of place.

"Hey, lady, how about having a drink with me?" said the man in the red T-shirt.

He was smiling at her, with large, irregular white teeth and a toothpick clenched between them. His right eyebrow twitched with a surface tension. He seemed like a coiled spring of barely controlled energy. He frightened her.

"I'm waiting for someone," she explained.

"Aw, come one, gorgeous, give me a tumble. Of course you're waiting for someone, only you don't know who you're waiting for beforehand. Know what I mean?"

He winked at her. Actually winked! It would have been amusing, had he not pressed his body against hers, his face so close she could smell the beer on his breath.

"Ross is my name. Stan Ross. But everyone calls me Bebop. I play the horn, you dig?"

"Excuse me," she tried to leave, but he had her wedged in.

"Honest, sweetheart, under this rough exterior beats the heart of a working musician. How about it?"

"No," she screamed with a shrillness that cut through the surrounding noise. The general level of conversation dropped. All eyes fell on them. The man in the red T-shirt pulled back, as though shocked by an electric current.

"Well, I'm sorry for breathing'!" he called after her as she raced out the door.

Annie turned her steps back toward the apartment. More than anything else she wanted to be up there now, out on the terrace looking down on all this. It was so much easier from up there. Nose to nose, face to face, it was too much for her to handle. Neither of those men had been bad guys, she guessed. But no matter how lonely she was, she just wasn't interested in that kind of company. Yet it wasn't as though she could just write those people off. Not when they involved you, when they got familiar so quickly. Not like country people, who maintained a well-practiced distance. No, these people didn't waste any time. They dug around inside before you even knew them. How could she even begin to deal with them? Where was Rick? Why had he lost interest? What was she going to do now, when two relatively casual encounters had left her feeling so intimately violated!

CHAPTER
TWENTY-SEVEN

Annie had waited two more days for the phone to ring. Finally she called Rick at his office, anxious to learn the board's decision about her article. But the secretary said he was in conference, and would return her call later. He did not. That night she called him at home. He had been cordial, but distant, explaining that it was a particularly busy time, and, while he had meant to get back to her, he had found himself too rushed to do so.

Her article, he said, had been approved, but his voice conveyed impatience rather than congratulations.

"Is anything wrong?" she had asked him.

"Oh, on the contrary," he'd replied. "I have another assignment that might interest you."

"When can we meet to discuss it?" She couldn't help but note the desperation in her voice.

"After the holidays, Annie. In the meantime you've got the world's greatest playground at your feet. Use it."

But she didn't go out. Her response to the events the other night at the singles bar had been more profound than she had guessed. She'd thought a good night's sleep was all she'd need to recover from the experience. It never occurred to her that when the sun went down on the following day, the very thought of going out into the street, or into a restaurant, would fill her with a bone-chilling dread.

Annie had never been frightened like this before in her life. Or perhaps she'd always been frightened, and hadn't known it. Had she insulated herself from her fears of the world by running into marriage? Whatever the case, she now found herself a virtual prisoner in Philip's apartment.

Sunday she woke before the sun came up. In those spectral hours, when the sky turns slowly light like a piece of iron in a fire, she felt the irrepressible impulse to run for cover. She needed a bit of comfort . . . something familiar. . . someone to talk to.

Throwing her things into an overnight case, she taxied down to Grand Central and was aboard the first train to Albany. All the way upstate, as the Hudson river picked up the reds of the burning ember balanced in the eastern sky, she told herself that later she would make sense of everything. Her needs, at the moment, were too powerful to be reckoned with. She felt like a youngster returning home after having left to seek her fortune in the world; a youngster who had spread her wings prematurely. Yes, she told herself, that is how I feel: premature.

She caught a bus in Albany to Whitingham and from there, another to Sherbroke. Getting off at the depot on Main Street, she had to admit the town looked enchanting, nestled into its hamlet, surrounded by slopes of evergreen. It was a sleepy little place, and on Sunday morning, besides a dog running free, and an occasional stroller out to inquire if the morning paper was delivered yet at the general store, everything was still.

It was hard to believe how much she had disliked

280

Sherbroke, its tight little ring of gossip, its provincial view of the world. So hostile had she become that she'd ceased to see it. Standing at the intersection of Main and Pearl, she viewed it as for the first time, and found it comforting.

Mr. Sloan, at the general store, arched his eyebrows when he greeted her, commenting upon her long absence, and the wonderful "baby-sitter" she'd chosen. There was more than merely innuendo in his description of Vanessa, but Annie smiled, refusing to rise to the bait.

Mr. Sloan picked up the phone and woke old Mr. Barnes, who drove the local taxi.

"You back for good?" asked Mr. Barnes, steering his ten-year-old Plymouth Duster. The last in a long line of native Vermonters, Mr. Barnes was not known to mince his words.

"Why?" responded Annie. "You think it will make the front page of the *Star-Ledger?*"

"No, ma'am." He shook his hoary head. "Wouldn't even make the local page. Just askin'."

That was the end of their conversation. It set Annie's teeth on edge just enough to increase her anxieties about returning home, unannounced, at eleven in the morning.

He let her out at the beginning of the driveway. She approached the house slowly, attempting to view it with the same clarity she had viewed downtown Sherbroke. Already the leaves had fallen. A plume of smoke rose from the chimney, suffusing the air with the fragrance of pine.

At the side of the house she looked down on the meadows to see the Colbys' barn, charred but otherwise invincible. Beneath the bucolic order of the landscape

281

there was a disorder, the forces of which she had tapped when she'd left home.

She felt like Jonah, now, more than the Prodigal returned. Trouble followed her. Those she touched were destined to bear the brunt of the chaos inside of her. If she could have been invisible, she would have floated into the house to watch those inside go about their business.

But her solid flesh would not melt, and she braced herself on her way to the front door.

Once there, however, she couldn't knock, or even ring the bell. The act of doing so made her feel like a total stranger, more alone than she'd felt in the city. She turned the knob and let herself in.

She heard voices in the living room. They were light, punctuated by exclamations and laughter. She found them spread out on the floor, in front of the fire, playing Chinese checkers. They were in bathrobes and pajamas still, so engrossed in their game that they didn't see her for several seconds. Just long enough for her to notice the toe of Mark's foot resting against Vanessa's leg.

"Mama!" Danny was the first to notice her.

He didn't run to greet her. His big brown eyes shone more stunned than surprised, and he looked back and forth between Mark and Vanessa to confirm the apparition in the doorway.

"Annie?" Mark rose, slowly, gathering his robe around him, as if it were armor.

"Hello." She smiled self-consciously.

"Say hello to your mother." Vanessa urged the youngster forward.

"Hello, Mama." Danny padded over to her in pajamas

that covered his feet. "I didn't know you were comin'."

"Give Mama a kiss." Annie bent down so the child could throw his arms around her neck and peck her cheek.

"How about some coffee?" Vanessa was halfway into the kitchen before anyone could answer.

"Sure," Annie called. Was she mistaken, or had she caught a look of anger in Vanessa's eyes? If she had, it was gone by the time they were seated at the table, over coffee and the frozen croissants that Vanessa had heated in the oven.

"How have you been, Annie?" Mark's voice was kind but aloof, his best professional manner. Vanessa, also, seemed distant, as if stepping back from the conversation, waiting for Annie to speak.

"Fine. Adjusting to big-city living." She tried to smile, to make her visit seem casual. But it wasn't working. She had nerves written all over her, and she knew it. It occurred to her, for a second, to make some kind of lame excuse, such as that she had just stopped by to pick up some clothes or toilet articles, but she knew that would only make things worse. "It's not as easy as I thought it would be," she confessed. "I'm sorry I didn't call, but it was all spur of the moment. I wanted to . . ."

"Retreat?" Mark filled in the word when Annie's pause grew perilous.

"That's right. I needed to retreat for a moment."

"And are you back for good?" His tone was still dispassionate.

"No." She shook her head.

"For the day, for the night?" He needed to know.

"I don't know!" Her voice rang shrilly before she quieted it. "I don't know. Maybe this was a mistake, to interrupt you. You all seemed so happy when I walked in."

"I'm going to get dressed." Vanessa rose. "We'll take a walk, Annie. How does that sound?"

"Fine." She was grateful to her friend.

"Can I come, too? "Danny asked.

"If you are dressed and ready by the time we leave." Vanessa answered before Annie could decide. "Run."

Mark said little to her while they waited.

She smiled, sipped her coffee. In spite of her own condition, she could see he was prospering. The worry lines around his mouth and eyes had all but disappeared. She was glad for him, but found she had nothing much to say.

If they had been strangers, she would've been tempted to confide in him: his attentiveness, his gentle manner encouraged confidence; but he was all mixed up at the root of her problems, and she couldn't talk to him about anything important.

Nor was it much easier with Vanessa, she discovered to her surprise, and frustration, as they walked through the woods on the other side of the road.

"Are you all right?" Vanessa asked her, keeping her eye on Danny as he ran ahead of them.

"No." Annie shook her head." I'm not."

"What's wrong?"

"I'm frightened."

"Of what?" They walked over the fallen leaves. To their left the river, swollen with a recent rain, coursed over rocks slippery with moss.

"Of being out there," Annie managed. "Of growing up.

"Join the club." Vanessa smiled. She watched Danny

gather up an armful of leaves and throw them high into the air.

"My coming up here was a mistake," Annie volunteered. She waited for a response, but there was none. "I came running back like a child, to be in the bosom of my family, of my husband, son, and best friend—but in fact, I feel like an intruder."

"This is still your home." Vanessa stopped, faced her. "Mark is still your husband, and Danny will always be your son."

"Perhaps. The reality is more like the picture I walked in on. Very cozy." Annie shook her head against the note of bitterness in her voice.

"It's what you wanted," Vanessa reminded her.

"I know. I can't blame you. I asked you to stay with them."

"You did. I had reservations, as you know. After all, you are my best friend. But you asked me to do it with such conviction."

The blond woman nodded, then fell into step beside her raven-haired friend. She watched her son amuse himself with the mounds of fallen leaves. "I don't recall the last time I saw both of them so happy," Annie commented. "The three of you made a complete picture, Vanessa. I might as well have been looking through a window from the outside. What I saw was a happy family."

"We do get along well," Vanessa responded simply.

Annie nodded and turned in her tracks. "Come on, Danny, it's time to go back."

Mark had been visibly relieved to hear that his wife had decided to return to New York City the same day, and Vanessa had driven her back to Albany, but the two had said little. For Annie, saying good-bye to her son had been the most difficult. She regretted opening the wounds, and wished again that she'd never come up. "I don't know when I will be back. Maybe I shouldn't even write to Danny."

"Use your time to think about what you want," Vanessa had responded. "But I think Danny does need to hear from you. Don't hold back your feelings for him."

In her first letter to Daniel, Annie told him about a mime she had seen perched on one leg like a stork in front of the Metropolitan Museum. As October drew to a close, she recorded the more outlandish costumes in the Halloween parade in Washington Square Park: the huge giraffe, the eerie skeleton on stilts, the band of three-year-old fairies, and a variety of wicked witches. Danny responded to her letters with pictures, which Annie attached to the refrigerator with magnets. The drawing she liked best was of a plump pumpkin with skinny legs.

At the beginning of November she received a picture of a scarecrow, and the artist's signature, "Danny" Just below the inscription he had penciled, "I love you, Mommy."

Annie took the letter out on the terrace and let her sobs float into the rising sounds of traffic. In the constant din of white noise her cries rose into the universe unheeded.

"Will you be up for Thanksgiving?" Vanessa asked her over the phone.

"No, I don't think so."

She wasn't ready yet. After the last time she tried to retreat into the bosom of her family, it had been more difficult to return to her new life. Think about it, Vanessa urged her. She would, Annie responded, but already she was certain of her decision. Since she had begun moving closer to her goal of self-sufficiency, she found it easier to be alone than a stranger in the midst of her family. She didn't think she could stand to watch Mark hide his feelings for Vanessa or hers for him. She understood their closeness, but it wasn't something she wanted to experience firsthand. She hadn't put it exactly that way to Vanessa, but it was what she thought. And as Thanksgiving drew near, and turkeys made their way into the store windows and the public consciousness, Annie maintained her normal routine, except for the additional phone calls to her son.

Of course, there were invitations. She didn't have to be alone if she wanted company. She had made an adjustment to city living, and even the singles scene, which had terrified her, was now only an amusement. Not that she'd spend her Thanksgiving nursing a beer at a bar. She had one invitation from a woman she'd become friendly with at the yoga class she attended twice a week in a loft off Union Square. Another invitation came from Vanessa's collaborator on the Bowery piece, the writer Ched Royales. He and a number of other artists without family commitments were getting together in SoHo. She had thanked them for thinking of her, but declined both offers.

The one invitation she might have accepted never came. She'd waited until the last minute before asking

Rick what his plans were, then was forced to settle for an evasive answer about relatives in Kingston.

On Thursday she walked to the bank on Broadway and Ninetieth Street only to find it closed, and to realize the holiday was upon her. The streets were conspicuously empty. Most of the city's population were either on their way to, or sitting in front of, sumptuous meals. She walked down to Zabar's and bought herself several *pains-au chocolat*, then returned to the apartment. A light snow had begun to fall, and quickly the late afternoon disappeared into darkness. She couldn't get over how quickly the days were ending.

Determined to bear up, she made herself some coffee, then sat at the table chewing on one of the light crusts mined with pockets of sweet chocolate.

Her mind had begun to fill with images of her son on the day of the fire, when the telephone rang. A voice on the other end croaked a greeting.

"Hello, Vanessa?"

"No, Vanessa isn't here."

"'This is the number I have for her. Who am I speaking to?"

"Annie Abrams. Who is this?"

"Why, Annie, it's been so long, I didn't recognize your voice. You sound so womanly!"

"Who—"

"Clemens, Clemens Ansel."

"Clemens, hello!" Annie felt a sudden wave of relief at the familiar voice. It was as though a hand had reached out to calm her. "Vanessa told me you were in Peru."

"I was, until yesterday. Now I'm in New York, and after the Alto Plano, boy, does the city look good!"

288

"I'm so pleased to hear from you."

"Yes, good to hear you. I called because I didn't know what Vanessa had planned for the holiday, and thought, well, if she wasn't doing anything, we'd spend some time. I guess you're busy. . . ."

"No, not at all. I'm just sitting here with a cup of coffee," she confessed. "Would you like to come over? I mean, there's no big feast or anything. . . . I haven't even thought about dinner—"

"I'd love to see you. I'll be over in an hour."

She gave him directions to the apartment, then hung up, relieved she wouldn't be spending Thanksgiving alone after all.

An hour later she was overwhelmed by gratitude, as if he had saved her from a terrible disaster. He stood in the doorway, an avuncular figure with his mane of distinguished gray hair, those gray eyes sunk deeply into the weathered cheeks visible above the beard. He hugged her warmly, and her need to be comforted overwhelmed her greeting. Soon she was sobbing into the breast pocket of his Harris tweed sport coat.

"Now, now, dear." Clemens stroked her head and held her until she decided she was ready to let him go. "I haven't received a welcome like that since the time I returned to photograph the Tasaday."

"I'm sorry, Clemens." Annie wiped her eyes, laughing through the tears. "But I am awfully glad to see you."

She reheated the pot of thick vegetable soup on the stove. Annie loved to prepare large portions of soups, to eat throughout the week; a holdover from her days of domesticity. There was some white wine in the refrigerator, and a loaf of French bread in the cupboard. She served him soup, bread, and wine, taking only a small portion of each for herself.

"Happy Thanksgiving." Clemens raised his glass.

"And to you," she returned the toast.

They talked by candlelight, the lights of Manhattan and the Jersey cliffs winking at them through the fine veil of snowfall.

He'd returned last night, he told her, and had been calling the house all afternoon. Vanessa was up in Vermont, she told him, with Mark and Danny.

He paused for a second, his soup spoon full of vegetables, before completing the motion to his mouth. "Mark and Vanessa and Danny?"

"That's right," Annie continued. "Vanessa's staying up there with them while I figure out what to do with myself."

"I see." Clemens nodded. Suddenly Annie's tears made sense to him.

Embarrassed, she hastened to change the subject. "How about you?"

"I'm afraid it's too late for me. Every time I try to figure out what to do with myself, I get into trouble. I had to give up trying, and become a leaf in the wind. Wherever it takes me, there I stay, until the next gust picks me up and takes me someplace else."

"Yours seems like a good life, Clemens."

"I don't know." He shook his head. "It's been all right for me." He swallowed a spoonful of vegetables. "But I'm not sure how good it was for my daughter."

"Vanessa's a solid, thoughtful human being."

"You two always were thick as thieves." He winked.

"Now, what about your trip?"

His trip, he told her, had been an artistic success, although, high up, at the heights of the Andes, he'd had an attack of arthritis in his hip that just about crippled him. "I'm getting old."

"Not you, Clemens. That gray beard doesn't fool me. I can see the youth in your eyes."

He thanked her and went on to talk about Mexico, the president's family, the great Aztec capital they were unearthing at the very heart of the city.

"You see, that's the way they built things, the new city's right over the old one. Eventually it resembled a series of Chinese boxes. Maybe that's the way we build our lives, too," he speculated. "Sometimes, right in the middle of my new one, a chink opens up, and I'm looking smack at the life before that, or into the depths of my childhood."

"Does it get easier, Clemens?"

The candles flickered. Ansel sipped his wine, pushed away the empty bowl, and leaned back in his chair. "For some of us, it does. For the ones who are finally able to accept themselves as they are, and can live with it."

"What if you can't find out who you are?"

"Then you get buried under what everyone else expects you to be. You spend your life trying to please those around you. Some people can live like that, I guess. But whenever I tried, and, believe me, I did try, something deep inside rebelled, and made my life miserable."

"Are you happier now?"

"I am." He dabbed his lips with his napkin. "I've made what I could of my life. And where I fell short, well, I've learned to accept that part of myself, too."

291

"But you've been successful at everything you've done."

"Not true. I was a lousy husband and father."

"Your daughter and your wife loved you madly. Vanessa's kept me up late at night talking about you."

"Of course they loved me, and I loved them. But I loved my work more."

"I see." Annie let his words sink in. "That seems all right to me when you say it, but it sounds terrible when I hear it in myself."

"Because you still care too much what other people think of you."

"I've left my husband," she told him, "and my child."

"So I gathered," he said. "Let's move into the living room, shall we? Do you know what you're going to do?" asked Clemens, sitting on the sofa.

"I've been doing a little writing," she told him. "I like it."

"You could do that within your marriage." He sipped his wine.

"No, it won't work, Clemens. I can't go back to it."

"It sounds as if you've already decided. Then, what is so difficult for you?"

"Leaving my little boy." She poured them both a snifter of brandy and carried it over. "And I'm having difficulty– being alone."

"That's because you're not used to it yet, and the holidays are the hardest to adjust to. Give yourself a chance." He accepted the snifter and took an appreciative sip. "I'm sure you'll even grow to like it."

"Have you?" She sat down beside him.

"Indeed. Some of my most enjoyable moments are

spent that way." He took another sip, and then set down his glass. "Some people are built for constant intimacy, Annie. Vanessa is one of those people. She craves a family, a husband. That's why I finally had to cut the cord between us. She would have followed after me the rest of my life, and always longed for something else. By the time I had passed on, she might have been too old. I didn't want that. Cutting her loose was one of the hardest things I've done."

"For her, also."

"You, on the other hand, Annie, may not be so constructed. It's harder for women to find that out about themselves than men because women are supposed to be the nurturers. To be honest, Annie, some of us need a little space around us. There's nothing wrong with it. We love, in our own ways, and nourish in our own ways, too."

"Like apples and oranges."

"Exactly. Give yourself time to find out."

"I'm trying." She sat at the foot of the sofa. "Mark and Danny are very happy with Vanessa."

"How does that make you feel?"

"I'm not sure. I think Mark and Vanessa are lovers."

"You should be pleased."

"What?" She stood and stared down at him. "How can you say that?"

"Doesn't that make things easier for you? You should feel less guilty for leaving. It frees you. For myself, I feel less guilty knowing she's happy."

"Why, you sly old fox." Annie felt herself smile.

"Now you're beginning to understand."

CHAPTER
TWENTY-EIGHT

Ever since Annie had called, wanting Mark to come down to talk, Vanessa had known her dream world was on the brink of disaster. She'd always known the day would come when Annie would recognize her mistake and want to reclaim her family. How ironic! Just when Vanessa had felt secure enough to let her guard down, Annie had phoned and shaken her to the roots of her security.

"I'll be glad when it's finally settled," Mark had admitted. If the uncertainty of his wife's return bothered him as much as it did Vanessa, he took great care to hide it.

Mark turned in his sleep and without waking, wrapped his arms around her more securely. His lashes cast long shadows over his cheekbones. He looked at peace, Vanessa thought, and wished she could close her eyes awhile longer and forget her troubles. Yet how could she sleep when today might well be the last time she could lie with Mark? That very afternoon Annie could draw an abrupt end to their life together. Vanessa might never again know the sweet taste of his lips against hers or the gentle pressure by which he held her closely to him. They'd be forced to discontinue the passion they'd claimed as their own. There would be no more burnt breakfasts to laugh over, no more lazy lovemaking at the end of a well-spent day. Danny would forget her as quickly as he'd accepted her. She closed her eyes, her brow creased. Each thought was more painful than the last.

Maybe she could still see Danny? Maybe he could come into Manhattan and visit her? Perhaps Mark would bring him—? She stopped herself. The temptation to continue their love would have to be removed altogether. She'd never do anything to interrupt Annie's attempt to re-establish her family. There would be no stolen moments with Mark, no hushed long-distant phone conversations. She'd do whatever she must to avoid contact. At first it would be hard, on all of them, but the only way they'd succeed would be if she erased herself completely from the picture, and let them pick up the pieces of the life they'd led before she'd dropped in to confuse things.

Where would she go? She could stay at Philip's, she guessed, but only for a few days. She could call Rick. Possibly he'd have work for her, something that would take her out of the country, someplace far away, where she'd have time to forget, to heal. Who knew, maybe Ansel would consider taking her along on just one more assignment. She'd have the chance to ask him in a few hours. While Mark was talking with Annie, Vanessa and Danny would visit with her father. Mark had wanted her to come with him to New York, as if they were going on a holiday!

She should get up, before Mark or Danny awakened, and pack her things, so she wouldn't have to return for them. Then, when Annie lowered the boom, there'd be no need for her to come back. She'd already have made the separation, without dragging it out any longer than it had to be.

Lifting Mark's hand from her waist, she tried, as quietly as she could, to untangle herself from his arms. He opened his eyes and smiled at her. "No, stay," he said, his voice as unguarded as a child's. "We don't have to get up yet."

He rubbed her arm softly and closed his eyes, trusting she'd stay longer.

What the hell, Vanessa thought to herself, sliding back under the covers. There'd be plenty of time to think about the future, so little time actually to enjoy the present. Annie could always ship Vanessa's things south. It was still too early for Danny to wake, and another hour in Mark's arms would fortify her to get through the day.

"Can't you sleep?" He was awake enough to feel her tension.

"I guess I'm pretty awake already. But you sleep. I won't go away."

He closed his eyes again and smiled. He looked so at ease that Vanessa wondered how he escaped worry. Men are so different, she concluded. She remembered how calm Ansel had been at their separation while she had been devastated. This wasn't exactly the same thing—Mark wasn't sending her away—but something was keeping him calm.

He laid his leg over her, and the weight felt good, like a baby confined in swaddling clothes. There was something tender in the way he stroked her thigh, and a quieter kind of intimacy replaced the passion that had kept them both aroused for months. In the countless nights of zealous lovemaking, he'd come to know every line and curve of her body, as she had his. Now he traced the familiar paths, as if he knew without looking where he wanted to go. Like a dancer who knew his partner too well to bother asking for the next dance, he started moving, understanding that she'd pick up the step. It was music they both were accustomed to. And like dancers at the end of a long party, when the orchestra is tired and closing up, wanting to go home, the couple lingered, hardly swaying to the final bars. They clung to each other, holding out for one last refrain. Even after the music stopped playing, they continued their embrace, unembarrassed by their need to hold on for another moment. The golden hour had passed. What Vanessa had thought might last only one night had gone on for months, like the oil that had burned eight days longer than anyone had expected.

She squinted to see the alarm clock in the early morning light. It was time for her to go back to her own bedroom. They had been careful every night to set the alarm. No point in confusing Danny at the end of her stay.

She put on her robe and looked in on the boy. He was starting to stir. "Time to get up, honey."

"Is Daddy awake?"

"We'll let him sleep a little longer, until we've had our baths."

"Didn't I have a bath Tuesday?"

"Yes, you did, but today's a special occasion," she whispered, leading him out of the room. "We're going to New York City." She turned on the hot and cold water and stripped off his pajamas. "We're going to see my father."

"Your father?"

"Yes, I think you'll like him. Step in, now."

She washed her face and teeth while the boy bathed. She helped wash his hair, and rinse it, then left him to dry off. While he was in his room, dressing, she showered. Her hair was wet already when Mark pulled back the curtain and stepped in to join her.

"Mind company?"

She started soaping her hair. "Not yours," she said, handing him the shampoo to hold.

"Step back for a minute." Mark ducked under the spray and started to lather his hair. She had set a quick pace, and instinctively he picked it up, without being told they should hurry.

As if they'd been showering together for years, they both managed to shampoo their hair and get all the soap out, without taking longer than they would have spent in individual showers.

"Squeaky clean." Mark rubbed his hand over her shiny stomach.

Vanessa glanced down and saw he'd grown excited by the touch.

He grinned sheepishly. "It won't matter if we're five minutes late."

"Your son is waiting for his breakfast." Vanessa tried to sound insistent, but wasn't very convincing.

"No, he isn't. I sent him to Colby's for eggs. Besides, you missed a spot."

"Where?"

He spread a palmful of soap suds over her breast and down her belly. "In fact, you look like you could use a thorough rubdown."

299

Her breath caught as his hand disappeared from view. There was no chance of pretending further indifference. She was aroused, if less visibly than he. Danny wouldn't be back for a few more minutes, she thought, reaching for the bar of soap.

Their fingertips were wrinkled from too much water when they stepped out of the stall. Vanessa wrapped her hair into a turban, and Mark dried her back, leaning down to kiss it.

Before she was dry, he stopped, to take her again in his arms. Either she didn't notice, or didn't care, that he was still dripping wet. In the last of their time together, nothing mattered more than that they should enjoy each other.

Mark cooked breakfast while Vanessa threw things together. She straightened the living room, not wanting Annie to have to return to a mess. She didn't want her to think they'd lived like total slobs while she was gone. Careful to take all Mark's possessions out of the guest room, and her things from his room, she was almost ready to go when Mark announced breakfast. Put on your cheery face, she told herself in the mirror. By the end of the day it will all be finished, and then there will be time for tears.

She rushed them through breakfast. "Let's finish that piece of toast in the car, Danny," she urged.

Mark knew she was nervous, by the way she was rushing around, but he couldn't calm her. True, Annie might throw their lives into further disorder, but he didn't intend to fret about it until it happened. Besides, regardless of what Annie had to say this evening, he had ideas of his own. He'd had two months to consider what he wanted, time to outgrow some wild fantasy about what it would be like to live with another woman. The truth of the matter was that he loved Vanessa, now even more than ever, and what once had connected him to Annie had long since disappeared. He had told Vanessa that something would have happened to his marriage eventually. It might have drifted along for another few years, vaguely dissatisfying but both parties unwilling to instigate the change. If not Vanessa, some other incident would have brought them to their feet. For *him* there was no doubt about what he wanted. He wished he were the only deciding factor.

What would Mark do if Annie wanted her son? It would kill a part of him to give up the boy. Since Annie had left, they'd grown even closer. They had a family again, and it was with Vanessa.

"Ready, Dad?" Danny yanked on his hand. "'Nessa wants us to hurry."

"I just need to phone the hospital. Go ahead." He patted his shoulder. "I'll be with you in a minute."

CHAPTER TWENTY-NINE

Danny, dressed in his bright yellow sweater and blue down vest, sat in the backseat with his feet stuck forward into the space between his father and Vanessa. As they reached the city limits, he suggested. "How about a movie?" When his suggestion was not immediately picked up, he elaborated. "We could see *Spiderman* again."

"Maybe, Danny, if there's time," replied Mark.

"Don't worry," Vanessa reassured the boy. "You're going to enjoy yourself."

She would make sure of that. The child would find the day memorable. Perhaps she would, too, in an altogether different way. The prospect of Mark's meeting with Annie loomed like the storm clouds on the horizon.

Danny settled back with his copy of *Where the Wild Things Are.* He loved the book and it always touched Vanessa to read it with him. Watching him curl up with his book, she found herself hoping that there was a place of refuge in Danny's world. She was sure there was. He had handled everything so well—even his mother's departure—at least on the surface. After the fire there had been few signs of rage or grief in the child. But who could tell, finally, what the currents were beneath the surface?

Was she worrying about Danny as an extension of herself?

Yes, perhaps she was. It was Vanessa she was worried about, the woman whose need to love, and be loved, found reward in the bosom of this family. She was about to be thrown back out on her own again. Surely it was Vanessa the waif, the child with a too large bag of camera equipment, that looked up at her with bewilderment, asking why she felt in such jeopardy.

Mark was trying to play it light, taking Annie's call in the spirit of an outing, an excuse for a day in the big city, but she could tell that he was worried. She never doubted his love for her. In the way he held her, or touched her cheek, there was no mistaking the feeling behind his gestures.

But Mark, like Danny, had a depth in which the currents that ran counter to each other never showed on the surface. Annie was still his wife, and he'd had years of time shared with her to account for in the emotional ledger.

Why was her happiness founded in such confusion? Vanessa hadn't lived a sheltered life. More than most children, she'd been out in the world moving among a cross-section of sophisticated people. But she had viewed their lives as a soap opera, a fantasy, something not quite real. Their affairs, divorces, and remarriages had always seemed to her to have been scripted more for her entertainment than her edification. So this is what it was like to be an adult, she thought. Finally to become a part of the dream: to wake up to find that it is very serious business.

They got off the highway at Seventy-second Street

and drove east through the park at Sixty-sixth, nearing their destination. Mark would drop her off, with Danny, at the Pierre. They would visit with Clemens until Mark had finished talking with Annie. Annie hadn't asked to see either Vanessa or her son, and Mark thought it best not to tell the child of the plan until he had spoken with her. Danny, as if intuiting the delicacy of the situation, hadn't yet raised the question of his mother. For this Vanessa was grateful. It would be difficult to bring everyone together until there was more clarity. But what if that clarity meant the reunion of the family, the exclusion of Vanessa? She would just have to accept that. As a matter of fact that was just what she was doing, preparing herself for this eventuality. In order to do it, she had to anticipate it over and over again until the pain was dulled, and she could accept that outcome.

"Oh, boy, look at the horses, 'Nessa!" yelled Danny, pointing at the hansom cabs that moved slowly but elegantly in the right lane on Fifth Avenue.

"Would you like to ride in one later?"

"Could we?"

"Sure."

"Wow."

She watched as he lapsed back into a fantasy. Perhaps he was now Danny, the Wild Boy, driving a horse-drawn cab down Fifth Avenue with Mark and—who would he tuck safely inside? Herself or Annie? No, it was unfair to the child to ask that question of him, even in the privacy of her own imagination. Whoever he drove in the safety of his carriage was his business.

"Here we are, folks," said Mark, pulling up in front of the Hotel Pierre.

"We getting out here?" Danny peeked out the window. A uniformed doorman approached and opened the back door.

"This is it," said Mark. "Don't look so alarmed." He turned to Vanessa as Danny was sliding out into the street. "It will be all right."

"One way or another." She forced a smile.

He leaned over and kissed her lightly on the lips. "I'll come over as soon as I'm through."

"Okay"

"I hope everything goes well with Clemens."

"Me, too." She got out and closed the door behind her. "See you later."

"Try to enjoy yourself." He shifted into drive. "If I'm going to be longer than an hour or two, I'll call."

She waved, standing with Danny at the curb, feeling more like another orphan of the storm than a responsible adult.

There were already the beginnings of the Yuletide in evidence. Wreaths of myrtle hung on the doors, and sprigs of pine decorated the wooden panels of the lobby. Danny was entranced with the uniforms; he regarded the doorman and the bellhops as if they were officers in the exotic army of his dreams.

Like Little Nemo, he would reveal himself as their secret commander-in-chief, tonight in Slumberland.

Clemens Ansel was waiting for them in his suite. He looked more like a robust Santa in his red vest and shirt-sleeves than the patriarch of Vanessa's recollections. His gray beard seemed bushier, his cheeks redder, and his greeting was warmer than any she could remember.

"Vanessa." He held her at arm's length and looked her over. "My dear, how good it is to see you."

"Good to see you, too, Dad." She let the words rise spontaneously in her throat. She was glad to see him, and believed him when he had said the same.

"And Danny, I don't know if you remember me. We've only met once and you were so tiny, I could have held you in the palm of my hand."

"Which hand?" asked Danny.

"This one." Clemens opened his palm and held it toward him.

The boy examined the hand, then looked up at the man with something like awe. Indeed, from his point of view, Clemens must have appeared to be another of those mythical figures out of Slumberland. Perhaps that King of Slumberland himself.

"But what a fine young man you've grown up to be." Clemens put the hand gently on the back of Danny's head as the child entered the room.

Vanessa watched the two of them. It was amazing, she thought, what a little distance did for one's perspective. She felt like someone returning to her birthplace after years of absence, to find out that everything was exactly as she'd remembered it, only half the size. Clemens was of strictly human proportions. She realized that up until this second, she had considered him to be immense.

Watching the two of them, the obvious relish of his dialogue with the child, she felt a new warmth for her dad. Yes, she had called him that. He had been right to send her off on her own. And it couldn't have been easy, particularly when he knew his resolve would have to withstand her desperate plea.

He was sitting in a chair, bent over to examine the book of Sendak's Danny spread open on the floor. She walked over and laid her hand on his shoulder.

"I've taken the liberty of ordering up some food," Clemens told her, touching her hand in response. "It's in the kitchen. Danny—?" he looked down, "would you. . . ?"

"Hot dogs? Sure."

"Right this way."

The gray-bearded photographer led them into the kitchen of the suite, where two chafing dishes sat on a cart. In one there was Swedish meatballs, and in the other, pigs-in-a-blanket.

"Don't eat too many of them," warned Vanessa. "You'll ruin your appetite for supper."

"Ouch!" Danny withdrew the hand he'd stuck directly into the chafing dish. "It's hot."

"Wait, I'll serve you," said Vanessa.

She dished him out a little of each while Clemens poured him a cold glass of 7-Up. He then filled two glasses of chilled Pouilly-Fuisse for them. They sat facing each other as Danny spread himself out on the carpeted floor, with his food and his book.

"A wonderful child," commented Clemens.

"He is." Vanessa felt her eyes water. She was transparent. Clemens could see right through her, she knew. He was looking at the woman his daughter had become: the mother.

"And he loves you very much. I can see it in his eyes when he looks at you."

"He hasn't had an easy time of it," she confessed.

"No, life isn't easy, even for children."

Clemens's answer was a relief to her. She no longer felt as though she had to hide anything from him.

What had she been keeping secret behind her own desperate hope? The guilt of displacing Annie? Even though Annie had encouraged the closeness, the guilt was still there. In addition, there was the recognition of Danny's confusion, even if he never voiced it.

But her father's simple reply showed her that this was all a part of living—the physics of it. Vanessa had to accept that it was not an ideal world. They were all doing what they could, trying to discover what was best as they moved. All that could be asked was that there be love, and a healthy respect for the truth, when it was uncovered.

"I always thought it should be easier," she told him.

"For some, it is." His smile was wry. "For those of us who never set down roots but fly with the birds—well, it seems easier for us. But we give up something."

"What do you give up, Dad?"

"Intimacy, Vanessa." He placed his hand on her arm. "I'm not complaining, mind you. I've had a full life, after my fashion. And I was fortunate to have had you. You were my one sustaining link." She nodded when he paused, seeing there were tears in his eyes, also. "But I couldn't hold on to you for that reason. It would've been selfish. And, I'll tell you the truth, honey, I am one of those who are content to fly alone."

"I know that, now."

"There are those like me around, you know. It's hard for some to accept, particularly if they don't have something to fall back on, like a career or an art. But you're not one of those loners, Vanessa. I've always known that about you."

"I'm discovering that."

"You have the eye and the talent. As a matter of fact, you will probably end up being a far better photographer than I. But you also have your mother's need for people, and unless you satisfy that, you will be no good to yourself, even with all the career accolades in the world."

"I don't know." Vanessa gazed at him. "I'm scared, Dad."

"Everything will be all right." They let their eyes hold one another for a moment, then Clemens disengaged. "You're *my* daughter, after all."

CHAPTER THIRTY

"Are you ready to go?"

"Why don't you stop up, Mark?"

"Because Annie is in a rush. We'll meet you in the lobby."

Vanessa hung up the house phone and tried to compose herself. She dressed Danny, making sure he didn't leave his gloves, and gathered her own belongings. Clemens accompanied them down in the elevator.

As they descended, Vanessa tried to find some clue in Mark's words or the tone of his voice. *Annie was with him, and she was in a rush.* Was it because she wanted to take her son and her husband and be gone? Could it end like that, an abrupt good-bye in the hotel lobby?

She felt herself slump against the mahogany wall of the elevator car. Clemens regarded her and hastily she straightened up. In addition to everything else, why did this have to occur under her father's scrutiny?

And there was Danny. If he were not of her flesh and blood, he had become a limb of her spirit.

And Mark!

Please, she implored the unnamed power that presided over her destiny, please let this all pass in the wink of an eye.

The elevator door opened and she saw Mark and Annie silhouetted against the fading exterior light at the far end of the lobby. They were talking together easily, and while she couldn't see the expressions on their faces, the position of their bodies and the gesture of their hands were relaxed, fluent.

She had lost them, had lost them all.

"Mama! There's Mama!" Danny gave one brief, almost apologetic look at Vanessa, then raced around the bell-boys, luggage, and other hotel patrons, into the waiting arms of his mother, who bent down to receive him.

She watched Mark approach her, but she couldn't bear it; wanted to turn away and dissolve into the crowd. Her father's hand was on her elbow, and with the slightest pressure imaginable, he directed her forward. Vanessa moved mechanically, feeling the gates shutting down on her senses, like the sluice gates of a dam.

Still, he was coming to meet her, with unfaltering steps, one hand outstretched in greeting.

Clemens accepted the greeting, and the two men shook hands like old friends. The photographer patted the physician's shoulder with bluff good humor. Politely the younger man inquired into the other man's plans, and when Clemens answered that he'd be around for the holidays, Mark nodded and said that Vanessa would certainly be glad.

But she would not hang on to her father, Vanessa resolved. She had learned how to be alone, and when the grieving passed, as surely it must, she would learn how to be on her own all over again. God, how many times would she have to learn that lesson?

"Come—" Mark took her arm. "Annie wants to say good-bye."

She was caught between the two men now, approaching the woman and child who waited by the entrance.

"No, wait" Her eyes were dark with fear.

Mark stifled her protest. "It will only take a minute."

"Hi, Vanessa." Annie's voice was timid, as if they'd never been closer than acquaintances, but a smile softened the distance, and she stood on tiptoe to kiss her old friend.

Vanessa felt the warmth of Annie's cheek against hers, felt the tears well up in her eyes, and used every remaining ounce of will to hold them back.

"I wish we had more time," Annie said, "but we will talk later, after the dust has settled."

Vanessa could do little more than nod. She scanned the eyes of those around her but couldn't look at Mark. Numbly she watched Clemens bend down to say good-bye to Danny. She heard Mark saying something to Annie about last-minute arrangements. Everyone seemed so easy. She was the only one feeling the weight of the loss.

"I don't want to kiss you good-bye," Danny told Clemens. "Your beard tickles."

Clemens, still spry enough to hunker on his knees before the child, considered the dilemma. "In certain parts of the world, where everyone wears beards, it is the custom to give a man two little pulls on his chin whiskers, as a farewell."

Danny was delighted, and bearded the lion tenderly.

He reached up for Vanessa's hand. With his other he held on to Annie's and between the two women he walked out onto Fifth Avenue.

From where she stood, Vanessa could see the circuit lights blinking on the tree by the Plaza fountain. Distant store windows were decked out with silver foil, cutouts of chimneys and reindeer. A sidewalk Santa stood at the entrance to the park, ringing a bell in front of a large kettle.

"We'll see you later, Vanessa," said Annie.

And before she could respond, the doorman was holding open the door of a cab. Annie and Danny got in, and no sooner did the door close than the light on the taxi roof went off, and they melted into the downtown traffic.

She felt so alone. It was dark, and she shivered beneath her heavy coat. Then Mark was beside her, and Clemens, too. For a moment her father held them both in a huddle; then he melted into the background of the Pierre. In another minute Mark would also be gone. Then she could give in to her tears.

"That wasn't so bad, was it?" His face was close to hers, his eyes wide and brilliant.

"I don't understand." She sounded dazed.

"We have two hours to kill before we pick up Danny." Mark took her arm and started walking to the south end of the park. "Annie wants some time to talk to him alone over dinner."

"And then?" She forced her voice not to quiver.

"Then we'll drive home, the three of us."

"Annie?"

Mark stopped his walking, turned to look at her. "Of course not, silly—" He suddenly realized that she hadn't understood after all. "Don't worry, I'll tell you all about it on our drive home."

Suddenly she was no longer cold. Vanessa felt herself folded into the warmth of Mark's embrace. The gates of her senses reversed themselves and from their opened

314

chutes poured a flood of tears. For a full minute she let her head rest on his shoulder, and sobbed. Only after her tears were spent came a shudder of relief.

"We're going to be all right, Vanessa." He stroked her hair gently.

She couldn't speak, nor was there any need. He let her rest against him a bit longer; then, still protected in his arms, she walked with him across the intersection of Fifty-Seventh Street.

"Should we take that ride in the hansom?" he asked, studying her face for an answer. "I know it's a bit corny, and it won't be the same without Danny, but I'm sure we could force ourselves to enjoy it." He hailed the horse-drawn carriage and helped her inside. In the privacy of the cab, his lips found hers, and all that remained of the outside world—its demands and complexities—was the rhythmic cadence of the horse.

www.ingramcontent.com/pod-product-compliance
Lightning Source LLC
Chambersburg PA
CBHW050553260626
47157CB00002B/551